NAERO'S MASTERY

A Spacer Clans Adventure:

Book 4

NAERO'S MASTERY

Mason Elliott

A Spacer Clans Adventure:

Book 4

High Mark Publishing

High Mark Publishing
www.highmarkpublishing.com

Seattle & Portland, Los Angeles, Chicago, London

NAERO'S
MASTERY
A Spacer Clans Adventure:
Book 4
by
Mason Elliott
Createspace Trade Paperback Edition

Cover Art by
Mike Leonard
madmanmike.deviantart.com

Edition Notes
If you do not see this edition note here in this spot on the copyright
page and on the very last page of your eBook or print version of this title,
then you are not getting the final, polished version of this novel that the
publisher, editors, and author intended for you to receive. Please contact
either the publisher or the author via their emails or websites if you do not
see the following update code:

High Mark Publishing Update Code F0215A

Become a fan of my books.
Please join my Readers List:
http://bit.ly/1L2QpUL

Thanks, from Mason Elliott

1

If they got past her…

Naero woke up softly in the night watches, unable to get certain fears out of her head. She slipped out of their oval nanobed from beside Khai, in their private quarters. What was she so worried about? Her family was relatively safe on board *The Holy Ghost*, Admiral Naero's flagship of Fleet-1, of the One Hundred Fleets.

But for how long would her family remain safe?

"I'll be here when you return," Khai whispered. "I know how you like to pace sometimes, my heart. Get it out of your system and come back to us."

"Go back to sleep," she whispered to him with her half-smile.

Naero transported directly to the large, empty observation deck.

Then she recalled that she was still quite naked.

There wasn't much chance that anyone would come by at that time of the watches, but she clothed herself in Nytex flight togs with barely a thought.

The primary observation deck was an elongated, almost rectangular oval, three hundred meters long and thirty meters wide. With the blast shields withdrawn, it provided onlookers with an unparalleled vista of the Alpha Quadrant stars up in space, like bright jewels.

Spacers belonged to the stars.

Naero did pace back and forth down the middle of that long, open chamber. She glanced up into the Unknown Sectors where she had lost her parents.

She and Khai were back once more in the Alpha Quadrant, sliding peacefully beneath more familiar stars, on their way to an important conference between the Alliance and the Gigacorps.

The war in the Gamma Quadrant had finally backed off considerably, after more setbacks for the enemy.

The enemy retreat and cessation of hostilities gave many a chance to make the return trip. They had arrived none too soon.

Back home, trouble was brewing big time in the Gigacorps Sectors. The Corps were making a concerted attempt to re-instate their dominance once more over lander humanity. The landers resisted bitterly, especially after what happened to many of them during the Ejjai Invasion and the High Crusade.

It had been the Spacer Alliance, not the Corps, who had saved them from the vile Ejjai invaders. While the Corps had unwittingly invited the rapacious Ejjai and their alien overlords among their worlds in the first place. So many trillions paid the price for that stupid miscalculation.

Yet in the present, the Corps were not yet ready or willing to be diminished and surrender all of their power.

High tensions could very well lead to countless, intense civil wars in many regions that might cripple lander humanity for decades, if not centuries to come.

For all of humanity, it would be a self-inflicted disaster that they could ill-afford.

There were far greater problems looming large out there on their galaxy's horizon, and very few persons besides Naero knew exactly what they were, and had stared them in the face.

In the next galaxy over, their advanced alien enemies had already amassed an Armada, an enormous invasion fleet. They lacked only a way to cross over the vast distance between the two galaxies.

One attempt to do so had already been foiled.

There would no doubt be others. The enemy would eventually find another way. They always did.

Even more frightening than that, Naero had literally gazed into the Abyss of Desolation, and issued her challenge. And the Abyss had answered that challenge and swarmed straight back, nearly destroying her.

She had witnessed firsthand many fell things that were as yet, much stronger and more powerful than herself. She had barely been saved from their clutches, and the gateway to that grim prison dimension was destroyed and sealed shut.

But for how long?

For the first time in her young life, Naero questioned her own strength, and wasn't quite sure what she might do next.

How could she combat all of these multiple threats, these legendary beings, monsters, and powers–Destroyers who stood greater than herself?

Naero needed to get stronger, but how?

The faces of her family, her husband, her beloved children, Jan and his two wives, Baeven and Jia and their crew, Aunt Sleak, Zalvano, and the their kids, her friends, her Clans flashed before her.

If she fell. If she perished…it was certain that most, if not all of them would die next, defending themselves and the same things they all loved as best they could.

From what Naero foresaw in her dreams and visions, eventually she was going to come up against one of these super lethal threats on her own, unprepared, and she was going to die.

She had been plagued by strange dreams and nightmares for a long while. Most recently, almost every one of her dreams was about her fighting in various places, always against sinister and considerable threats.

In almost all of these dark dreams, she went down fighting to the end, but that did not matter.

She perished, nonetheless. Dead was dead. And her death doomed all of the people she loved and fought to protect to face destruction without her thereafter.

A few of dreams still remained where she became a monster herself, just another of the deadly threats her friends and allies would face. She couldn't handle watching herself spin out of control, and murder those she loved with her own hands.

That dire possibility remained as well. A part of her was still potentially her own worst enemy. She must also stay on guard against that.

Thus, what could be done in the end? What could she do?

Om finally commented, the Kexxian Data Matrix entity embedded deep within her own mind.

Naero, some have long suggested that you take time to finish your Spacer Mystic training. You have never finished exploring the full range of your abilities, or the extent of your sources of power. Perhaps that is a proper place to begin.

Thanks, Om. I've thought about that too. Perhaps it is time for me to do just that. The High Masters and even Baeven and Jan finished their training. They both have told me that I remain out of balance, not in harmony with myself or my abilities–or the universe for that matter. But this isn't the best of times to do so.

There is never a good time to pull back and train, or meditate and seek enlightenment. Yet doing so has always benefitted you immensely. You have always emerged far stronger, wiser, and self-aware.

Om, the dangers remain all around me, circling like baevens to pick my bones clean. And there are also many dangers in training as well. What if I don't make it back?

You face dangers whatever you choose to do, N. You might as well pick which dangers, threats, and challenges you will confront first.

That sounds right, but how can I leave my children? Khai?

Even if you choose to do nothing, eventually, you will be forced to leave them one way or another, and by death for certain. You and Khai have taken time to start your family. Next, your primary goal is to grow stronger and more skilled, so that you can defend them and yourself better. At least Mystic training offers you that possibility. Strive to become whatever it is that you can be.

You're right, Om. I think that is the path I need to follow. I'll talk it over with Khai ASAP. Spacer Intel and the Mystics have hinted that they have many missions that the Mystic Enforcer must see to. We can stand to be apart for a time.

Naero, do not forget. We still have much work to do with deciphering and mastering the Kexxian Data Matrix. Those efforts must continue also.

I agree, Om. But no one can help us with that. We'll have to tackle all of the KDM as we go along.

Our enemies are never going to wait for us, in any case, N.

I know that very well, Om. We can only do what we can, and that will have to be enough.

Naero was definitely more focused and determined now that she had hashed things out; she was going to find a way to keep pushing forward.

Even if there was no guarantee that she would ever make it back to hold her children in her arms again.

Everything in life entailed some degree of risk.

Doing nothing would solve and prevent nothing.

*

The large nanosparring room was like a small arena and rang with the sounds of fighting and laughter.

A two-year-old Spacer child all but flew and zipped and wheeled through the air as if she were made of white flame.

Her long, blazing white-gold hair was pulled up in a high ponytail with an antique, golden hair clip, Spacer battle style. Her radiant hair matched her ivory skin and set off her dazzling blue eyes–as blue as pulsars.

She punched and kicked and snapped combinations lightning fast, driving back even the large green Mystic Enforcer who was her father. Her tiny blows from her small fists and feet cracked and struck with force. She flattened Khai and put him on his back.

Shetharra Lythe Maeris planted one small foot on his large green chest, clenched her little fists, threw back her head and shouted her cry of victory.

Then her father scooped her up and they wrestled together, as he tickled her into submission, made raspberries on her little belly, and they continue to laugh. The tiny spacechild squealed with joy.

Naero could not resist, and came down to wrap her arms around both of them on the practice floor. She kissed her daughter, and then her husband, looking into his golden eyes as they all smiled together.

Their small daughter kissed Khai, and then her mother.

"Mommy, I beat Daddy again. I want to fight you again now. Please, please?"

Naero hugged her and patted her on the back, regaining her feet and holding her close. "No, practice is way over for today, my little duck. It's way past time for your nap. Come on, Shetharra."

Shetharra rubbed her eyes with a tiny fist. "Don't need a nap," she protested. Then she yawned.

Naero held her close and kissed her daughter's head. Khai followed after them.

"Will you sing to me, Mommy?" Shetharra asked.

"I always do, don't I? I will always sing to you, my sweet girl."

"Yes. But sometimes Daddy sings to me, and sometimes Aunt Sharrah, when you aren't there. She sounds a lot like you."

"They like to sing to you, too, Little Duck."

"Quack-quack!" she said, followed by giggles. "I know…I want you all to sing to me."

"Sometimes we can," Naero said.

5

Khai and Naero brought Shetharra back to their quarters to put her down for her nap.

Naero made the mistake of putting her child on her feet. Shetharra squealed and ran up to the secured statue of the knife fighting girl.

"Hello, sister!" Shetharra jumped up and planted a kiss on the statue's face. Then she ran giggling from her father, who chased her around the room.

"Shetharra, quit running around and come take your mist shower," Naero said.

The child peeled out of her togs and came running to her mother naked and laughing, and leaped into Naero's arms.

Naero bathed her child quickly and then combed and brushed her long, glittering white hair.

Khai assisted where he could.

Naero teknomanced little togs back on her daughter and pweaked the presets to soft, white pajamas with twinkling holographic pink stars and the Maeris Clan logo on them. The stars faded on their own.

"I wanna sleep naked like you and Daddy, Mommy. I don't like to wear clothes."

Mommy and Daddy smirked at each other and rolled their eyes.

"Mommy and Daddy wear clothes now, Little Duck. So you need to wear clothes too."

"Aww…"

She laid down beside her daughter on the big nanobed, with the little nanobed right next to it. Khai got in on the other side, smiling at them.

"What shall we sing today, Shetharra?"

The little girl giggled, wiggled, whispered, and turned over on her belly, kicking her little feet. "The one little duck."

Naero rubbed her tiny back and began to sing softly. Then she made her first three fingers walk slowly up Shetharra's spine.

One after another, the little ducks went out to play, over the hills and far away.

When Mother Duck quacked, fewer and fewer ducks came back

Shetharra began to laugh and scream in anticipation.

Then Mother Duck quacked really loud, and all of the little ducks hurried back.

Naero used three fingers walking across, "The third little duck…"

Then two fingers walking, "The second little duck…"

Shetharra howled, "No, no! Not the one little duck!"

And finally one finger walked, and poked, and tickled unmercifully. "And the one little duck!"

A few short minutes later, Shetharra breathed easily, deep in sleep.

Naero brushed her daughter's glowing white hair from her angelic face, just enjoying gazing at her little star. Then she glanced at Khai who watched both of them very intently. "Go ahead and move her to her bed, sweetie,' she told him. "You never seem to wake her."

Khai scooped his daughter up in his big hands. He carried her over as gently as could be, and tucked her into the child's small nanobed. He and Naero both kissed their first child.

Four small female guardian Shai softly approached, and took up their positions around the bed, glowing pink and almost white with the deep love they felt for their Spacer family. The mantid warriors looked small, not much bigger than the child herself.

But woe unto anyone or anything outside the family who approached their little girl without permission.

Khai called to them. "Krin, Mizha, Jintil, Ethra–you're on duty."

They all nodded their mantid heads. Sometimes Shetharra slept with her parents in their quarters, on other nights she stayed in the nursery, the next room across the corridor.

Naero sighed and leaned her head against Khai. He wrapped a big green arm around her.

"Now let's go check on the twins," Naero said.

They crossed over through the corridor, leading to the quarters across the way. There in the nursery was their nanny, Naero-3. She had now taken the name Sharrah, had long, dark brown hair and lavender eyes. She also nursed the oldest of the twins, Daeyen Wallace Williams, who was three months old, only a few hours older than Kathron Zhentisa Maeris, his sister.

They talked about the kids for a bit. Everyone seemed to be doing fine.

Sharrah had an assistant nanny, Kyra Apache, plus another set of four Shai guards, stationed in the four corners.

When Naero and Khai hesitated and looked at the floor, Sharrah came out and asked them straight. "All right, just come out and say it. Are both of you leaving this time, or just one? I don't mind. I just want to know. And while you're at it, please tell me how soon you need to leave, and how long you'll be away this time."

Naero sighed heavily and a sick look washed over her face. "That's the problem, Sharrah...we don't know if we'll be coming back this time."

Sharrah rolled her eyes. "Yeah, you guys always get misty and say some crap like that. But then you sneak back for a while and the whole

7

process begins all over again. Eventually, one or both of you is needed somewhere. I'm surprised you were able to stay away on leave this long."

Khai hugged her and kissed her on the cheek. "You are the very best, Sharrah. We couldn't do anything without knowing that you have everything well in hand back here at home."

She pushed him away, laughing. "Yeah, yeah. The both of you always tell me that as well."

Naero hugged her like the sisters they had become. "We only say that because it is true."

Sharrah smiled. "I do love my work. You needn't worry. Kyra and I and the pink ladies of the Shai will see to them. Uncle Jan and his wives come by to see the girls regularly. So do Great Aunt Sleak, Zalvano, Tyber, and all the rest. You should see how big little Gallan is getting. Shetharra just loves him so. They play so well together. Go on then. Save the galaxy as you do. Things will be just fine here."

Naero and Khai said their great thanks a final time.

2

The conference negotiations with the Gigacorps were being held on Rillian-4. All fifteen of the Gigacorps, including Joshua Tech, had high level emissaries there, along with many representatives and delegations from many important regions, sectors, and worlds.

Khai had departed that morning to take counsel with the Mystics.

Naero was happy to be reunited with her good friends and family, Lady Shalaen of the Yattai, and Tarim of Fleet Maeris Security. When the three of them were together, it seemed as if they never stopped laughing and hugging each other. But they had to be sober during the negotiations.

These meetings were incredibly serious and important.

At present, the Gigacorps were bent on reclaiming their right to enforce and bring back their ironclad tyranny on the lander worlds of humanity.

The Alliance argued that they had forfeited those rights and all claims to authority and dominion when they blindly unleashed a hyper-violent, uplifted alien species and other alien enemies upon humanity–which came close to wiping out said humanity.

And although their lackeys and slaves had been defeated, those alien masters still lurked out there somewhere in the galaxy and beyond, poised and planning to renew their attack on humanity and restart the grim wars all over again.

As usual, the Gigacorps lined up their goons and lackeys to make their threats and spew their ridiculous lies, denials, and delusions.

Jibben Denlevy of Stellar Corps: "Left to themselves, these reeling worlds are once again falling into the expected and predicted chaos of local planetary and mob rule. The Corps only wish to restore proper order!"

Admiral Nathan Joshua responded. "All troubles created and exacerbated by offworld Corps agents, thugs, and agitators sent down to those worlds to cause just such problems to erupt, as a pretense and an excuse for the Corps militaries to launched brutal subjugation campaigns against their own populations. Populations who have seen fit to reject and defy Corps dominion and enslavement. We have hundreds of hours of vid proof and confessions to prove every one of these accusations many times over."

Mya Gringold of Chikara Corp. "The human worlds are lost without the divine guidance of the benevolent Gigacorps and their mastery at management and solid economic structures. Only rebels, revolutionary radicals, and deluded fools are resisting the reinstatement of Gigacorps power, driven by outside influences who want these worlds for themselves. These worlds must be pacified, and re-educated in order to return them into the fold of associates. The Alliance has no right to take them."

Aneko Kimura piled in, before a response could be made. "The truth is that the Gigacorps worlds are lost without Corps control and management governance. The populations of these worlds are screaming and begging for the gentle, unseen hands of the Corps to return with their control, their guidance, and wisdom to make these worlds profitable again within the Gigacorps sphere of influence, and law and order. Order will be restored once again, at all costs, against rebels, rioters, and hooligans of every stripe, both local and invaders. The Alliance and their spack backers need to back off. This is none of their affair. We own these systems and their populations."

Nathan Joshua rose up. "That is an utter fabrication and a lie. Independent Webnet polls show that by far, the human worlds demand local autonomy and an end to the harsh, arbitrary strictures of Gigacorp subjugation and the defacto seizure of virtually all wealth and resources on such worlds."

The Gigacorps emissaries blinked in abject horror.

Trennen Gormen of Krupp Corps responded in stunned disbelief. "But as we have proven, we own these worlds and their populations. They are ours. How can our property be denied us? This is wrong. Their resources and profit and wealth structures are ours to manage as we see fit. Such is our due for the benevolent management of these worlds, who would be lost without our wisdom and our guidance. These people cannot effectively and efficiently do all of these complex things on their own. They are like the cattle of Old Earth, and we but herd them as best we may."

"That is exactly the point," Carrie Sommers of Gelden Corps stressed. "By what right does the Alliance or any of these persons presume to dictate to us, the owners, what should be done with our property? We do not answer to any of you or them. The owned do not have any right to question the owners or deny the owners any of their sacred rights of ownership and control. This is against all of our most sacred, cherished beliefs. By what right do you force us to give up our rights and beliefs?"

Nathan Joshua grew insistent. "We can argue these follies until the stars go out. But hear this declaration: From this point forward, the Alliance and the humanity of the human worlds declare openly and emphatically that by the Rights of Sentient Liberty, no sentient being can be held as property."

Trennen Gormen of Krupp Corps laughed. "As illegal and impossible as that is, then the Gigacorporations will still have ownership and control over these physical worlds, their wealth systems, and all of their physical property."

He smiled knowingly. "And quite soon, without ownerships access to habitation, or even to air, water, and sustenence, the ignorant, human cattle will quickly capitulate to the old ways, and freely contract themselves and their children to become willing associates to the Gigacorporations once again, in perpetuity. And once those contracts are renewed, they can never be broken, and things can get back to normal. A normal that is inevitable."

"Wrong," Joshua stated. "The Time of Corporate Dominion and Tyranny is at an end, whether you like it or not—whether you admit or not. The bulk of humanity are not cattle, as you claim. And no longer shall defacto, Gigacorporate Aristocracy, in any of its forms, be allowed to use contracts to force free beings to enslave themselves or exist in perpetual slavery. Under the explicit laws of the Rights of Sentient Liberty, any such contracts are automatically null and void, wherever they exist or are found, into the future, while humanity and sentients exist in our galaxy!"

A groan of disbelief and shock rose up from the Gigacorp delegations.

"Blasphemy!"

"Sacrilege!"

Joshua gripped the table with both hands and leaned forward, continuing to speak calmly and rationally. "I repeat, corporations are a business structure, not a dogma, religion, or cult. So, tell me then; tell us all. How will the Gigacorps respond to a world such as Lyrion-5, who have openly declared and established a democratic republic after the Ejjai invasion? How exactly will the Corps go about reinstating their rights?"

"That is easy for any sovereign state to answer. If rebellious worlds to the legal and benevolent Gigacorporate authority are not willingly re-established, then such worlds shall be pacified to an acceptable level."

Nathan Joshua folded his arms in front of them all, standing defiant. "Pacification sounds like such a harmless word, ambassador. Come now, enough Corps doublespeak. Isn't pacification code for military assault and subjugation by force–to the point of death and slaughter?"

"The Gigacorps are well within their rights as legal governing, sovereign authorities. Defiant rebels who will not bow to reason must be dealt with and reduced to proper, manageable levels for the good of the population of each world."

"So, ambassador, at last were getting to the point. When you say reduce, you mean kill. And what percentage of the population of each world is it acceptable for the Corps to kill–for the good of the people of each world?"

"An acceptable percentage of reduction, I assure you, all for the good of the population to bring them to see reason and accept Gigacorporate will and rule once again. All for their own good."

"Ambassador," Joshua said, "we actually have that percentage of acceptable reduction planned by your military. We intercepted those orders and decoded them as they were being transmitted. In fact, it is eighty-seven percent. Let us make this clear to the entire galaxy, and to all of the worlds threatened with such 'reduction.' The Gigacorps, in their gracious benevolence, are fully prepared to kill off eighty-seven percent of the population of any world that resists their tyranny, and their naked aggression. That is nearly nine out of ten of every person living on these worlds! Even the Ejjai could not kill so many."

"Admiral Joshua, you are clearly twisting the facts. In most cases, it is believed that these worlds will surrender to reason after only a forty or fifty percent reduction. Then everything can go back to the way things were. Back to being normal. We think it will be a small price to pay, and give us a chance to weed out any other troublesome elements on our worlds, such as the impaired, and those who are too old to be of use. Our populations will be left docile and obedient after a good culling of any troublemakers and undesirables."

Joshua knitted his hands together, after bowing his head. "You blithering, fanatical quisling. You vapid, horrific, mouthpiece. Do you not even have the wit to see that this is exactly one of the worst forms of tyranny ever exposed, that must not only be confronted and exposed, but also destroyed?"

The ambassador huffed. "How you continue to twist our logic. It is not tyranny if the cattle are forced to see reason, and willingly agree to contract themselves and their offspring to us!"

"No! It is exactly the worst kind of tyranny if that is the only logical choice you allow them, in order to stay alive–after killing half or more of them off!"

"That's not our problem. If they agree to such a contract, then they are bound to it once they do so. A contract is the law! The basis of all law. Is the Alliance against the rule of law now as well?"

"You want a legal excuse to subjugate and exploit humanity forever."

"As is our right! We keep telling you, it is not exploitation if the cattle agree to it. That is freedom for all! It is a freedom that all must be forced to admit, accept, and agree to. Are you against freedom now?"

Joshua persisted. "Freedom does not give the Corps or anyone the right to enslave others by convenient legalism and corporate doublespeak, allowing populations of world after world no other viable choice. That is the worst license and sophistry ever created.

"That is precisely why the perverse and twisted law that you adhere to is now declared null and void by the very humanity you seek to enslave by it. In fact, the entire sick and oppressive corporate structure as upheld and envisioned by the Corps is now entirely defunct, and expressly illegal across all of these worlds. They are now declared free of Gigacorps law and rule. Forever!"

Corps people leaped to their feet and actually screamed and howled.

Nathan Joshua stood tall, behind powerful shields as debris and garbage showered the location where he stood.

He persisted, despite the near riot.

"The corporation was never meant or intended to be warped and twisted into a system of interplanetary governance or religion. It was an economic structure, developed to focus on managing profitability for a business. It was never meant to me fashioned into a gigantic system to rule over all of humanity, and deny them their liberty or freedom forever and ever."

Jibben Dunlevy shook his fists defiantly. "The cattle would be nothing without us! They cannot govern themselves or properly direct their economic or other affairs. Where will they be without us to manage everything for them? We are the best of them! We are the achievers. The leaders deserve to own and control everything!"

Joshua shook his head. "Not any more. The fact is, given a choice, the people of nearly every world reject the Gigacorporations and their tyranny wholesale. And humanity does not need parasite corporations; such corporations need humanity as their hosts to feed off of.

"There are proven forms of human governance that work, such as the democratic republic, that actively suppresses Tyranny. Joshua Tech uses corporate structures to form sustainable economies for all, not just a few. We have proven that it can be done. If a system can be rigged against humanity, then it can also be rigged to work for humanity."

"Die, blasphemer!" A chair bounce off the shield, just as several shots rang out from the Gigacorps delegation. A delegation that was supposed to be unarmed.

Naero had stood by too long as it was, scanning the Corps people and studying them carefully. Now her plan of action was clear.

She used the voice.

"ENOUGH!"

That single word was both a sonic and mental attack. Naero used it to partially stagger, stun, and disorient the Gigacorps delegation, almost a hundred in number.

Next, she reduced the weapons they brandished to dust and rose up in her Shetanna guise.

The vidstreams were still broadcasting the event across the entire Webnet for everyone on every world to watch.

She transfixed nearly a hundred corps people in glowing pods of scarlet Chaos energy, holding them still, doing them no harm as yet.

She used her gravwing and rose up above them in full-on Shetanna mode, blazing blood-red energy katanas. "THIS IS A DAY OF LIBERTY FOR ALL OF HUMANITY. THE POWER OF THE GIGACORPORATIONS HAS BEEN BROKEN, EXPOSING THEM FOR THE TYRANTS AND MALIGNANTS THAT WE HAVE ALWAYS KNOWN THEM TO BE. THE TIME OF THEIR SICK, DELUDED CULT OF GREED IS OVER. BUT LET US SEE THEM AS THEY REALLY ARE. HOW MANY OF THEM ARE EVEN HUMAN STILL?"

Half of the pods rose up in the air.

Naero put forth her Cosmic energies, causing them to writhe, transform, and expose them for what many of them actually were–advanced alien symbiot agents, posing as Corps delegates and leaders.

People everywhere screamed in horror.

Naero's voice rang out. "THE GIGACORPS MADE THEIR DEALS WITH THESE DEVILS AND INFLICTED THEM UPON HUMANITY! HOW MANY

HUMAN WORLDS SUFFERED FROM THE ALIEN INVASIONS AND HAD THEIR CHILDREN FLUNG SCREAMING INTO THE SPINNING BLADES OF THE EJJAI MEAT SHIPS?"

Viewscreens showed feeds from hundreds of important lander homeworlds

Scores of Shetanna's replicants hovered over the gigacities, exposing the alien symbiot shapeshifters who had infiltrated the Gigacorps leaderships and power structures.

People on those worlds chased the horrid, alien things out into the streets and cornered them for all to see.

"THE AUTHORITY OF THE CORPS HAS BEEN COMPLETELY INVALIDATED, FOR THE SIMPLE FACT THAT MANY OF THEM ARE NO LONGER HUMAN. THEY ARE ENEMY ALIEN AGENTS, SHAPESHIFTERS WHO HAVE INFILTRATED THE CORPS AT THE HIGHEST LEVELS, IN ORDER TO PIT ALL HUMANITY AGAINST ITSELF. THEY WANT US TO WASTE TIME FIGHTING EACH OTHER, WHILE THEY PLOT TO DESTROY US AND ENSLAVE WHAT IS LEFT!"

On the vidscreens and in those streets, masses of people swept over the exposed aliens and dragged them down. Many of those people recalled the grim losses they had suffered during the Ejjai Invasions.

Now they wanted vengeance.

Shetanna sent her swords away and continued to speak. "AND WHEN YOUR WORLDS WERE SHATTERED AND WITHOUT HOPE, AND THE FILTHY EJJAI MURDERERS STALKED YOUR STREETS AND HUNTED YOU AND YOUR FAMILIES AT WILL, WHO WAS IT THAT CAME TO YOUR AID WHEN YOU HAD NO HOPE, AND CRUSHED THE INVADERS IN THE DARKNESS? WAS IT THE GIGACORPS?"

She pointed an accusing finger straight at the Corps. Lackeys.

Crowds and massed throngs all over the Alpha Quadrant roared in answer. "No!"

"YOU'RE DAMN RIGHT IT WASN'T. DESPITE ALL THAT YOU HAD BEEN TAUGHT TO HATE THEM, DESPITE A CORPS PLOT TO DESTROY THEM, IT WAS IN FACT THE FORTY-NINE FREE SPACER CLANS AND THEIR FORCES WHO DROPPED EVERYTHING AND CAME TO YOUR DEFENSE, BLED AND DIED FOR YOU, AND SAVED YOU FROM OUR MUTUAL ALIEN ENEMIES. VALIANT SPACER FLEETS ROARED IN AND BLASTED THE ALIEN FLEETS TO DUST. COURAGEOUS, UNSTOPPABLE SPACER MARINES HOPPED FROM WORLD TO WORLD, OBLITERATING THE INVADERS WHEREVER THEY COULD BE FOUND. AND THEN THEY LEFT, TO DO IT ALL OVER AGAIN ON ANOTHER WORLD. SPACERS WERE YOUR CHAMPIONS, HUMANITY."

Across the known worlds, billions of people took up the chant.

Shetanna! Shetanna! Shetanna!

Naero raised both her hands to speak again. "No, SHETANNA WAS THERE, BUT SHE WAS ONLY A SMALL PART OF THAT GREAT VICTORY. WITHOUT THE FREE SPACER CLANS BACKING HER UP, AND LEADING THE BULK OF THE FIGHT, THAT VICTORY WOULD NOT HAVE COME. AND TELL ME THIS. DID THE SPACERS COME TO YOUR WORLD AS CONQUERORS, OR LIBERATORS? SHOW ME ONE OF YOUR WORLDS WHERE SPACERS CAME AND DID NOT LEAVE—WHERE THEY ACTED THE TYRANT AND TOOK OVER EVEN ONE OF YOUR WORLDS?

"IT CANNOT BE SAID OR DONE, BECAUSE IT NEVER HAPPENED, EVER. SPACERS BELIEVE IN FREEDOM. IN LIBERTY. YOUR WORLDS BELONG TO YOU, AND IT IS UP TO YOU TO GOVERN AND GUIDE THEM AT THE LOCAL LEVEL. HUMANITY AND ALL OF THE OTHER SENTIENTS IN OUR GALAXY ARE FREE TO MANAGE THEIR OWN AFFAIRS. AND THERE IS NO LONGER ANY NEED FOR THE TYRANNY OF THE CORPS TO CONTROL YOU. IT IS ALL OBSOLETE. ESPECIALLY NOW, SINCE MANY OF THEM HAVE BEEN EXPOSED AS BEING INFESTED BY AGENTS OF OUR MUTUAL, ALIEN ENEMIES. THE CORPS HAVE BEEN COMPROMISED. THEY CANNOT BE TRUSTED."

Waves of cheering erupted. Naero had to wait for it to die down.

"THE ALLIANCE OF FREE WORLDS STANDS READY TO BOTH HELP AND PROTECT. IF YOU AND YOUR WORLDS WISH FOR A BETTER LIFE FOR ALL OF YOUR PEOPLES, WE WILL SHOW IT TO YOU. WE CAN SHOW YOU WORLDS WHERE SUCH THINGS ARE BEING ACCOMPLISHED THIS VERY SECOND. NO PERFECTION OR UTOPIA, BUT GOOD SYSTEMS THAT WORK WELL, AND HAVE PROVEN TO BE SUSTAINABLE. THESE THINGS CAN AND DO EXIST, IF GOOD PEOPLE FOCUS THEIR EFFORTS ON WORKING TOGETHER TO MAKE THEM SO. ANYTHING CAN BE MADE NOT TO WORK IF PEOPLE TRY HARD ENOUGH. THAT IS FOLLY AND STUPIDITY. THE CORPS NEVER ALLOWED ANY OTHER SYSTEM BUT THEIR OWN. THERE ARE OTHER WAYS THAT WORK FAR BETTER, FOR EVERYONE."

More applause and cheering.

"YOU ARE FREE TO JOIN THE ALLIANCE, OR NOT JOIN THE ALLIANCE. THE ONLY THING THAT WILL NOT BE ALLOWED IS FOR THE ARBITRARY AND INSANE TYRANNY OF THE GIGACORPS EXTREMISM TO CONTINUE TO SHACKLE HUMANITY AND HOLD IT BACK. THAT IS NOW ILLEGAL. NEVER AGAIN WILL THEY DOMINATE AND ENSLAVE OTHERS AS THEY ONCE DID. HUMANITY IS NOW FREE TO TRULY FACE THE CHALLENGES OF THE FUTURE. BUT WE MUST REMAIN CAUTIOUS AND VIGILANT.

"AS WE HAVE ALL WITNESSED, WE HAVE CUNNING ALIEN ENEMIES WHO ARE STILL OUT THERE IN DEPTHS OF SPACE AND EVEN LURKING IN OTHER DIMENSIONS, HI-TEK FOES WHO CONSTANTLY PLOT OUR DEFEAT

AND DESTRUCTION. IF HUMANITY IS GOING TO SURVIVE SUCH THREATS, THEY MUST LEARN TO WORK AND STAND TOGETHER IN THE DEFENSE OF THIS GALAXY AS NEVER BEFORE! THESE MONSTERS HAVE CLEARLY INFILTRATED OUR WORLDS AND OUR LEADERS, BUT NOW WE HAVE THE MEANS TO EXPOSE AND TAKE THEM OUT. WE WILL NOT ALLOW THESE ENEMIES TO MANIPULATE AND DESTROY US FROM WITHIN!"

Another round of tumultuous cheering erupted.

"IF WE STAND TOGETHER, AND CONTINUE TO ALLY OURSELVES WITH OTHER SENTIENT RACES WHO RESPECT AND HONOR FREEDOM, WE CAN RISE TO THE CHALLENGE AND FACE THE THREATS AND POSSIBILITIES THAT THE FUTURE WILL BRING TOGETHER. WE CAN EXPLORE OUR GALAXY AND EVENTUALLY BRING FREEDOM, REASON, AND PEACE TO EVERY PART OF IT!"

She shook both of her fists in a gesture of triumph and challenge.

"LIVE FREE OR DIE, HUMANITY!"

With that, Shetanna turned and swept away, floating the remaining captured shapeshifters along with her to turn them over to Spacer Intel for questioning or eradication and further study.

Cheering and celebration continued over multitudes of liberated worlds, now basking in the uncertain glow of new freedom.

Naero knew full well that the declaration of liberty was just the easy part up front. Taking responsibility for one's freedom and managing and sustaining liberty for planet after planet was going to be the hard part.

Doing so might take generations.

But at least now, humanity had the opportunity to do so.

With the delegation completed, Naero would contact the Spacer Mystics. She had already spoken to Khai before he left, and he was in full agreement and support with her decision.

She had put these things off far too long.

Naero checked in with Khai, and then with Sharrah. Fleet-1 happened to be one sector over by coincidence, but Naero wasn't planning on going back. Just a daily call to see the kids and everyone.

While she and Sharrah were catching up, the alert warning erupted in the nursery.

"What is it, Sharrah. What's happening?" Naero demand.

Sharrah remained calm, checking with the bridge and ship security. "I have to go Naero. We're under heavy attack. Enemy phaze teams are boarding us. Get here if you can! We're going to be all right."

Sharrah pweaked her combat armor up, drew a blaster, and summoned a blazing katana with a purple energy blade in her other hand.

Then enemy jamming cut off the link.

Naero instantly phazed into battle mode herself and sealed up.

She contacted Khai and told him to get to the flagship if possible.

She left a message for Ty through Alala and Om, and then they transported out into space. Naero startapped until she was topped off with Cosmic energy.

From there she focused, got a lock on *The Holy Ghost*, and transported directly to it.

Fleet-1 was engaged and fully involved in heavy combat against ten alien fleets. Naero's Fleets-3, 4, and 5 busied themselves carving up the invaders and waiting for reinforcements on their way.

But the flagship was covered with enemy stealth and phazed boarding craft that now showed themselves and who troops penetrated the ship proper to duke it out with the crew.

Starfighters blasted off the boarding vessels, like removing ticks from a hound, but by then it was too late. The enemy boarding teams had already inserted.

Clearly this was a suicide mission trying to take out Naero's family, once she and Khai were gone.

The largest concentration of boarding craft were clustered closest to the flagship's nursery.

Naero and Om analyzed the situation, noting where the highest concentration of foes were.

Of course, they were on all sides of the nursery, fighting with the crew response teams, ship's troops, and doing everything they could to break into the nursery itself.

At one key point they were about to do just that.

Naero ignited her swords and transported straight in.

3

The first thing Naero and Om noticed as she sliced through the initial dozen or so assassins with her blades was that these were not the same, freeze-pop Ejjai shock troops.

These were second generation, enhance killers, larger, faster, and stronger. Even smarter, dare she say it. They weren't as stupid as regular Ejjai and they thought and performed with greater military and tactical discipline and precision.

Explosions rocked the nursery and the flagship up ahead. Naero nearly panicked.

She raced in.

Anything that looked like an enemy she exploded with Cosmic force, nearly reducing them to ash, whether they were moving or not.

She was not fooling around.

Naero, fifty three enemy dead. They resorted to suicide fusion bombs, taking out most of the nursery blast shields, chambers, and themselves in an attempt to gain entry.

Where are my kids Om? Fuck these slashers. Cut to the chase. Are my babies all right? Because I'm about to lose it.

Stay calm. Everyone's fine, for the moment. Sharrah transported herself, the kids, and the entire staff into the large greenhouse and hydroponics chamber in the adjacent green zone. But the enemy is tracking them somehow, after the explosions, and giving chase. I count three hundred and twelve enemy boarders closing in from several directions, including heavy meks and flying gunsuits. Response teams engaging from the other ends.

Naero transported into the greenhouse and saw Sharrah and the staff using a shield generator to protect themselves and hold the enemy off.

They were already under fire from multiple enemy incoming, smashing their way through the plant pods and decorative trees and flowers.

Gunsuits opened up with autoguns.

Naero incinerated twenty three of them in seconds

Then she impaled all of the meks on Cosmic energy rods and caused them to implode, reduced to hyper-dense balls of hot scrap.

Another corridor blast shield door exploded off its hinges, and more foes poured in.

Little Shetharra stood up and extended both hands. Here glowing hair became so radiant that it was blinding.

A beam of white hot force as wide as she was tall arced through the room, destroying everything in its path.

The beam went straight down the corridor packed with assassins, and annihilated them, blasting what little remained of them straight through several bulkheads and out past the ruptured hull of the flagship.

When the squad level shield generator disrupted, Sharrah stepped in defiantly, shielding them all with her own energies.

The raw firepower smashing into her shields continued to build.

Little Shetharra stepped in front of Aunt Sharrah, and the shield instantly pulsed and became completely impenetrable.

Naero raced down the middle of the attackers, gutting them, exploding their heads as she passed through them with her swords extended.

From the corner of her eye, Naero saw several small things scuttling through the greenery of the chamber at high speed.

Eight Shai mantids suddenly rose up behind the packed flanks of foes, foes concentrating on firing their weapons or hurling bombs at their targets. The Shai warriors towered twelve meters in the air, and their mood colors had switched to near jet black with fury and rage.

The enemy was in for a very harsh surprise.

Naero focus on transporting and phazing bombs and grenades outside into space, beyond the ship.

She grinned, knowing full well what was about to happen.

The Shai mantid warriors hit the enemy and sliced through the attackers faster than the spinning blades of an Ejjai meatship. They literally mowed them down like a buzz saw passing through a field of wheat.

A wounded attacker rose up behind Naero and tried to set off a huge fusion charge on its back.

Kyra Apache leaped on the monster, a blazing blue energy blade in each hand. First she sliced off its arms, then she leaped into the air and severed its head with both blades slashing in opposite directions.

Her war cry echoed throughout the chamber.

She wheeled and kicked the enemy corpse away. It was over twice her height and mass, but it was also dead.

"Mommy!" Shetharra yelled.

Naero held up a hand and shouted. "Stay where you are until the ship is secure, sweetie. Stay with Sharrah." She floated in the air and opened her third eye.

She startapped and systematically hunted any other foes nearby with psyonics and exploded their heads, by the dozens.

They weren't getting any closer.

When she was satisfied that all of the nearby connecting decks were clear, she went over to hug her kids, and check with Sharrah and the staff.

Naero, the other ship battles are winding down. The Marines and the crew are quickly polishing the last pockets off. Reinforcements have arrived, and the remaining enemy warships are on fire, limping away.

Thanks Om. I want a full analysis of all of this new enemy gear, and their second gen slaves. We can't let them hit us the same way twice. When they adapt and try something new, we need to react and counter it quickly.

Already in process. They are continuing to radically adapt their tek to neutralize and get past ours. We'll try to stay ahead of them.

Naero heard some heavy crunching sounds around the greenhouse.

The Shai actually liked eating Ejjai, and helped clean up some of the mess on hand very quickly.

Then they resumed their smaller size, and gathered in protectively as well. Their mood color began to fade from blue to red violet, and then pink around their edges.

"No harm has come to our little ones?" Krin asked, her mandibles moving rapidly.

"Thanks to all of you," Naero said. She stepped forward and embraced each of the Shai mantids and planted a kiss on their heads. "many thanks to you, Krin, Mizha, Jintil, and Ethra." Naero kept going until she had thanked all of them by name, and gave them high praise.

All of the mantids bowed their heads and went from pink, almost to snow white. Each of them would have given their lives if need be, without question.

After that, Naero personally thanked Sharrah for her clever thinking and action, and brave Kyra and the rest of the staff.

Naero kissed her twins and the scooped up Shetharra in her arms. "You were very brave my little duck."

"Did I do good, Mommy? I couldn't let them hurt Sharrah or anyone. They were mean and scary. I had to stop them. You're not mad at me, are you?"

"You did very well, my sweet girl. I couldn't be prouder. Just, can you try not to punch holes in Mommy's nice new ship?"

"Okay, Mommy. I'll try not to do that."

Khai showed up seconds later, his face worried until he locked eyes with Naero. One look, and he knew things were all right. They didn't even need to exchange words.

Both of them worked with Om and the flagship's command staff in an effort to try and make sure that such a thing could not happen again. The outer hull and scanners were adapted, and special detector screens and onboard fixers were put in place to detect any kind of similar infiltration.

These protocols and new tek specs rapidly went out to the entire Alliance Navy.

Privately, both Naero and Khai were furious, and vented once they managed to be alone.

"They went after our family directly," Khai said, clenching his great fists, and hammering the hull until he dented it. "They clearly waited for us to leave before they struck."

Naero folded her arms in front of herself, experiencing a slow burn. "I'm so sick of reacting, just waiting for them to hit us again. We've lost track of them in the Gamma Quadrant, that's where their bases are. They've gone into hiding almost. We need to take the fight to them, and hunt down their leaders. Their slaves are pushovers without them."

Khai sat down and shook his head. "I'm worried about my father's people, the Oden. They've had to leave their homeworlds and go into hiding with the help of Intel and the Mystics. The enemy has a price on their heads, and are seizing Oden wherever they can attack and capture them. And we know all too well what they're being used for."

Naero sighed. "Of course, dammit. Hosts for the many varieties of the enemy's Darkforce generators, helping power the alien war machine and all of their vile plots. But we can't take them down if we can't find them."

"That's exactly what the Mystics want me to do–go hunting. But how can I? How can we go off and do anything while we're worried about something like this happening?"

"Don't worry. This time I'm leaving sixty of my best replicants to guard the Nursery in shifts. They can handle almost anything."

Khai let out a deep breath. "Well, I suppose that will do it. We'd better get going now that everything is under control. You don't want to be late for Master Tree. You know how he is about punctuality."

"Screw that anal tool bag. He can damn well wait after what we just went through!"

Khai burst out laughing.

Naero joined him the next second.

4

Naero kindly requested that Strike Captain Tyber, the living ship AI Alala, and *The Dark Star* to personally escort her to the Spacer Mystic Homeworld of Tae'ha.

A stealth ship should do the trick.

Alala and Om were great friends, and spent the entire time rapidly gabbing back and forth over many hi-tek, teknomancy matters through their networks of tiny spyfixers. They did so, so as not to bother Naero.

Naero suggested that the two AIs get a teknomancer room together somewhere.

Om got the joke and replied, *if only.*

Alala had no idea what they were babbling about, and perhaps that was a good thing.

But with Om busy and happy, that gave Naero days to catch up with and enjoy Tyber, and his and Zhen's young son Gallan, who was now four, going on five. Seeing the bright little boy almost made Naero cry, missing her two best friends from the past who had died well before their time.

More than that, Naero still had a promise to keep. Zhen's soul still resided within her, dormant, waiting for her to bring her friend back into existence somehow.

Thus far, such a way had eluded her.

He was never pushy abut it, but at some point, Ty would inquire, and she would tell him not yet.

Naero could do many amazing things, but the vast majority of the Lifespark's secrets of life and death still eluded her, and all other mortals.

Whenever she got the chance and the time was right, she sat little Gallan on her lap, and hugged and kissed him dearly, while the little boy laughed and giggled and hugged and kissed his Aunt Naero back.

Of course, she wasn't really his aunt exactly, but they always said that, just the same. I was what was in her heart that mattered.

Naero would tell him about his namesake, what a fine young man Gallan had been, how he was strong, and a loyal friend, and a brave Spacer warrior. How he was funny, how he liked to eat good food, and enjoy life with his friends. Naero told stories about all the trouble the two got into growing up.

Little Gallan surprised her by asking about his mom, Zhentisa. It should not have surprised her, but it did make her cry.

She showed him pics and vids of his pretty mother, and told him stories about her, how she, too, was the best of friends. And she was a healer, a great physician and surgeon who helped people. Even as a child Zhen had had a gift to heal things. When Naero and all of their crazy friends did something stupid and got hurt, Zhen was there with them, to patch them up and begin the healing process.

And even though she was not the greatest of warriors, she was still a fighter who believed in freedom, and stood by her friends and companions with undaunted bravery, until the very end.

When Naero cried, Gallan would wipe Aunt Naero's tears away and kiss her eyes as only a little loving boy could.

She savored dinner one night with Ty, Alala, and Jynel, Naero's replicant that she had stationed with Ty and his amazing ship to help advise and protect them.

Except for her same size, Jynel had altered her appearance as many of Naero's replicants chose to do. She had bright straight, shoulder-length orange hair with many shimmering highlights, cascading around her and halfway down her back, with green crystal eyes. Her skin was slightly darker and more tan.

Whenever Naero rejoined with one of her reps, she always upgraded them as much as possible, passing on any new powers or abilities that she could. She did so almost instantly when they embraced.

Naero could never pass on her greater Cosmic abilities, which always remained unique to her, yet many of her other powers and talents continued to grow, like her new ability to detect and expose the enemy shapeshifter symbiots. That was vital to pass on to the allies.

And just as Naero shared her memories since their last meeting, Jynel shared hers, like how she thoroughly enjoyed being a part of Ty and Alala's amazing crew, and her natural affection for little Gallan.

Naero smiled at her 'sister' as she had begun to think of them. "You know, you are always free to go off and live your own life, any time you want."

Jynel smiled. "Not a chance. This is my place, my ship and my crew. This is where I choose to be. Thank you, eldest sister. How I would love to see your and Khai's children again."

Naero spoke with her friends about their explorations, about their secret Intel missions hunting down the enemy.

They spoke of many things long into the evening.

Finally Ty caught her eye, and for once she saw his weariness.

"Any luck yet?" he asked her. It was a simple question, without pressure or demand. Ty remained grateful for what she had given them. He simply wanted to know.

Naero smiled and then sighed. "Not yet," she told him. "Sorry."

Ty would always drop the subject and then quickly move on to something else.

They spent five happy days together. Naero even took time to work out and spar with Ty, Jynel, and little Gallan, who loved all of the attention. Then he would go spiraling for hours with his little friends on board. What fun they had.

Even with their enhanced speed, they would reach Tae'ha on the sixth day. That was fine with Naero. She remained torn. Part of her wanted to get her Mystic training over and done with. Part of her still wanted to avoid it for some reason she could not fathom.

5

Tae'ha possessed two main continents, much like the hemispheres of the human brain. The slightly smaller continent, *Nama* was hi-tek and perfectly designed and organized. The slightly larger continent, *Aman*, was kept wild, natural, and untamed.

As a Mystic Homeworld, subject to the protections of the Time dilation Phazes, the planet had a small, highly advanced human and sentient population of only a hundred thousand.

As anyone might have guessed, the teks and mathematicians chose to reside on Nama, while the artists and other thinkers thrived living on Eden-like coasts of Aman. The vast, wild interior was kept pristine and uninhabited for Mystic training.

Naero would spend time finishing up her Order Wisdom training on both major land masses.

She was met at the Mystic starport on Nama by no one less that High Master Tree himself, a silver being in elegant blue robes, who seemed neither young nor old, stoic and wise.

Naero kept the anal tool bag thing to herself.

Yet Naero could also never forget that an enemy shapechanger symbiot had taken High Master Tree's place in the past, and nearly tricked her into allowing herself to be tried and executed by her own people.

Such things made a big impression Naero, and it was hard for her to forget.

Whenever she saw Master Tree again, she naturally scanned him with all of her abilities, to make certain that he was the real one.

"Yes, Prime Adept Maeris. I am the real Master Tree. Welcome. It is good that you have returned to us to complete your Mystic Training. Welcome. After you rest tonight, we can pick up right where we left off."

Naero forced a smile. "Grreat…"

"We've timed things so that you won't even have take part in the next Time Displacement cycle here on Tae'ha."

Naero blinked. "That was thoughtful. So how is this going to work?"

"Well, the training will be intensified, but you had all but completed the regimen as it was. With a few days of re-orientation, you'll spend one week on Nama, and then a final week on Aman. That should do it for Order Wisdom training. Then you're off to Master Jo on Oorrii. You'll be his problem then."

"I guess so."

"But on Oorrii," Master Tree said, "the Time Displacement will be unavoidable. To the outside universe, you will spend three months there, and yet within, three years will have passed by the time you depart."

"I understand, High Master."

Tree was accompanied by his two Prime Adepts, who acted as his bodyguards and aides. With Khai now busy serving as the Mystic Enforcer, Von Ramirez was still acting in the Prime Adept capacity, the young woman who literally glowed with intense blue energy in the Order Wisdom spectrum. They knew each other well enough to embrace and greet each other pleasantly. The second Prime Adept she knew somewhat– Raymon Cherokee.

Ray was one of the strongest Mystic telepaths ever known, who could use various mind tricks, psy-blasts, and sonic attacks in sparring and combat.

But they weren't friends yet, so Naero simply smiled at him, shook his hand, and made Mystic small talk.

Like all of the Mystic adepts of her age, she knew the best of the best, and had even used her quickening abilities to ramp up their powers, and even give some of them new abilities.

What made the Mystics stronger made the Free Spacer Clans stronger. Several of the adepts that she had originally trained with were now masters already themselves, and worked hard to help educate and train the next generation of Mystics. That also began to include other sentients, thanks to Master Jo, and no species objections from the Gaviok of the Shai, the new Chaos High Master.

Naero didn't have anything to do with any of that. Not yet at least. She had enough on her own plate to deal with as it was.

She was actually giving up time away from her young family as it was. And three years within the Time Displacement was still going to be three years to her, cut off from those she loved most. It was a definite sacrifice.

She had hoped to see her good friends, the twin sisters Chang Fu-han and Chang-Lijuan, but they were Mystic Masters in their own right now, in charge of the Mystics' Lo-Tek World Observation programs, providing adepts with experience dealing with more primitive cultures. From the papers and announcements Naero had read, which the twins sent her way on a regular basis, the entire program was evolving and continually trying to learn from its mistakes and triumphs.

Von and Ray brought Naero to a similar adept cubicle that she had used before. It was little more than a pop-up nanohut, linked together in the Prime Adept training center.

It made Naero recall her days as crew in Aunt Sleak's merchant fleet, and the small quarters she had been forced to make do with back then.

She spent that evening after dinner meditating and stretching, striving to stay in tune with her energies and abilities.

Funny. She was still such a dopey mess inside, but she always did a good job of keeping herself together and putting on a good front. Perhaps Tree was right. Perhaps she could use a little bit of order wisdom within.

Om chimed in. *I've been telling you that for years, you goofy, whacked out loon!*

Oh, shut up, Om, she told him with a laugh. I've seen you when you cut loose. You're even crazier than I am, you looney bastard.

I doubt that. And I've seen the proof firsthand. And, as you well know, I am quite parentless.

Really, Om? It's going to be a sad, sick day when you get loose and go off on the universe. I shudder to think."

I couldn't do any worse, or more damage than you have on the run.

Well, Om, I'm still just getting started. To my mind, I have a long way to go yet. We'll just have to wait and see.

Now you're scaring me, N.

She laughed.

When she went to sleep, she placed one of the mind crystals over her forehead, just as she had during her Chaos Wisdom training.

After she drifted off, she linked with Khai, and told him where she was and what was about to happen.

For his part, Khai was searching for both traces of the enemy, and for his own people, his father's people, the Oden. Many of them went into hiding on their own, before Intel could reach them. They still might be in danger.

Since the many open enemy attacks on the Alpha Quadrant, the advanced race of the Oden was now on the run. It was well-known to them that the enemy hunted them for use as hosts in the diabolical Darkforce generators.

Naero and her allies had run across several such vile devices, with Oden trapped inside of them, and even some Yattai. Naero had given a full account of those cases to Shalaen, who was herself a Yattai.

Once their business was done, she and Khai spoke about how much they already missed each other and their children. They spoke about having even more kids, and how much fun it was actually making them. That was one of the best parts of the process.

But watching them grow was pretty sweet and wonderful as well.

Both of them had always wanted a big family. For the time being they had three. Naero sighed and still could not believe that once she went into Change Wisdom training, she wasn't going to see Khai or her family for three years.

For her, that was going to be the worst sacrifice of all. Yet she knew that it had to be done. She was committed now, and there was no going back.

Khai tried to comfort her with words, but that did not work very well.

6

On Aman, waves of Mystic adepts on gravwings relentlessly tracked and hunted Naero as their quarry in the jungle, firing at her with live weapons. And not just any tropical rainforest jungle, but also a hi-tek jungle of highly sophisticated fixers, drones, scanners and detection tek that made it a gauntlet of deadly threats.

All the while, Master Tree used his symbiotic union with the entire planet to stay in her head telepathically, evaluating her performance and spouting philosophy.

Naero, you still need to embrace the power of Order Wisdom. You always seem to be resisting or somehow fighting it. Why can't you simply accept it? Some part of you always seems to waste time attempting to refute or deny it.

Part of her defense was to keep moving. That worked best. Whenever she tried to hole up somewhere, they always located her in the end and found a way to drive her out.

She even wondered if Master Tree was ratting her out to the others.

She wouldn't put that past the old tool bag.

Master Tree, I don't know if I will ever be able to embrace Order Wisdom entirely. It's far too rigid and black and white for me. I'm not merely resisting it; I'm actually disagreeing with it. That is not denial. I accept the power and value of Order Wisdom for what it is and what it does, but just like Chaos Wisdom, it is not the be all and end all. There are other ways of seeing and doing things than simply imposing a rigid, limited thought process around it, in order to control things. There is more than one way. More than one right answer.

Three attackers, swooping in on her right flank, weapons blazing.

How did they–?

No time. She banked back down into the thick jungle canopy, keeping herself phazed and shielded.

Maybe that was it. Perhaps they had a new way to track her Cosmic shielding.

She took a chance and dropped her shields, cloaking all of her power sources.

But if they hit her now, they could do damage, possibly even kill her in such a vulnerable state.

The attackers shot past her and came back, performing a zig-zag search.

That was it. They lost her.

Naero carefully slunk away.

Master Tree began again. *In a round about way, you're starting to make the usual standard arguments that the Three Wisdoms maintain against each other, Naero. It's simply the Great Debate all over again, same as it was three centuries ago. Chaos sees Order as too rigid, slow, and contemplatively pedantic. While Change is too flighty, manic, and cerebral after its own fashion.*

Naero joined in. Change sees Chaos as too superior, brutally simplistic, and coldly amoral and abusive. While Order is usually too slow and hesitant, actually resistant to any kind of change.

Naero slipped into a deep tropical lagoon, regenerating, processing oxygen, and drawing in energies from both the planet and its sun. She did her best to cloak them.

And as for Order, Tree continued, *Chaos is simply too indifferent and oppositional, even rude. While Change is by its own nature too impulsive, unpredictable, mercurial, and outright dangerous.*

Naero thought about her objective, to reach a certain place in an accepted amount of time, without simply fighting her way through. She was to utilize stealth, and not brute force. She could not replicate, nor could she simply transport herself there. She had to use her other skills.

But with the time limit, she also only had a quarter of a standard hour in which to reach the objective.

She transported herself high up in the atmosphere, forming an EV suit around her.

Isn't this cheating, Naero? Master Tree asked her. *You weren't supposed to transport."*

Wrong, Naero told him. The rules said I couldn't transport directly to the objective. They did not say that I couldn't transport somewhere else.

Trickery from a trickster, Master Tree said. *Why should we be surprised?*

Haisha, you old goofball. You guys wanted to see how my mind works. So go right ahead and observe. This is how. Wahoo!

If she dove down precisely, she could land right on top of the objective with a few seconds to spare.

But as she drew closer, her opponents weren't making it easy. With minutes left in the challenge, they had all of their forces stationed in layers around the objective. They were doing everything they could to keep her from making a mad dash at the end, just like she was attempting now.

She was just taking another vector.

Another possible solution came to Naero and she grinned.

On the way down, she created a swarm of mosquitos, all of them filled with Cosmic energy. The swarm would wash out, gum up, and defeat all attempts at scanning and detection.

They wouldn't be able to pinpoint her amid all of that Cosmic static.

She shrank down to bug size herself and plummeted down with the enveloping swarm.

The threescore or so adepts fired their weapons all around them, in hopes of hitting something, namely Naero.

She did almost get blasted to death, but she zipped down, regained her normal size, and was sitting pretty on the objective site with her legs crossed and a half-smile on her face.

Naero sipped a cold borbble of Jett and offered an ice chest of more to her comrades after their failed exertions.

"I slipped in last night and left the ice chest here, in preparation for my victory."

The Order geeks dropped their weapons and joined the festivities.

Master Tree came to her in person.

Like the stuck up old poop that he was, he didn't drink, not even soft drinks. Just fresh, tepid spring water.

"What is the HARM Contention, Naero?" Tree asked her.

"Chaos says: Do harm if you have to. Order says: Don't do harm if you don't have to. But Order still does harm if it must. Change asks: Does harm need to be done? Why, and to whom, how much, and in what way? Change also does harm. All three Wisdoms will do harm, but in different ways for different reasons."

Tree nodded, "Simplistic, but sufficient on the main points. Next, describe the Action Contention?"

"Chaos asks if we must act; only if we must. Order states that we must fully understand the ramifications of taking or not taking action. While Change asks: What is the best way to take action?"

"Good. State the Reality Contention. What is both Real and Important?"

"Chaos says: What is and what will be? The actual. Order focuses on achieving goals. What should be and what is workable now? The imposition of structure and order upon what merely exists. Change looks to the future and asks: What can be? What can be made better and how?"

Tree nodded. "Sufficient. Now demonstrate to me how you can balance the natural energies of all Three Wisdoms into the formation of the Universal Harmony."

Naero sat down, crossed legs, held out her hands, and opened her third eye almost without thinking.

She created a swirling orb of all three energies from the Three Wisdoms, red, blue, and yellow. They balanced out the Darkforce, the Lightforce, and the Lifespark of Creation and Destruction between them to form the Harmony which made all things possible in every dimension, in every universe, in every reality.

Such was the key to understanding all things. Yet even that was just a beginning of wisdom and further enlightenment.

Then Tree asked her point blank.

"Why do you despise Order Wisdom so much?"

His query jolted her out of her concentration.

Her small, functioning example of the Harmony disrupted in a puff, and vanished.

Naero recovered and gave his question proper thought before answering. "I don't despise Order any more than I do Chaos. It's just, for me, that I find them both limited and insufficient in their own way. Of course I see the value and the need for both of them. I accept the existence and even the need for Chaos and the eternal impetus at work, just as I desire Order and consistency in my own personal life–whether I will ever have it or not. But that is not enough for me. For me, there must still be more. And I have a gut feeling that I'm going to find it in Change Wisdom."

Master Tree raised his eyebrows. "High Master Jo is going to have his hands full with you, I am certain. Now, your week in Nama is finished. Tomorrow we will relocate to Aman. Once there, you will have only one more thing to accomplish."

"What is that?" Naero asked.

"You must use what you have learned about Order Wisdom to take control of your so-called, Dark beast, the fell creature that lurks within you. That will be your final test. When you have found an answer, then you can move on."

Naero's heart sank. "Then I'm doomed, Master Tree. I've tried all of my life to control my Dark beast, and it has nearly destroyed me several times. I can barely control part of it. That is the best I can do. This is a death sentence!"

Tree looked at her impassively. "If you are meant to die, you will die."

*

Aman was a continent of near natural forests, mountains, hills, and grasslands, serene, but perfectly controlled and and organized by Order Wisdom. If an entire continent could be structured and maintained like a huge garden, that was Aman. All was in balance. All was in harmony. No sentients were allowed on the interior of the continent beyond the coasts, only the Mystics when they trained there. There were native species of Tae-ha's fauna in all their variety, all in perfectly calculated and balanced numbers, of course.

All that week, Naero would be alone on Aman with Master Tree and his guardian Prime Adepts, Von and Ray.

Naero had meditated and prepared herself as much as possible the night before.

On the first day out, she struggled all day long, unleashing more and more of her Dark beast and trying to master it.

It defied her, it eluded her, and several times it nearly broke free.

Yet she failed in every single attempt.

Still she kept trying.

As darkness fell, Master Tree ordered her to stop, return to her nanohut, and rest and regenerate.

Naero could not walk. She was too spent even to recharge her energies.

Von and Ray had to carry her back to her quarters. Von fed Naero by hand and even gave her some healing that night.

Finally Naero recovered enough to be able to take in some energy from the planet, and then put herself to sleep so that she might regenerate the rest of the way, all that night.

She could startap in the morning and try again another day.

That night while her physical body rested, Naero took council with Om, going over everything they knew. Then she spoke with Khai, and explained to him what she was up against.

She thought about contacting Baeven.

Her outcast uncle was the only other Spacer, besides herself, who possessed or was possessed by a Dark beast such as hers.

The only thing that they could think of trying was to confront the Dark beast within herself, within her own mind.

In theory, it could work. Inside of one's mind, a person's own imagination and force of will was supreme and godlike. If properly trained, inside of the mind, an individual could accomplish anything in the controlled reality of the mind.

Yet the primary problem that Naero discovered very quickly the next day, was that her Dark beast remained a part of herself. Her Dark beast was her. It was not some outside force or being attempting to invade or take her over.

And because it was part of her, Naero's Dark beast had a will of its own, that was apparently just as strong as she was. It was less imaginative, but also more simplistic, motivated, and driven in order to compensate.

All her Dark beast wanted was to break free and destroy everything around it. All of its energies were devoted to that need.

In the end, Naero controlled it most of the time by limiting its access to energy, and keeping that side of herself in more or less, a lethargic, dormant state.

Even when she assumed her partial Dark beast, she had to carefully control how much energy passed through that form.

Master Tree was right in many ways. Order Wisdom and its powers should aid her greatly in such attempts. Yet it could not do it all, in a similar way that Chaos Wisdom and energy could not accomplish such a goal, all on its own.

The fact that Naero was more adept at manipulating Order energy along with Chaos energy together brought her closer. That much was logical. Yet her Dark beast did not function on anything akin to the basis of logic. It defied description and analysis, and fought directly against any attempt to limit or control it, whatsoever."

Naero spent that entire day wrestling with her Dark beast and fighting it back down again and again from deep within.

It could not be controlled.

It could not be reasoned with in any way.

Naero ended another day under Master Tree's silent, sober observation as she exhausted herself mentally, psyonically, and physically.

That night, she shut down her mind, and all that she could do was rest and recover.

With yet another day ahead of her, Naero received permission to take a different approach.

She spent the day in meditation, going over things with Om.

Then she joined with her Kexxian alter ego, Orean, and sought wisdom and possible answers from the Kexxian Data Matrix.

Amazingly enough, she discovered that even some of the ancient Kexx had also been plagued by such inner, Darkforce entities.

Each case was different. Some managed to destroy their entities, but tragically, doing so left them all but crippled and horribly damaged and fragile for the remainder of their broken lives.

The Highly advanced Kexx discovered that not only were these entities a unique and crucial part of these individuals, but they could not be removed or destroyed without doing great, irreparable harm to those persons.

The Dark beasts, as it turned out, were vital to those who had them, whether those people ever learned to fully control them or not.

Among all of the mighty, godlike Kexx–only seven of their advanced species ever succeeded in fully gaining control over their Darkforce entities.

They were the seven Dreamers who defeated the six Champions of the elusive and horrific G'lothc at the very end of their long, and bitter war. They sacrificed themselves doing so, and they did so willingly without question when their moment of truth came. They did so without hesitation or lament, for the sake of the universe, and all that they loved.

The Dreamers were capable of miracles, unique and astonishing even among the Kexx, the closest thing to gods the universe had ever seen. According to the lore of the Kexx, the Dreamers could will things into being with but a thought. They could alter reality itself. They controlled the very laws of Creation and Destruction.

Whereas the G'lothc seemed only to have mastered the power to destroy.

In the end, the Kexx defeated the mighty G'lothc by overwhelming them with imagination and creativity.

Each of the seven could create entire armies and navies, complete with amazing ships, crews, and advanced weapons that made the current tek level of Naero's universe look feeble by comparison.

Together they could move entire worlds, even stars, and control their energies and existence.

Each time the mighty G'lothc thought themselves invincible, the Kexx and their allies the Drians would rise up and crush them.

Naero searched and searched, in the endless sea of knowledge that was the KDM.

Nowhere did it say how the Seven Dreamers learned how to fully gain control of their Darkforce entities, only that they had.

All that was said, was that each case was unique, and that each Dreamer found their own personal path of enlightenment in order do so.

It was something each of them had to discover within themselves, on their own.

One, the mightiest of the seven, even managed to do so as a mere child. But the other six did so in various time frames, some over the course of many years.

All of that knowledge and wisdom and lore turned out to be a mixed bag for Naero. True, at least now she knew for a fact that such could be done. Yet it still did not help her much in her current predicament.

Or perhaps it could.

She had in fact gained several valuable insights into herself and her Dark beast. Both Master Tree and Om were correct.

Enlightenment was always useful, and brought her closer to greater understanding.

The only problem now was in applying them in some way that was useful to her dilemma within her current time frame of need.

Naero still did not know if she could accomplish such a great task, in the space of only a few days.

She gathered all of her strength once more.

The next day, after explaining her intentions, she started with her partial Dark beast form.

From there she incrementally attempted to unleash a little more, and then a little more, and still retain control of herself and the Dark beast as she went along.

At first her efforts seemed to work, and showed promise.

Yet at a certain point, her Dark beast simply awoke and did what it always did.

Twice she tamped, and rammed it back down into submission and dormancy.

On the third attempt, Naero let her guard down barely for a split second. Disaster.

Her Dark beast finally broke out and seized control.

For the next two days, she fought with it nonstop, trying to regain control.

For two standard days, her Dark beast ran amuck and laid waste to half of the continent of Aman, deep within the interior.

The damage and the paths of destruction could be seen glowing from orbit.

There was even talk of evacuating the costal cities, if she came too close to them.

But Naero and Om were able to study and observe her Dark beast and its mindless actions from within, also gaining valuable insights.

Master Tree, the Mystics, and their military and naval forces bombarded Naero's Dark beast from orbit, only enraging it and making it bigger and stronger. It fed off of destruction and conflict and absorbed energy.

In the end, it was Naero and Om who discovered how to gradually siphon off her Dark beast's energies over time, and cause it to grow tired and then slip back into dormancy.

They could outwit it slowly, over time.

Then Naero could take control again, and contain it within herself once more.

Naero proved that the Dark beast could not be unleashed or controlled gradually over time. At a certain point, it simply broke loose and had its way.

The exercise was both terrifying in scope, and very costly to the continent as a whole. She and the Mystics regretted that.

Yet Naero did come to understand her Dark beast more.

But that didn't mean that she was any closer to controlling the damn thing. It was just as wild and destructive as it always was. That much seemed to be the undeniable norm.

Naero ended her experiment completely exhausted, and no closer to her original goal than she had been before.

She reported her failure to Khai that night.

Naero felt as if the fates were trying to tell her something.

Perhaps they were.

She went straight to High Master Tree the next day with the only plan she could go with.

He smiled at her, as stoic and maddening as always. "So, Prime Adept Maeris. What scheme do we have in mind today?"

"Nothing. I'm done. There's nothing left to try."

He raised an eyebrow. "Surely you can't mean that."

"I am. Right now, there is no answer, no solution to this problem. For the time being at least, there is no way to completely control my Dark beast. The best that can be achieved is what I'm already doing. I'm containing it as best I may."

He huffed indignantly. "And you think this is acceptable?"

Naero put her hands on her hips. "For right now? Yes. It may not be the answer you want to hear. But it is an answer, logical enough. Not all things have an answer or solution at a given time. Perhaps some will never have one. We both must accept that fact that I can't be forced to produce a solution, just because you want me to."

High Master Tree laughed for joy and clapped his hands together.

"Haisha! You finally got it right!"

Naero gaped. "What? That's it? You gave me an impossible task, an unsolvable problem from the very start?"

"And you figured it out right, just like a true follower of Order Wisdom, even though it took you a while. Not all things can be ordered or resolved, and must be accepted as they exist. Bravo. Well done, Maeris!"

Tool bag! Naero was so pissed, she wanted to kick him in the balls with one kick and then stove his head it with another.

And she was just the gal to do it.

Om jumped in. *Better just smile and nod, N. Take the win while you can. Grit your teeth and be gracious. No testicle kicking or head stoving.*

"So, you just let me bash my head against a rock all week for no reason. How enlightening."

Tree clapped her on the shoulder. "I had to. You should have seen yourself struggling. But you had to come to the proper conclusion on your own, and you especially are so driven to win, to succeed, to do what has not been done. It was so hard to keep a straight face most of the time.

"Of course, it would never occur to you that failure was also an option, that sometimes, nothing can be done. A solution cannot always be found, and you cannot always succeed or win. Well done! You pass Order Wisdom training. You even have an extra day before you need to depart for Oorrii. I suggest that you and your friends celebrate your accomplishments somehow before then."

"Thank you, High Master Tree," Naero said behind set teeth. She bowed slightly.

It took all of her strength to walk away with her hands clenched into fists, and not kick Master Tree's silver butt and his biscuits, right then and there.

7

One slight problem arose, even with the extra day on Tae'ha.

For once, none of Naero's ships were close by or available. *The Dark Star* had been called away on a mission a week before. There were strange signs of enemy movement along the borders of known space in both the Alpha and Gamma Quadrants.

The Alliance was spread thin.

Even Fleet-1 was ordered back on patrol with the rest. None of the scans and sightings made any sense.

She could hop one of the merchant traders departing before the Time Displacement took affect, but none of them were going anywhere near Oorrii.

Even Baeven couldn't be reached.

Naero would have to charter a vessel, or try to borrow one from the Mystics, or perhaps a swift courier from the Spacer Marines.

With enough fixers, she could teknomance a ship for herself in time.

But then she studied the Intel listings of Spacer ships in the area.

One vessel caught her immediate attention.

Naero sent out a personal request.

If she was being stalked and tracked, this might throw off her mysterious pursuers.

Within a standard day, *The Bookwyrm* docked at the Tae'ha starport in all of her bright pink and orange glory. Naero stood ready with her duffle of gear, and entered within as the hatch opened.

Pretty Chime Fox nearly knocked her down by surprise, wearing Nytex flight togs that were bright green.

"Naero! It's so good to see you. Come on in and meet everyone. Oh, crap. Should we call you admiral or something? Haisha, this is so great!"

Chime hadn't changed much. Short blond hair, brown eyes, spunky and cute, even if she remained a bit of kook.

"Naero's just fine," she told Chime with a grin, allowing herself to be led by the hand. The outer hatch irised and sealed behind them.

Naero scanned the ship almost instantly with teknomancy.

Om still beat her to it.

Stellar Industries Reliant Class, Four hundred ton merchant trade vessel. Spacer mods, Jump-5, Level 3 shields, 30 mm spinal gun, four defensive turrets. Stellar K551 engines. Crew of thirty-six. Plenty of room for guest quarters, trade goods, and the ship's extensive library of physical books, book fabricators in most of the popular languages, and webnet download ports for ebooks and publications from throughout the Alpha Quadrant.

After the High Crusade, Naero had personally helped Chime Fox and Peter Cooper find the soon to be christened *Bookwyrm* at an amazing price. It was a wedding present to the couple.

Naero paid three-quarters of the cost for the vessel ahead of time.

Another hatch snapped opened before them and they passed inside.

They entered part of the ship's quasi, bookstore, library, which took up several decks, and half of the ship itself. This looked like a meeting or event room.

"We travel from world to world doing book events for authors and local to regional tours. It doesn't bring in as much credits as regular trade, but we have that as well, and the book stuff is much more fun. And Pete still has his own writing under his pen name."

The hatch at the other end of the chamber opened, and Pete Cooper came in with two little blond girls in his arms, about three years old, and a slightly older little boy hiding and peeking out from behind his father.

Naero flung her arms around Pete and hugged him dearly, both he and Chime from Company 36, the Marine company that she had been attached to as a Mystic Liaison, in her role as Shetanna.

"You look good, Pete. Chime taking good care of you?"

"Better than I deserve," Pete said happily.

Chime pointed a finger. "Who takes care of whom around here, mister?"

Pete laughed. "It's a mutual thing. And look, we keep finding these rare beasties about. They keep popping up, and we don't have the foggiest idea what they are, or where they've sprung up from!"

The kids all giggled at that.

Naero was so enchanted that she reached out and touched the girls' faces with her hands. "Oh, Chime, Pete, they're so beautiful. Like little fairies, I expect them to have pointed ears and shining wings.

Pete shook and tickled the two little girls and they burst out in more explosions of giggles and laughter. "This little troublemaker is Kelsey, and this other little sprite is Violet. And the ringleader of this invasion keeps hiding behind me. Come on out Jonny."

The five year old boy stepped out from behind his father, wearing dark green togs and holding a book in his left hand.

Chime came over, swooped up the boy into her arms, and kissed him on the cheek. "Naero, meet little Jonny Fox, named after my cousin Jonny, as you well know. He even looks a little like Jonny, doesn't he? But then, you never knew him as a boy like I did."

"I guess not," Naero said. The boy did have medium brown hair and bright green eyes, just like his namesake. She held her hand out to the lad, and he took it. "Hello, Jonny. I'm Naero Maeris."

He kept staring at her while they shook hands. He continued staring at her even after they let go. "It's very nice to meet you. Is it true? Mummy and Daddy said so. Is it true? Is it her? I won't tell anyone, honest."

Naero knitted her brows and thrust out her bottom lip slightly, scanning Jonny's parents for a clue. "Chime, Pete?"

Pete sighed. "We're Sorry about this, N. We kinda, sorta told him we knew…Shetanna."

Oh, so that was it.

Chime gasped, "Oh, N, you likely don't know, you're so busy. There are several popular new book series featuring Shetanna flourishing across numerous sectors and worlds, for all age groups, as wells as many vids, and vid shows. They range from stories for kids on up to adults. It's quite the industry, really. Pretty amazing"

Pete nodded. "Yeah, you really should look into getting a piece of that action."

Naero smiled and transformed into full on Shetanna mode, sans her blazing scarlet swords.

She used the voice.

"I AM SHETANNA, THE DARK ANGEL OF DEATH!"

"Haisha. Haisha!" little Jonny squealed, clapping his hands together. "Please, please tell me about some of your adventures."

Shetanna held her arms open, and little Jonny sprang across like a Tocharian yellow monkey, wrapping his arms around her neck and hugging her close.

Naero closed her eyes, smiled, and patted the boy's back.

"I'll do better than that, Jonny. I tell you stories about the brave man you were named after. He who is your blood, on your mother's side. This is the blood you come from, Jonny. And then I will tell you stories about your parents, and how all of us were mates, and fought side by side together. We saved each other's lives many times over."

Jonny pulled back and his eyes were wide and his little mouth hung open. "Really? Is all of that true?"

Shetanna nodded. Then she used her powers to cast transparent holo images of Spacer Marine armor and arms around Chime and Pete. "See, Jonny. You never knew that your parents were such heroes, did you?"

"Haisha!"

"They were elite Spacer Marines of Bravo Command, the best of the best. They were all my best mates, my abani, like family to me. And they were mighty warriors. They fought the Ejjai to save all of humanity, their valor knew no equal, and together with all of our allies, we won a great victory to save many lives on many worlds."

Naero allowed the holos to dissolve, fading away with her Shetanna look. Jonny stared at his parents and was speechless.

"Thanks a lot, N," Chime said in mock anger.

Pete grinned. "Now we'll never get the little bugger to shut up!"

Naero smiled her half-smile and nodded. "You're welcome. I just though the lad should know that his parents were heroes."

Together they brought the children into the mess hall, or on *The Bookwyrm*, what they referred to as the Café.

There they heard raised voices. An older Spacer woman, who could only be Chime's greatgran, was arguing with two landers in expensive clothing, one male and one female. It sounded as if they were talking politics over the latest blow up with the Corps on the INS feeds.

Chime and Pete came over with the kids and Naero in tow. They pweaked up a play area for the kids from the nanofloor, right next to the nanotable and seats.

Little Jonny walked with them, holding his mother's hand, and joined the girls.

"Naero Amashin Maeris, meet my greatgran, Thelian Lygia Fox."

The older woman was old even by Spacer standards. Her face and her skin were wrinkled and her limbs atrophied, signs that only showed themselves during the last ten to fifteen years or so of a Spacer life. Her hair was a shock of bright white fluff, almost as white as Naero's Shetharra.

But her green eyes still twinkled with life and energy.

Naero bowed her head in great respect. Elders were living history, legends in themselves, and they were so few. "All honor to you, Elder Fox. It's a great pleasure to–"

Thelian cut her off. "Now don't give me any of that Elder crap. You just call me Theli, or Greatgran, like everybody else. You're Naero, Naero Amashin Maeris, are you? Daughter of Lythe and Tarthan?"

"I am," Naero said. "They are the blood I come from."

The old woman suddenly held back tears. "Bless you, child. Chime told be how you were mates with my boy Jonny, and the way you honored him after he passed. Thank you for all of that. Let me kiss you, spacechild. They never told me you were so pretty, just like your mother."

Thelian kissed her on both cheeks, and then kissed both of Naero's hands and began to cry.

Naero was a few seconds away from crying herself.

"You honor me and my blood greatly," Naero said. She kissed Thelian on both cheeks and then her wrinkled, but still powerful hands.

"Our Clans have known great sorrow and loss, have they not?" the Elder said with a very deep sigh. "For one hundred and thirty nine years, I've seen so much. So many idiotic wars, so much loss. Yet I still have pretty little Chime, and she and this good man of hers have blessed me with sweet Jonny and my little angels of light. I'm so fortunate to have them in my final years. I'm very thankful for that."

She knelt and the kids came to her and covered her with hugs and little kisses. Greatgran closed her eyes and was in paradise for a few seconds among them. Then she told them to go back to playing, and she returned to the adults.

She sat down. "Well, this is a merry meeting, indeed." She banged the table with one hand. "Come along now, let's all sit together and have some food and drink. Tonight we'll have to get drunk after the kids are sleeping. I've got a whole cooler of Spacer Poteen we can raid, dammit!"

Chime chided her in part. "Greatgran, we told you to lay off the sauce, you old reprobate. The ship's doctor says your boozing days are done. It's not good for you."

45

"To hell with that," Thelian protested. "It's the only vice I have, and I'll be hanged by my tits and skinned if I give it up now! Whenever I do go on the next adventure, I'm good and ready. It'll be nice to see Jonny and all the rest. If they have Poteen in the Beyond, we'll all get good and blitzed over there."

The two landers just stared, eyes wide.

Thelian point at them. "Let me introduce the writers traveling with us on our book tour, bestselling authors in thirty systems, Renni Clooney and Myke Bickels. They write great books, but they only pretend to know something about interstellar politics. They're still too young and dumb to know runny shit from hand soap."

Naero grinned and shook hands with the two authors.

"Renni Clooney," the thirtyish woman with dark brown hair and brown eyes said, as they shook hands. "Do you read like, Chime?"

Naero smiled. "Nobody reads like Chime. But I'm a reader, when there's time. What do you–"

"Mostly romance and young adult romance-adventure. I've tried my hand at a few mysteries. And this is my counterpart, Myke Bickels."

Bickels was stocky and dark brown of skin with black eyes. "It's a great pleasure to meet you, Admiral Maeris. A high honor."

"Just call me Naero," she corrected.

"Got it. I write thrillers mostly, but I'm branching out into middle grade SF and Fantasy. It's huge market."

Greatgran and Chime went off to fetch food and drink for their little party. Chime kept a loving arm around Thelian as they bantered back and forth. They seemed to know each other so well.

"Thelian's something else," Renni noted. "Has she always been so feisty?'

Myke laughed. "Feisty? She's a total kook!"

Naero shook her head. "I knew Chime and Pete from the service," Naero said. "I just met greatgran. But she is what my dad would have called, 'a real pistol.'"

Within minutes, they were feasting and drinking and sharing treats with the kids, everybody gabbing all the while. Crew came in to eat and watch, and to meet Naero.

But it was still more or less a brunch, so Chime was adamant about greatgran not unleashing Poteen on everyone this early.

Thelian cornered Naero at one point. "Naero, I never knew much of your family, but I did know Thackery Ramsey for a few years. Some of us Foxes were on the same trade fleet ship with the Ramseys."

Naero blinked. "You knew my great, great granddad Ramsey on my father's side?"

"Yep. I was fifteen and he was sixteen, just before he went off to serve his two year stint with the Spacer Marines."

"We're you guys good friends?"

"I hope to think so. We spent hours in the zero-G havens and the slider tubes. The kids call it spiraling now. Thack was a pretty good swoocher, let me tell you. Lovely boy. My first love, really. But I never saw him again. I always regretted that."

"Haisha, Greatgran. No way. You and Thackery Ramsey...were an item?"

"I know it seems amazing now, Naero. But back then, I was as glorious as you and Chime. And Thack was the most handsome boy in the universe to me. But he was kinda handsy, if you know what I mean. Things got so hot between us that I had to kick him away a couple of times. If he hadn't gone off to serve, I might have ended up part of your bloodline."

"I would have been honored," Naero said.

It was funny and strange to think of one of the great elders of her father's family as nothing more than a horny, lovesick teen at one time in the past.

Every person grew up and had their moments.

When she had a chance, Naero checked in with Chime and Pete.

They would delay their book tour a few days to take her to Oorrii. Just a quick stop off. Then they would catch up on their schedule.

When they admitted that their ship did not have a cloaker, Naero stepped into engineering for a bit and teknomanced one for them.

Naero did not want to attract any danger to her friends, and it was better to be safe than sorry.

While she was at it, Naero and Om gave *The Bookwyrm* several other valuable upgrades, like jump-7.

Perhaps Naero was just being cautious, but ever since she had left Tae'ha, her sense of warning had remained on the verge of going off, and there was no telling what that meant.

Her friends did put on their drink that night, after dinner and the kids were in bed. But Naero did not let herself get tipsy.

Just in case something did happen.

She felt much better once they were in jump, on their way to Oorrii.

8

Om woke her early the next day. Naero had slept well for once. It was almost nine bells.

Haisha, she never slept in that late.

Nothing seemed wrong, her sense of warning wasn't going wild. Om couldn't even say exactly why he woke her up.

For some reason, I just felt like I should.

Naero used teknomancy to go from naked to suited up and ready for anything in less than two standard seconds.

Sitrep, Om. Where are we? What's happening? It feels like we're out of jump.

We are. In fact, we've made an unscheduled landing on Mikril-6, a far flung earthlike with not much around it to lure in anyone from the trade routes. It's scheduled for exploration, but there's no one and nothing there yet.

Someone or something is doing this, Om.

She called out throughout the ship. "Chime? Pete? Greatgran? Please respond!"

N. Wait...I'm having troubled concentrating myself.

Naero's warning sense spiked, big time.

Things grew creepier by the second.

Naero used teknomancy and all of her abilities to shield them every way that she could think of and prepared for for a fight. Om said he felt better.

Scan the ship Om. Where is everyone? What's happening?

They're gone, Naero.

Naero shuddered. Her mouth went dry. Gone, Om? Where the hell did they go? Almost forty people on board, and they just land in the middle of nowhere, for no reason, and just walk out—"

That is exactly what everyone did, N. Every hatch and exit is wide open. Cold trails lead off into the jungle. Various ore samples in the rock deposits and outcroppings are limiting further scans.

Naero scanned for psyonics. No traces. If the enemy was using one of those weird psyships, she would know it.

This was something completely new, and far more dangerous.

Clearly it was all a set up, an elaborate trap. And whoever was in control were clearly playing the game as if they had already won.

They were just jerking her around now, making her worry.

Where are our fixers, Om?

Asleep or disrupted. I can't seem to activate or awaken them.

Extend our shields to them and try again. I'm checking the ship's log, vids, and systems for any signs of an attack.

The shielded fixers are coming back online. Attempting to isolate the shielded component that is shutting everything down.

Stranger and stranger, the logs showed nothing. No warnings. Nothing. Normal scans did not detect anything.

Naero suddenly wondered why whatever it was didn't just zap her as well and have done with it? Perhaps it couldn't.

Whatever this was, why didn't it work on her? Was she immune somehow? Even Om had started to lose it. Why didn't she suffer any effects?

What were their shields keeping out that could take control over an entire Spacer crew, Om, and even their fixers?

No direct connections yet, N.

The vids simply showed the crew going about their duties. Then, as if it were completely normal for them, they proceeded to divert and land on Mikril-6.

Then everyone calmly stopped what they were doing, proceeded to this location, flung the starship wide open, and proceeded to wander off into the jungle with no supplies, equipment, or weapons.

Chime and Pete did carry their kids with them.

The entire crew was now at risk.

Send out our shielded fixers, Om. Scan and the sweep the entire area and try to locate our people, on visuals if need be, and anything else we need to know.

In process. Fixers spreading out in a standard, low-level detection pattern, grid by grid.

This was bad. Whoever took the crew could just as easily kill them all–with ease. Such possibilities troubled Naero something fierce. All she had wanted was a simple ride, and now something very sophisticated and dangerous was turning that journey into something far more sinister.

She and Om had seen and faced a great deal, but nothing like this, thus far. Was it the G'lothc? Had some of those evil spirits escaped the cusp of oblivion somehow and acquired hosts? Or perhaps this was the work of a full grown, Dakkur Black King, seeking vengeance through powerful psyonics.

Baeven and Jia had both warned her about such formidable and lethal beings, and she had barely triumphed over an immature Dakkur prince. The psyonic powers of such creatures were nearly on par with the G'lothc themselves. Or worse, what if the G'lothc managed to possess a Dakkur king?

Naero shook herself. Speculation was worthless and disheartening. Focus. Find her people and save them, if they could be saved.

Anything on those scans, Om?

Sorry, N. Nothing thus far. Continuing.

Wide scan, Om. Send out all of our fixers. Extend the range.

Naero created a skeleton replicant crew for *The Bookwyrm in minutes.* Keep everyone and everything shielded and protected, and now cloaked. Naero wasn't taking any chances. She wouldn't let the enemy use the ship and its weapons against them.

Where were the damn crew? That much was starting to freak her out. Her friends. The little kids. How could all of this be happening, and she and Om had no warning, awareness, or control?

No attacks. No signs of anything.

What could do this?

Something barely warped the air just behind her.

Naero whirled and slashed at it with her Chaos katanas.

Nothing.

Haisha. Now she was tilting at shadows.

She asked Om if something had actually been there.

Om wasn't sure.

Something was watching them. Something stalked them. Naero could feel it.

Whatever it is, they finally figured out that it was interdimensional in nature.

They couldn't attack it. They could barely even see it.

Just glimpses, flashes, and flickers of movement here and there as whatever these things were, barely showed ripples of themselves in the Prime Material plane.

Whatever these creatures were, they hovered and moved just outside of reality, most likely peering in at Naero's dimension.

If they possessed such vast powers and abilities, what possible interest would the Prime Material plane be for such advanced beings?

Why would they even bother to intrude or dabble in the boring normal realities?

Om did find the missing crew finally. One hundred kilometers to the west, all huddled together as a knot. They had either been stunned or psyonically paralyzed.

Let's go spring this trap and meet our hosts, Om.

They transported directly to the location.

They transported right into the middle off a vast, savanna grassland, with rivers and streams, and tall grasses, vast patches of which soared over ten meters high.

When Naero first spotted them, the forty or so crew stood gathered together in a clump, standing up to their elbows in thick, grayish black mud in a large mud hole.

She spotted Chime, Pete, Greatgran and the kids among the rest.

Everyone of them had their eyes closed. They appeared to be standing there in the mud, asleep or paralyzed.

No harm has come to any of the hostages yet, N.

Let's keep it that way, Om. The first chance we get, let's get them out of here.

Will do, if possible. Our fixers can't actually touch them right now. I'm guessing we can't either. They're shielded somehow.

Naero stepped out into the open savannah and used the voice, her words rolling out across many kilometers. "ENOUGH OF THIS. I'M HERE. YOU'VE GONE TO ALL OF THIS TROUBLE ABDUCTING MY FRIENDS AND DRAGGING US OUT HERE. WHAT DO YOU WANT?"

Something like a dust storm erupted from the northwest and swept their way, twenty klicks out.

What is it, Om?

A complete, hi-tek army just popped in out of nowhere, N. Moving fast. Ten thousand strong, converging on this position fast.

Naero looked back at her friends.

She startapped, and kept startapping, ramping up her energies.

If nothing else, mastering Order energy taught her how to increase, harness, and store her base energy by a hundredfold.

Thank you, Master Tree.

Let's go out and meet them, Om. We can't fight them around here with the hostages. We leave some reps to watch over them while we go boogie.

Naero, I don't know what the hell boogie is, but against ten thousand advanced foes we have not engaged yet, it better be good.

Have I ever let you down, Om?

Hmmm...trying to count.

Stop it. Let's ride. Head for those mountain foothills to the northeast, with all of the rich mineral deposits.

N, cloak all of that energy. You'd probably glow in the dark. They'll be able to track you for sure.

I want them to track me, Om. Let's draw them away.

Oh, I understand, now.

Naero shot away at top speed, blazing a trail across the darkening sky as a massive series of thunderheads blew up across the savannah. They must be in a rainy season.

Below, a myriad of animals unique to that region stampeded, hid, or otherwise took shelter from both the growing storm, and the rumblings of the mysterious, advancing army.

Just as Naero hoped, the strange force tracked her with ease and moved to intercept.

She'd have less than an hour to prepare to make her stand.

She did not move any further, and focused all of her efforts on preparing herself for combat, but she had at least succeeded in selecting the site of the battle on her terms. And she also drew them away from her helpless friends.

Now the real contest could begin.

9

Naero stood calmly in the middle of a cracked, dried lake bed, with the storm winds rippling past her.

Dimensional vespers, and enemy cyphers flashed and flickered around her like lost, taunting souls. They could not touch her. She could not touch them.

Yet the hi-tek army the enemy brought against her was real enough.

One psyonic voice attempted to penetrate her defenses. It was not an attack. She let it through.

It was the fell voice of a G'lothc spirit.

We come for you, insect. You who think yourself so mighty.

The voice broke off.

Naero scanned the host closing in to encircle her.

Time to show off some of her new and improved powers.

She and Om scanned the enemy forces one last time: ten thousand strong, mostly second generation Ejjai troops, but a mix of the enemy's slave races, including the Dakkur. And three hundred possessed for good measure, already beginning to transform.

Naero encased herself in a cocoon of layered, protective energies.

Within a kilometer, the forward elements unleashed torrents of interlocking fire that ravaged the entire area all about Naero.

They sustained their fire and swept in to overrun her position from several directions.

The storm of ordnance, artillery, and direct fire were so great that the position was reduced and enveloped in a cloud of smoke and burning destruction. The enemy elements even began to inflict damage on one another as they bunched together, but they kept up their attacks.

A rapidly spreading disk of blue and scarlet force detonated out from Naero up to two kilometers in every direction.

Anything those energies came into contact with was reduced to blasted, burning, glowing chunks. She took down one quarter of the army, and the majority of the battle armor infantry in one stroke.

Naero rose up, towering over them fifteen meters high, in her partial Dark beast form, with *Heartcleaver* resting on her shoulder, the Cosmic weapon stood taller than she was.

Two of her eyes blazed scarlet, he third eye flared blue.

Three beams from her eyes raked entire battalions of hypertanks, causing them to cook off and disrupt.

She ignored concentrated fire that would have vaporized an entire naval fleet of warships.

Even as the enemy swept around her, Naero sprung her own trap.

Forces made up completely of replicants, two thousand strong, exploded out of the ground and took the remaining foes unaware, complete with Allied advance hypertanks, meks, min-gunships, and close assault starfighters.

Within five minutes, the enemy's second-generation army was reduced to burning slag.

Yet Naero knew that all of this was but a test, perhaps one of many.

Then the fell voices came back–like droning insects in her mind, like invisible hornets swarming all about her–and their sting was in their words, whispering, threatening, predicting doom for her and all of her allies.

We're coming for you, Naero.

Coming for you and all that you know and love.

You can't stop us, Naero. You'll never be able to stop us.

Not if you were ten times stronger–a hundredfold stronger than what you are now.

You had but a glimpse of what we are.

But a taste of the horror we will unleash.
Entire galaxies have fallen before our might.
Who are you? What can you do?
You cannot hope to stop us.
Did you know that we were behind your parents' deaths, Naero?
Yes...we were there when they died.
We watched them and all that they loved perish and burn before their eyes.
One day, we will show it all to you.
As we shall be there when you fail.
And when you fall, you shall join them in the great wheel.
Yet another trophy. Another prize, put on display.
As all who oppose us are destined to fail.
What will you do, Naero?
What will you do?
Against that which cannot die?
Against that which knows not defeat?

"I will find a way!" Naero shouted back at the fell voices, shaking her upraised fist. "You have been defeated before. One day, I will find the way to destroy you all!"

Om, have you figured out how they are doing this? It should take massive amounts of Cosmic energy to do what they are doing. Where the hell are they getting it?

Keep them busy a while longer, N. I'm very close to pinning it down. It's all around us. I need a little more time. Behind you. Look out!

Naero sprang away and summoned her swords.

The fell voices laughed and chortled.

How will you fight them, Naero?
When we take them over and send even them against you?

Naero continued to slowly retreat.

They had control of little Jonny Fox, age five.

He held a knife in his tiny hand and lurched forward at her like a drunken puppet. His eyes stared forward like one drugged, head slumped to one side. He shambled at her, swinging and swiping at her with the blade.

Their control over the captives isn't so good, Om. Clumsy, pitiful, really.

Watch out, N. There are many others.

She turned to see Chime, and Peter, Greatgran, the two authors, and the rest of the crew staggering out at her from all sides, faces slack, knives moving in their hands.

Naero rose up into the air on her gravwing to avoid their attacks. The enemy knew that she would never harm them.

What about possession wyrms? She scanned them all quickly, knowing how to detect and deal with their presence.

If they had been infected, she would need to act fast.

Yet none of them had been infected. Not a single control wyrm.

You have done this, Naero.

You have made all of this possible.

Om, what are they talking about?

I don't know, N.

Naero circled about in the air.

The controlled captives started flinging their knives at her. She brought up shields to deflect them.

See how utterly helpless you are before our powers?

What will you do when we take control of your allies?

When we send your own family against you?

What will you do then Naero?

You can protect yourself.

How will you protect all of them?

We will send you friends to destroy you.

The Oden half-breed...we will take him over and have him kill you.

How will you sleep?

Whom shall you trust?

We will send your own children to kill you.

Your crews will willingly drive their fleets into the nearest stars.

How will you stop us, Naero?

Om, get ready. I'm going to startap more and take the hostages back by force. If this is some kind of mindlink, I'll go person to person and–

Stop, N! Wait a moment. Don't do anything just yet. I think I've got a handle on what they are doing, and how.

But Om, we have to–

Listen, damn it. Every time that you grow stronger, they grow stronger as well. There's some kind of connection. Think about it, N. Your Cosmic energy levels shoot off every known scale every time you startap. You and your firstborn are walking Cosmic Phenomena. Look at the energy flows all around you.

Yes...yes, very strange. Am I their power source, Om? Is it me? Have they found a way to turn my own energies against me?

It would seem so, Naero. Energy floods out of you at immense levels. It emanates all around you, and yet you maintain control of it so that it does not harm you or others around you. Just how is that accomplished? That is a major feat on its own.

Hmmm...Cosmic energy by its very natures exists in two places at once. Yet like an iceberg in an ocean, it has natural outlets in stars, or in the user, and only reveals part of itself in the Prime Material Plane until more is called upon. Most of it exists in the Astral Plane, which is the dimension of pure Cosmic energy in all of its possibilities, feeding into the other planes and dimensions.

Can you sense where these Cosmic attacks are coming from, N?

Naero rose up higher for a moment and concentrated with the sight of her enlightened third eye.

She almost gasped. How had she not seen it before?

Om, the enemy is attacking from the Astral Plane somehow. They're breaking through enough even to affect things here. That is where they are latching onto my Cosmic forces at the source, like so many leeches. They're using my own powers and energies against me to fuel their efforts and commit these things in our reality. They're using me.

Good. Now, how can we cut them off and stop them?

I–I don't know. I can drain myself down to a level where they could not sustain their efforts, but how will I ever startap again without them feeding off of me and doing things like this, or even worse? You heard their threats.

Naero, let's stop them now and end this before another enemy army or fleet shows up. We'll figure the rest out later.

Right. Save the others and make it to Oorrii. That's more than enough to achieve at the present.

One of the vespers came at her again. *So, Naero. You'll risk your lives for these useless ones? They are so weak. They are nothing. Forget them.*

I will die defending them.

Yes, you probably would at that.

Naero quickly shunted the bulk of her energies into the nearest star. She cut off all Cosmic access to the Astral Plane.

All signs of the enemy voices and vespers fell away. Good. She had cut them off from controlling her friends and their crew, who tumbled to the ground, stunned.

Originally she had intended to transport them all back to *The Bookwyrm*. Yet to do that she would have to startap again.

She settled for summoning *The Bookwyrm* and her reps, who had kept busy with the fixer cloud, teknomancing a troop transport out of the wreckage of the enemy hi-tek army.

As soon as her reps finished loading Chime's crew in, they all said goodbye and good riddance to Mikril-6. And none too soon. Several enemy fleets quickly converged on the system, jumping in just as Naero and her group was jumping out.

Naero reported the enemy fleet positions and data as they fled, and then went about with her reps to revive the captives and explain things.

But the major problem still stared Naero in the face like a dark reflection in a mirror.

How was she going to be able to fight the enemy face to face without them using her and her energies against her allies and loved ones at the same time?

How was the enemy escaping into the Astral Plane from their own dimensional prison that had held them for so long? Once more, her unrelenting and opportunistic foes had effectively devised a way to defeat her, and she had no idea how to stop them.

10

Naero said farewell to her friends with great affection and sorrow after they reached Oorrii. She would miss them, but she also regretted placing them in danger at the forefront of her cunning battle with her vicious, ruthless foes.

She hugged and kissed pretty Chime, and Peter, and their three little ones–and even loopy old Greatgran. The authors and the entire crew thanked her for saving them and all bade her safe journey.

The ship would be fully shielded now.

She left one of her replicants to join Chime's crew and help protect them, as much as possible in a dangerous universe. Let them return to their simple lives and raise their children. They had done enough, and already lost far more than they should.

Let them be.

Naero smiled as *The Bookwyrm* departed.

The experience had taught her a valuable lesson.

Her friends and allies would always do their duty according to their skills and abilities. Yet she would strive not to bring them further into harm's way, against foes that were beyond them.

Foes that were still beyond her.

The deaths of so many of her friends and comrades still weighed very heavily upon her heart.

Naero kept half of her reps with her and sent the other half back to isolated Mikril-6, to perform a rare thing for any Spacer.

They reported back that the enemy had fled or been chased off.

Naero's forces promptly claimed the planet in her name and re-named it Naero-6. All of the legal stuff could be worked out later.

Beneath a modified planetary shield, her reps and fixer clouds would construct a naval base, a shipyard, and training facilities.

A small handful of these replicants would possess the ability to replicate even more reps, to crew fleets and entire Marine Divisions.

Naero was going to spearhead the efforts to defeat the enemy. And she was going to create the elite forces to do just that. As yet, the enemy had proven incapable of taking over her mind.

In order to forge ahead, she still needed to complete her Mystic training. That was her task. Perhaps in mastering Change Wisdom, she would find some of the answers she sought.

That was why she came to this place. Naero looked across beautiful Oorrii in all of its exotic splendor. Over forty percent of its surface was land mass across seven continents and several major archipelagos.

In a way, the entire planet could be seen as one ginormous zoo. Oorrii boasted multiple major shielded habitats and protected enclaves, home to nearly every major sentient and animal species known to exist. The former agreed to live there or even contracted to do so, despite the effects of the Time Dilation. It was a very sweet arrangement. All of their needs were met, and they knew no want of any kind. Within reason, they governed their own affairs and lived on a world that was very close a well-managed paradise.

The sentient inhabitants and their offspring could leave Oorrii if they so wished, and even have visitors under certain conditions, but once they left Oorrii, they could never return. They were contracted to be sample populations of their kind and species and could not make such decisions lightly. There were plenty of sentients waiting in the wings as reserves. They knew a good thing when they saw it.

But all of the Mystic Homeworlds remained closed systems with tight security, for many good reasons. With the grim realities of the universe they all existed in, it simply couldn't be any other way.

Naero left her other reps behind at the starport to purchase or construct another ship, maintain contact with Naero-6 for as long as possible, and to await any further instructions from her. She would work out a place for them on the planet with High Master Jo.

Never again would she travel so lightly, without a full force of her reps to back her up in a tight spot. Doing that would also reduce the risk to others.

Nothing left to do but meet up with the Spacer Mystics.

Oorrii's greenish sun and particles in its turquoise sky lent a subtle, blue-green hue to both the air and the lush land. On the continent of Fahar, they were in a hot, humid subtropical rainforest region with both walled and domed structures and communities on the vast coast of an ocean out to the east and south.

The wind from the sea, wafting over the mid-sized, Joshua Tech starport brought cool breezes and many scents upon the wind, from starships, people, and local plants and food. A small city of various locals lived around the starport and maintained markets there.

She noted what the locals were wearing, and programmed her Nytex togs to match the soft, comfortable jumpers of pastel white, blue, yellow, green, and orange. She did so even as she kept walking. The shorts only extended about twelve millimeters down the thigh.

Her Spacer hairstyle and her many weapons still made her stand out. And instead of the ubiquitous local sandals or even bare feet, she still preferred high, open-slitted sandal boots of soft material. She colored her pweakable attire in local pastel yellow.

She stopped at a local street vendor run by meter-high Piettos and purchased a local flatbread wrap, complete with Spum, Durro cheese sauce, and veggies, plus a four-pak of Jett to wash it all down.

The wrap was so delicious, that she hurried back to the stand and bought two more for her walk outside of the starport area.

It suddenly struck her that she was famished and tired of food bars.

She tipped the wrap stand owner big time. The Besh woman in her middle years was stunned. According to the scale of the local economy, she could probably retire and live well.

What the heck, Naero had creds to spare. And the amazing wraps were worth it.

It was a nice day for a trek, the sea breezes were cool, and she had plenty of time. She did not always have to transport or fly directly to her destinations.

She got her bearings via Om and their invisible cloud of spyfixers. The vast Mystic Compound lay off to the south and west for many kilometers into the lush, jungle interior.

Wide, white marble and plasteel roads lined with intriguing statuary marked the roads, and as she walked further away from the starport, the foot traffic faded to nothing. It was still in the morning on Oorrii, and most likely, the Mystics were busy training, as she would be the next day.

The yummy wraps were soon history, and she still had one frosty borbble of Jett left by the time she reached the nearest set of gates to the compound, guarded by Mystic Intel Marines. They saw her coming, apparently recognized her, and snapped to attention, summoning the officer on duty, a Marine captain.

She was pretty well known by now, and did carry the rank of fleet admiral.

The Captain who saluted her was a young woman with shoulder length, violet hair and gray eyes. All of the Marines were in combat armor, jungle mode to help them keep cool.

"Captain Mitchelle Ramsey, Admiral Maeris. Welcome. We weren't expecting you until tomorrow, we were told."

Naero smiled and returned the salute. "You and your Marines be at ease, Captain. Thank you. I am a little early, please excuse me."

"Not at all, sir."

"Captain Ramsey, are we related in any way, through my father?"

"I sure as hell hope so, sir. But my folks tell me it's pretty distant."

Naero shook hands with the woman. "Blood is blood, cousin. I just called the main compound a minute ago. You should be hearing something back from them shortly. Mind if I go in?"

"Of course, Admiral. Shall I send an attachment with you as an escort?"

"No thanks. I think I can find my way. They'll meet me on the inside in any case. Just stay at your post here. A pleasure to meet you, Captain Ramsey."

The captain bowed slightly. "You honor my family, and our Clan, Admiral."

"The honor is mine."

She left the Marines at the gate and kept walking within, entering the wide Mystic labyrinth that drew all guests and travelers into the center. There were many patches of manicured forest, garden, and meditation pools, waterfalls, and outlooks along the path she chose. Very scenic.

This entire area was clearly designed for serenity, contemplation, and enlightenment.

You certainly need all of that that you can get.

Quiet, Om. I need to focus.

Yet in the distance, she could sense the shocks and blasts of Mystics training in earnest to develop their various powers and talents. They trained at the very highest levels of strength, speed, endurance, and Cosmic might.

Around the next bend, another white marble gate awaited her and more.

Along with the Marine guards and an entire Mek unit, two beings stood at hand.

High Master Jo sent his Prime Adepts to greet her and bring her into the fold.

Tess Fae, one of the greatest Biomancers and shapeshifters ever known to exist, stood upon a low hill inside the gate. Naero knew her. She shifted form every several minutes, from one creature to the next, many of them the most unique and dangerous of their kind from throughout the known galaxy.

On Oorrii she had countless specimens to observe and practice with.

"Greetings, N," Tess called out, returning to her base form. "Glad to have you among us here finally."

"Thanks, Tess. Glad to be here. I still have so many questions that need answers. I hoping to find some of those answers here."

"You may find answers to questions you never thought you had," another voice said. "Or simply more questions that you never thought possible."

"Don't get too cryptic, Den." Naero told him. He was the hazy energy form, a shifting, shapeless miasma with blue eyes flickering out from its amorphous midst. "You might scare me off."

Den Kurtz laughed. "Nothing scares you off, Maeris."

That enough might be true, but she still had many fears all her own, whether they stopped her or not.

"Let's go, Den," Tess said.

"Yeah," he snorted, "can't keep the big goofball waiting."

Naero chuckled. "So irreverent. Is that how you refer to your High Master?

"With affection," Tess added.

"Wait until you see it first hand," Den said. "He contains himself outside of Oorrii. But once he returns home, his true nature reveals itself, the little imp."

Tess rolled her eyes in her current form. "Yes, he thinks himself quite the trickster. Jokes, pranks, goofy tricks–an endless stream of them at times, completely without warning. His sense of humor and whimsy are near limitless."

"Yes," Den said wearily, "all the more annoying."

"Well then," Naero said with her customary half-smile. "Let the games begin."

"Be careful what you wish for, Naero," Den warned.

They flew toward the center of the Mystic compound, with Tess and Den as her escorts and guides.

She could see the smart labyrinth from the air and even note how it shifted with time, revolving, evolving, and never the same thing twice. Yet within, the shifts were so subtle that most did not notice them while inside.

They had no idea that what they walked ahead into had not been there before, and that what they had seen behind them was most likely gone.

At its center, the Mystic compound was a series of artistic buildings, built out of various materials, and set upon several disks or within interlocking, moving wheels, walkways, platforms, and movers.

Part of the center was a gigantic, working clock with certain buildings in great proximity and congress with each other at certain times of the day. All seemed to be in motion.

Towers rose and extended and collapsed like living telescopes of shining metal, plasteel, and smartmaterials.

One gigantic building alone was like a huge, transparent oblong melon. The top parts flexed and irised and collapsed inward at a rate of fifty-percent reduction, revealing the flat expanse of a vast floor of training stations, kilometers wide and long.

If a tropical storm rushed in, various parts of the clear ceiling and its superstructure could be raised to keep out the elements and collect water for the compound's use.

All highly efficient, N. A marvel of modern, hi-tek Spacer engineering and art.

A series of smartdomes and smarttowers worked their way up the low mountainside, looking out to sea to the south and east. Different portions of their surfaces could be programmed opaque, clear, or tinted, for windows, ventilation, or wide open views and gravwing ports. Several persons flew outside over the compound and back within.

Master Jo's private compound was the highest of all the structures, placed upon the summit of the mountain itself. It consisted of a series of cylindrical dwelling pods of various sizes and purposes, stacked and nestled together in a rough, vertical pyramid structure that looked as if they could be shifted about for any purpose from an open party, to enduring a major military assault.

Naero and her escorts actually flew through an open wall on one of the upper levels of the largest, top cylinder.

Within, the levels were part clear, and part opaque. Programmed color changed walls, floors, and ceiling panels in a shifting pattern. Stairs, flight shafts, and movers came online or collapsed randomly or as needed.

To Naero, the interior seemed almost fluid, rather liquid in its design and function–amazing both as art and as utilitarian structure. It was a complete smartdwelling made of highly reactive smartmaterials that literally flowed, shifted, and interacted with and around the users.

Naero relished it, but to others, like High Master Tree and the former Master Vane, it would have most like proven distracting, if not maddening.

When Master Jo appeared, he did so speaking to her and flashing from place to place, every few seconds or instants.

That did take a little getting used to.

"Naero! So glad you made it. Welcome to Oorrii!"

Master Jo's physical form was that of a glowing, golden Spacer boy between the age of eight and ten, both eternally young and wise.

A holographic storm of brightly colored birds passed around them and out of the open walls and windows. The screeched and shrieked just like the real thing.

Thankfully, he didn't have them holographically poop, at least not this time.

He's still nuts.

Quiet, Om. He's eccentric.

Okay.

Stop it.

Master Jo laughed. "I was born with the gift of constant, hyper teleportation at age ten, when my further physical development was arrested by the energies inside of me. Much to my parents' concern. My mind still continues to expand. Around others outside of Oorrii, I suppress those abilities since becoming a High Master. But here on my world, I can let them run free and relax."

Naero thought that she would start right in. "Master Jo. I have a complex problem involving the enemy and my Cosmic energies. There have been strange occurrences and then a serious incident on the way here. I hoped that you might help me."

"Of course. Sit down and explain it to me. Tess, Den. Stay or go as you please. I can always summon you."

Tess left them. Den hung around, floating about at will. He seemed to enjoy the transitioning structure in a way that Naero could not fathom.

Naero told Master Jo about all that had happened, and explained her concerns about her Cosmic energies and abilities, and her fears about the enemy and them somehow escaping into the Astral Plane.

65

He agreed with her. That would be very bad. Together they would explore her fears and concerns and all that they entailed.

Of course he did not have any ready answers for her. Her situation was particularly unique to her. But there was one big consolation. Once they went into the Time Dilation, that should cut them off from her, and she should be able to train freely, without limits.

11

Even the Mystics wore the simple Nytex, smartmaterial jumpers for practice, garments that were common on Oorrii. Perfect for the tropical jungle, form fitting, utilitarian, in Mystic whitish gray.

The very next morning, Naero mindlinked with Master Jo and they spent much of the day meditating together, exchanging thoughts and insights on Change Wisdom in general, and the differences between random change and enlightened change.

With Master Jo's natural abilities, he flitted about the labyrinth at will and even out into the wilds. It was Naero's physical task to track and follow him wherever he went, through their link.

That was not as easy at it sounded.

Master Jo psyonically drilled her constantly, no matter what else was happening.

What is the nature of Change, Naero?

She strove to remain composed, sitting lotus fashion just like him, hovering over a small, tinkling waterfall among floating, pulsing, Cosmic energy crystals.

The crystals occasionally collided and rang like finely tuned bells.

Change is constant and Eternal, Master Jo. Things change as long as they exist.

What stay's the same?

Nothing. That is an illusion of Order Wisdom. Yet there is value and logic in sustainability, and seeking to maintain harmony and balance. One more enlightened view takes into account that Change has always taken place in the past, things are currently changing in the present, and they will continue to change in the future. To deny those facts is not logical.

Must everything be logical?

No, of course not. Sometimes things are random or simply the way that they are in a current state. But logic can be very useful in maintaining balance, seeking rational sustainability for a purpose, and guiding Change as it comes.

They switched to sitting on the edge of a sea cliff, while below the waves of the mighty ocean crashed again and again against the rocks and crystals piled up against the shore.

What is the basis of the pursuit of Change Wisdom, Naero?

Questions that probe inwards and outwards. What kinds of Change are inevitable and must be accepted? For example, eventually, all things come to an end: sentients, stars, even universes. Change Wisdom examines things closely through many questions and seeks understanding.

What Change can we control, entirely of in part? In what time frame? Why or why not should we seek to control matters? In each instance, what is the best way to attempt to control Change? Should Change be resisted or suppressed? What is possible and feasible, and what is not? If change is desirable or going to occur in any case, what is the best way to guide or direct Change?

Change is not always good or desirable, master. Sometimes it is destructive and chaotic, like a hurricane, a volcanic eruption, or some kind of natural–

War is an upheaval, a destructive event caused by sentients trying to seize territory or treasure, or enslave and eradicate other sentients.

Yes, certainly. But wars can also be ended. War can only accomplish so much. Eventually, the costs become far greater than what can be achieved through acts of war. The only exception is the war for survival, like the ones we face with our enemies. All things have a right to exist and defend themselves against aggression bent on wiping out their existence.

They flipped to floating slowly over the jungle canopy with the wind in their hair and faces.

Thus, what is the difference between unenlightened and enlightened Change?

Unenlightened Change is left to itself to do whatever it will in its rawest form. It is random, thoughtless, and anarchistic. It is Change left to itself, Change for the sake of Change by dumb, indifferent chance.

Enlightened Change has at least in some part been examined, considered, and directed by sentient thought and will. It is an attempt at change for the better. Yet caution must be applied. Even the best of intentions for Change do not guarantee better results. For example, on Old Earth, ancient cultures built water systems and learned to preserve and store food, but they mistakenly used lead in these processes due to ignorance, and poisoned many.

Yet there as well, in the course of history, sentients have learned from their grim mistakes, and changed for the better, as progress continued. Should we change something? Do we have a right to change something? Look at the Kexxian fixers you have introduced into the Galaxy. They are revolutionizing everything around us as we speak. Did you have a right to unleash this Change on our Galaxy, Naero? What will be the end result of opening up the wisdom, knowledge, and tek of the Kexxian Date Matrix inside of you?

Master, I understand now that the KDM is a gift to the universe to help sentient races of good will and harmony defend themselves against threats just like the enemies we face today. Some of the same enemies the Kexx and their allies faced down long ago and defeated.

Again, the enlightened mind asks, who decides these issues? What Change is resisted? What Change is allowed to go forward? Who decides these issues and why? By what authority? These questions always need to be asked and answered.

I agree. But the way I see it, master. Enlightened Change should give the wise sentients of that place and time the best chance to examine the situation and come up with the best way to implement or direct Change. Change can be imperfect in any number of ways. Change may benefit a majority and even harm a minority, even against their will. What should be done to reduce or limit such harm? If Change creates winners and losers, what is owed to the losers? How do we honestly and fairly decide what Changes go forward and how they affect others?

The Gigacorporations always say to let the markets decide, but that is a canard and a swindle that is far too elusive and evasive. The Corps always rig and control the markets to decide matters in their eternal favor, and against their populations. If nothing changes on those worlds, their various brands of corporate tyranny will only continue to enslave humanity and other sentients for as long as they are allowed to do so. They will never stop doing so on their own volition.

Naero nodded. I agree. That is why the power of the Corps over humanity must be broken by the Declaration of Liberty of free sentients. The Corps were never meant to subjugate and rule over people. The economic systems put in place must serve their populations, not the other way around. That is where the landers went wrong. The Corps became a myopic cult of dogma and enslavement, for the good of no one but the entrenchment and perpetuation of Corps tyranny.

When and where there is Change or lack of Change, the systems in place must be constantly tested and questioned as they go along. Liberty and enlightenment both require constant skepticism, challenge, and vigilance.

Master Jo transported them both far away without warning, into a deep snow bank upon a distant high mountain somewhere.

Naero gasped at the sudden cold temperature shift. But she recovered quickly and warmed herself.

Master Jo thrashed about in the deep snow, laughing like a child. *Ahhh...a snow bath. How refreshing and invigorating, is it not?*

I would have rather had a little warning or choice in the matter, master.

Nonsense. A pleasant surprise is never–

Naero knocked him head over heels with a sixty millimeter snow ball. He grunted at the impact and toppled down the mountainside.

The snow fight was on, raging back and forth, until they triggered a massive avalanche that swept down that entire mountainside.

Both of them transported back to the compound.

Master Jo clapped her on the shoulder, the only High Master who was normally shorter than her. She liked that.

"Excellent, Naero. The Time Dilation kicks in at Standard midnight. Starting tomorrow, we'll be testing all of your powers and abilities to their limits. That's going to be quite dangerous for all of us. So enjoy a good meal, get good rest, and prepare yourself. Good night, adept. Glad to have you here."

With that he vanished.

It was evening by that time, and a spectacular sunset filled the sub-tropical sky. Tess came around to take her to dinner with the rest of the Change adepts, where she met old friends and made new ones in the elaborate dining hall.

Everyone seemed anxious to give her trouble and ask about her many adventures, and about her marriage to Khai, and next about their children.

Many of the adepts had heard amazing things about her daughter, Shetharra.

"Such a Cosmic prodigy," Vaeshen Taylor asked. "When will she begin her Mystic Training?"

"Not for a while, yet," Naero said. "I want her to have time to be a little girl, as much as possible, without so many expectations being placed upon her."

Yet Naero admitted to herself, that one day her little duck would indeed train with the Mystics, and find her own path. Perhaps all of her children would.

The next day, Master Jo assured her that she was now free to use and explore her powers and abilities in every way possible. He even encouraged it.

He transported them to the continent of Nezma, a desolate land currently devoid of any sentients and larger lifeforms by design. There were small birds, other lesser animals, and insects, yet even they were scarce. There were kilometers of mountain, rock, and many dormant and active volcanoes and planes of ash and waste over many kilometers.

This was a place to unleash destruction, if need be, on an intense or wide scale, similar to the one that existed on Tae'ha. The Navy and Marines also came here to test even their largest, most devastating weapons.

Large stretches of enormous craters dotting the landscape attested to that.

Hollowed out under an entire mountain range, there was also an entire underground dome set in the very bedrock, the largest of its kind in all the known galaxy, simply called, the Arena.

There the entire underground complex was formed to trap and contain all forms of Cosmic energy in abundance. Only the highest level adepts who could transform into energy forms could survive and train there.

Master Jo had his own energy form, and when they went there to practice, Naero transformed automatically into one of her energy forms as she entered within.

It was like swimming within the Cosmic flows themselves, like moving through a gigantic Cosmic battery. Instantly she was forced to fight off the hungry desire of her own Dark beast to feast upon all of that intoxicating power and use it to break free.

Master Jo cautioned her. "This place will prove to be quite the paradox for you, Naero. I can sense your turmoil. Here you can channel and make use of all the energy that you could ever want, and yet all the while, the allure of all of that power will constantly threaten to overwhelm and destroy you.

"Here you shall be tempted to your very limits as you struggle to refine and perfect your abilities and master your control over them. Such efforts bring their own severe risk, and you will constantly endure being an intense danger to yourself and everyone else on the entire planet. Do you accept these challenges?"

Naero bowed her head slightly. "I do, High Master. I must gain control over my powers and abilities, before they consume and destroy me, and many of those around me whom I hold dear. If I do not try, such will eventually be my fate."

Master Jo waved his hand. Before them, three naked, faceless humanoid opponents took shape: one red, one blue, and one gold. They were superb athletic specimens. The red one was vaguely male, the blue one vaguely female, and the gold one indeterminate, although on visual inspection, none of them possessed any overt genitalia.

She tried a quick scan of them and sensed nothing. They were not alive. Did they even exist?

Naero went straight up to the golden one and attempted to touch it and use biomancy or teknomancy to scan it.

"Master, what are these things? Holos? Robots?"

The thing wheeled and struck with astonishing strength and speed. A sweepkick knocked her back. Naero quickly flipped and recovered, assuming a fighting stance.

Master Jo smiled. "They are the latest training partners: psyonic constructs. They are similar to replicants, but they are formed psyonically, at will. They were designed for the highest level adepts, Naero. Those such as yourself, Janner, Khai, and High Master Gaviok. Perhaps even your oldest daughter and your other children one day."

"Let's leave my children out of this for now. These things feel solid enough. They hit back like a skilled opponent. Amazing."

"Yes. But they can only be formed here in the Arena and a few places on Nezma where the Cosmic energies are equally focused and intense. And unlike training against another living adept, you don't have to worry about hurting or killing them. They are not alive. They are simply energy, constructs, directed against you by my mind. You don't need to hold back. You can go all out against them."

Master Jo waved a hand at them, and they shifted shape and size as he spoke. "I can form them into anything I wish by the power of my mind. They can be tiny, or gigantic. They can switch to any known form of attack or technique at will."

Naero watched various weapons shift and meld in their hands. They could make use of any known form of armor, shielding, weapons, or tek. They could use any psyonic talent.

Suddenly the three became three hundred, assembled across the Arena.

"They can be one, and they can be many. Prepare yourself, Naero. When I said we were going to challenge you to your limits, I meant just that. This tek was originally design to help train Khai to become the Mystic Enforcer, and then your brother Janner and Master Gaviok, but it has since been modified and upgraded to deal even with you."

Naero's felt her own eyes twinkle. She loved a good fight, a good challenge. She loved it like the breath of life itself. Other than the enemy, who were always trying to murder her, there were only a few persons she knew in the galaxy, such as Baeven, whom she did not have to hold back against.

If Master Jo was correct, this was going to be both dangerous, and a helluva lot of fun.

"Bring it!" Naero Amashin Maeris almost snarled through her trademark half-smile.

"When do we begin?"

Master Jo grinned back at her. "Right now!"

Red came at her shooting energy blasts and beams from his hands. Blue used a 150 millimeter energized jo staff, and Gold used energy blades.

Naero fought them across the Arena all throughout that first week.

It was a thrilling joy not to have to hold back against them.

She could splatter the constructs with massive punches, rip them in half with kicks, and crush and obliterate them with sonics, with eye beams, and all manner of energy effects.

Master Jo would just as quickly reform the constructs and send them at her again in new combinations of threats and assaults, surprising her with different types and increased numbers out of nowhere.

He did everything he could with the constructs to overwhelm and overtake her that he could.

She practiced all of her skills and attacks, every one of her techniques and combinations of those techniques. She continued to explore and expand the full range of her powers and abilities.

Naero also suffered serious wounds of her own, and spent most nights using biomancy to regenerate herself for the challenges of the next day.

Each week that went by, Master Jo stepped up the threats.

He began to give the constructs some of Naero's own powers and abilities. The battles grew fiercer and more deadly.

73

At one point the constructs closed with her and nearly slew Naero. In response, her Dark beast nearly broke free.

Naero barely tamped it back down, allowing her partial Dark beast form to emerge as a release valve.

Master Jo increased the size and abilities of the constructs in an attempt to compensate.

The battles increased in magnitude.

Suddenly they faced another danger. Time after time, Naero increased her powers to such levels that she was at risk of either unleashing her Dark beast completely, or reaching critical mass and exploding, potentially taking out all of Oorrii, or at least a good chunk of it.

She could not release her energies fast enough, as her powers expanded exponentially, threatening to annihilate herself and everything around her. She had fought that same problem ever since she could channel energy.

Finally, Naero sought help from every source available to her. One of the keys came from the KDM.

In the end, she was able to configure a way to shunt and store Cosmic energy directly into the flows of the Astral Plane interdimensionally.

The Astral Plane was in a sense, an entire universe of proto-Cosmic energy all at once, waiting to act. Naero could use it as an outlet to release energy, if she took in more than she could control.

Naero continued to become one with the flows of Cosmic energy throughout the universe and its interactive dimensions. She continued to expand her mind and her awareness. She understood the complex interrelationships more and more. The various dimensions were all paradoxes. They were separate, and yet they interacted with each other in a myriad of important ways. They did affect each other.

And the enemy had found a way to cheat the very laws that bound them in their eternal prison. They were using dimensional energy to slip out into the Astral Plane and through it, to bend their will even into the Prime Material Plane itself.

She began to see how the enemy tracked her by her energy traces and signatures. She had not been attuned enough before to see it. When she startapped and expanded her energies without containing or shielding them properly, energy flooded out all around her in great quantities. Advanced beings with ancient knowledge could not only detect those flows of energy, but capitalize upon them as well.

Naero still didn't know how to fully stop them yet, but at least she could perceive the problems involved, and in what directions she needed to keep exploring.

The evolving matches with the psyonic constructs in the Arena kept her hopping.

Then one day, Naero emerged into the Arena, and Master Jo smiled at her like never before.

"What the hell are you up to today?" she asked, backing away slightly.

"Something new, taking into account all that has been gained from observing you and your astonishing powers."

"So what is it?"

The three constructs took shape, slightly modified.

They all looked just like her.

"That doesn't make them me," Naero said.

"As close as I can imagine them to be," Master Jo told her. "Get ready for an entirely new level of competition."

Naero smiled and went straight at them.

12

Naero rose to the challenge to battle the new improved constructs, tailored more and more to be just like herself.

Most of the time she still won, but the damage she took also increased. Sometimes she required days to regenerate from the fierce combat sessions she endured.

One time, Master Jo had to stop the match, step in quickly, and save her from dying. Eventually, she was going to be unlucky, if nothing else. The factor of raw chance was always involved when fighting at such extreme levels.

While Naero recovered, she woke up one day on *The Xanadu*, the starship that she had ordered her reps and fixers to build.

Not only that, but to her great wonder, Khai and Sharrah appeared, bringing the children to visit her in Medical.

Naero burst into tears at such a happy surprise and held her children to her, ignoring her pain as she repeatedly kissed them.

Khai could still wrap his enormous arms around his entire family and hold them close.

"How did you manage it?" she asked. "What about the Time Dilation? The kids?"

Khai shrugged. "We wanted it to be a pleasant surprise, once you got yourself situated. I convinced the Mystics and Intel that this was important. You need us, our presence and support. What's three years? At least we'll spend them all together, while only three months passes on the outside. They can do without us for that long. Janner and your uncle said they'd do their best to keep an eye on things while we're out of the mix."

Naero stared up at him, wiping her eyes. "I love you for doing this, Khai. I couldn't be happier. You always seem to know just what I need. Thank you, my heart. Haisha! How I've missed you all, and you've been hiding here all the time?"

Khai grinned. "Just waiting for the right moment. I brought Sharrah and the team, and replicated the Nursery on board *The Xanadu.*"

Naero called out to her medteks on hand. "Hey you guys, get with the biomancy. I want a full recovery and pronto. Let's make this happen. I have things to do, and people to see!"

*

Having her family with her gave Naero increased hope, support, and encouragement as never before. With them to stumble home to every night, she continued to work very hard and make good progress on many fronts.

Seeing her children daily for almost three years straight was going to be a joy she had never known. Naero loved it. And raising their children together deepened the love between her and Khai. Everything in her life just seemed to come together and mesh.

She could bounce ideas off of Khai, discuss them with Master Jo and Om, or go deep within herself to go over matters with her Kexxian counterpart, Orean.

Together, they all determined that she would develop greater control over her powers and abilities and even expand them, once she found and learned to master her on-the-edge center. This would be her own personal harmony, of all the forces and powers that roiled inside of her.

It was up to her find that and sustain it.

Taming the mess that was inside of her was the real trick, just as difficult as the never ending task of trying to control her Dark beast. Most likely, the two we're going to turn out to be related. The issues were definitely a very deep part of her own existence.

The first year passed quickly, and she learned all that she could learn through perfecting her combat skills and Cosmic powers and talents. Yet even Master Jo said that were many paths to Mystic wisdom and enlightenment.

Master Jo became adamant that a study of shapechanging would provide her with many opportunities to understand herself and the universe further. Shapeshifting was a Mystic ability Naero did not actually possess yet. She had mentally transformed into a Kexx within her own mind, and the skill was closely related to biomancy and replicating.

By now she was the foremost expert on replication.

Thus in the second year of her Change Wisdom training, she would focus on shapechanging.

Tess Fae, their best shifter around, would work very closely with Naero.

There were many dangers involved. She was warned that pain and injury were quite common–including mental agony due to shifting to and from many forms and different neural nets, structures, and patterns.

"We'll start with the other sentient humanoids," Tess told her. "They're the closest to us physically and mentally. You don't want to start right off with something far removed from your current lifeform, like an animal or an insect or such."

"How about just a regular lander?" Naero suggested.

Tess nodded. "An excellent place to begin. Ramorans, Besh, Silesians, Piettos, Naivatch, and even Matayans would all be good genetic choices. We have enclaves of them all on Oorrii. We can study them with biomancy before you make the attempt."

Naero laughed for old times sake. Haisha, transforming into a Matayan. What would Emperor Ellis say?

Yet in the end, they chose standard, Old Earth strain humans, close to Naero's genetic markers.

They took a small courier ship and visited the proper enclave and performed biomancy scans and studies of several human women Naero's own age.

Shapechanging into the male form or someone of a different age range involved other unwanted complexities that she did not need to deal with at first.

Tess cautioned her. "We'll keep it simple for your first transformation, N. The first one is often the most difficult, and usually very painful, going back and forth. Sorry. That's just the way of it."

Naero grimaced and sighed. "I understand. It would help me if I mindlinked with you and observed you transforming a few times. I've learned many psyonic powers that way, by observing someone who already knows how to use an ability. I can see the types of energies at work and gain an understanding of the paths those energies take."

Tess seemed highly impressed. "I don't know of anyone else, except for perhaps the High Masters, who can do anything close to that."

A young human woman their age, a lander from one of the enclaves, volunteered for the experiment. Tess had her brought into one of the Mystic medical clinics. Behind closed doors she had the woman sedated on a medbed. There was no risk to the host.

Naero linked with Tess and studied the first transformation as it progressed.

Tess in her turn was an expert. She linked with the woman by touch and used biomancy in very adept, specific ways to change herself into a copy of the test subject in almost every facet.

Even biomancy and the most advanced genetic and medical scans showed her to be an exact duplicate physically.

The only slight differences were psyonic, and only a handful of sentients in the galaxy could detect such things, given time.

Naero understood more about the shapechanging process, and felt slightly relieved.

Shapechanging was a form of replication, or at least very closely related version of it. Naero felt a flare of pain on Tess's part at the height of the process, but it was nothing that could not be endured.

She had experienced far worse.

The entire process took seconds, much less than a minute.

Then Tess shifted back to her neutral form, her base form, in about the same time.

"That was amazing, Tess. Can you do it again, and is there any way to slow the process down more?"

"I can," she said with a frown, "but that causes more pain. It's better if you do it quick. For your sake, Naero, I'll take the pain. You need to learn. Notice also how I keep myself anchored to my base form in my mind. That is very important. If you lose your focus on that, you won't be able to shift back. Some lifeforms can be very distracting, alluring, and exhilarating. You aren't much good as a shapechanger if you can't change back. Always remember that–who and what you really are."

Tess performed the transformation again, going slow, grinding her teeth and grunting and hissing at the ramped up pain. Naero nodded when she had seen enough, and Tess quickly shifted back.

Naero was curious. "When you copy another person or creature, do you gain all of their thoughts and memories?"

"Somewhat," Tess said. "Not their deep memories and emotions. Those are hard to reach. Mostly just their surface knowledge, attitudes, ideas, opinions–short term, superficial stuff. But it usually works enough for you to impersonate them for a while. That can come in handy, and you will be a match for them on genetic and other bioscans."

"How far does it go? Do you gain their skills and abilities? Can you do what they do? Can you operate weapons or vehicles they are familiar with? Do you know the people they know? If they have a specialized skill such as dancing, or surgery, or speaking a certain language, does that transfer?"

"Sometimes, but not always. Languages can be learned from the mind, but art forms and high performance skills are more difficult. For example, if the host is an accomplished painter or musician, or athlete, you can't gain such capabilities, because most of them are improved over time by practice. But if the host likes blueberries for instance, you might crave them as well."

Tess stepped away for a moment, and then turned around. "Now let me show you something else, Naero. When you become more adept at shapechanging, you don't have to copy a host completely, unless you need to look exactly like her or him or it. If you just need to blend into a crowd, you can settle for what I call, generic approximations."

In a flash, Tess transformed into a young lander woman very similar to the test subject, but still different in many subtle ways. "In many instances, approximates can be faster and easier, because you aren't trying to duplicate someone's appearance, personality, and genetics completely.

"But at the same time, you have to keep appearances within an acceptable range, so that they do not look freakish or call undue attention to you. It all takes experience and practice. Do you think you're ready to give it a go? Remember, most shifters don't get it on the first try. Stop if the pain becomes too much and back off."

Naero linked with the test subject and attempted to do everything that Tess had done.

It was much more difficult than she thought.

She gasped and almost cried out. Tess transformed from the ground up, from feet to head. Naero attempted to do the same, and was up to her ankles in the shapechange before she realized that the agony was akin to having her legs lit on fire.

Tess linked with her, sharing her pain.

Naero, go as far as you can go. I know it hurts. I've been there. You can get past it. Keep trying.

Naero focused, and pushed the transformation up to her hands and lower torso. Great. Now the bottom half of her was on fire. She resisted the urge to transform into an energy being to endure the heat.

Excellent. Keep going, N. the sooner you complete the change, the sooner the pain will abate. That's why you want to learn to shift as quickly as possible.

Naero pushed it up to her shoulders, shuddering and whimpering as she did so. The pain was agonizing, almost unbearable, even for her.

Almost there, N. Finish it. Go ahead and scream.

Naero did just that. She collapsed to the ground and nearly blacked out.

Tess dragged her back up to her feet. "Naero. Look in the holomirror."

The face of the young lander woman stared back at her.

"You did it," Tess said. "You completed your first shapechange."

It didn't feel like a victory. "I don't like it," Naero groaned.

Tess patted her shoulder. "No, it is odd and unusual, sometimes downright weird and even unpleasant, becoming someone or something else, and knowing what it is to be the other. As a shapechanger, it all comes with the territory. You just have to suck it up and deal with all of that. Now, let's get you back. That's going to be just as tough, your first time, so steel yourself to that fact. Change back to yourself, your base form. Do it as quickly as possible to limit the pain."

"Haisha!" Naero exclaimed, "Give me a few more minutes to prepare myself. That was rough. It took a lot out of me."

"Rest for a few minutes then. It's not a race.

"This isn't right," Naero said. "Is this what it's like to be a lander?"

"Remember, to them, all of these parameters are within their normal range."

"Tess, I...I feel so weak, so slow and vulnerable. Haisha! How do they manage?"

Her counterpart chuckled. "N, the average Spacer is far stronger and faster than the average lander human. Different lifeforms are going to be just that–different. Spacers forced themselves to evolve. And Psyonic talents are common among the Clans. And in your base form, you are something beyond even a Mystic Savant. We still don't quite know what you are exactly. Of course this would be a step down for you. If you don't like what you are, then transform back to your original self."

Naero pushed through changing back, slightly faster, and slightly less tormenting, by duration if nothing else.

By then she was done in, completely spent. She felt as if she were drifting into a coma.

They brought her back to *The Xanadu* on a medbed, and it took her three days to recover from the ordeal.

After that, things continued to progress. Shapechanging grew easier, faster, and less tormenting. Especially under Tess's tutelage. Sometimes Master Jo observed closely at hand, studying Naero's continuing progress.

It did go smoother with practice and progress. Weeks and months passed. Naero learned the variations of gender, and then age. Age was actually surprisingly tricky. Once again, her Chaos training with Master Vane gave her surprising insights, as she recalled her biomancy understanding of the life cycle from birth to death.

After she had mastered shapechanging into the various sentient humanoids, Tess and Master Jo agreed that it was time for her to explore the realm of animals and other types of near or non-sentient creatures.

Tess continued to be her priceless guide, explaining any complexities or concerns with various forms.

All shapechanging became a variation upon a theme.

"Animals are easier in some ways than sentients," Tess said, "and in some ways more difficult."

Naero frowned and sighed. "Of course they are. It's not like any of this could ever be easy."

"That's just it," Tess told her. "It's easier to transform into many animals. The hard part is in maintaining your focus on your base form– who you were, and being able to shift back to it. The allure of animal forms is that they are much more mindless and driven by base needs. It is far too easy and tempting to simply go wild, and never come back. That is the animal mind."

"Great," Naero said. "So, where do we start?"

"Something easy. Something closer to us, fellow mammals–primates and pigs work well for your first animal shapechange. Don't go for anything far fetched or exotic."

Tess had sedated test subjects brought in on medbeds. A variety of jungle ape, and a specimen of domesticated pig.

Naero mindlinked with Tess as the latter transformed into one beast, and then the other.

Naero, notice how much concerted effort it takes for me to maintain my own mind and consciousness. The impetus of my new form's mindset and neural net constantly just wants me to be an ape, or a pig, and nothing else. You have to maintain your center, your true mind. That is the only way to be able to find your way back to your base form.

Tess shifted back. "Your turn, now. I'll stay linking with your mind and help you if you drift off. It's easier than you think it is, so stay constantly on you guard."

Naero took in a few deep breaths.

She attempted the ape first.

Tess was right. In one way, the physical transformation was easier.

But immediately she felt the strong pull to simply give in to her form and its overwhelming desire simply to be an ape.

Tess gave her tips to focus on through their link. How to, in effect, maintain two minds: the animal mind, and her own mind, all at the same time.

You're doing well, Naero. Now let's bring you back and try the pig.

Sure thing Tess.

Yet that return was one of the most difficult she had ever faced, except for her very first.

Naero was forced to call it a day, and tackle the pig transformation the next.

Tess counseled her, "You're going to feel really weird, N. You aren't accustomed to this. Animal minds can linger in you head for a bit when you're not used to them. You don't get all of their influences out right away. I'll warn Khai to have you kept in medical and under observation, until the mind traces and imprint patterns completely fade. We don't want you going ape."

Naero stuck her tongue out at her friend. "Hah hah, how amusing."

Tess chuckled. "I couldn't resist. Just a little shapechanger humor. Want me to come by and groom you for fleas and ticks?"

"No, that's Khai's job. Although I do have a weird craving for mangoes."

Tess laughed. "I'll see what I can do."

From that day forward, Naero explored the ins and outs of various animals and lifeforms. She didn't enjoy becoming reptiles, amphibians, or bugs and insects, but she learned what she could when she had to.

Who was going to expect a bug? Yet they might swat her by accident.

Actually, being a pig was glorious. But becoming a dolphin was fascinating and liberating. Dolphins had amazing minds and very close relationships with each other. But all of their intellect was based and focused around being a dolphin and living their intense lives to the hilt. They were extreme athletes and animal world hedonists.

Birds of many kinds were intriguing, and the range of their powers of flight alone were exhilarating and staggering, let alone their many other powers and abilities.

Plants and trees were less than exciting, but there were still valuable insights to be gained from their long term view and perspectives. They were still living things, and they experienced life in bizarre ways that were completely foreign to other living things.

Then Master Jo gave her an extreme test.

He introduced her to Jati–a genetically and mentally modified Ejjai. The two were actually sitting together sipping Choolien violet tea with honey and lime in the gardens.

Naero's first reaction was to summon her swords and prepare to remove the Ejjai alpha's head from her shoulders the next instant.

"Stop!" Master Jo insisted, temporarily shielding Jati behind a golden screen of force. "Do not attack my guest, Naero. Jati is not like the hyperviolent slaves of the enemy. I have gone to great lengths to modify her much further to be rational, reasonable, intelligent, and even in her own way, quite compassionate."

"I don't believe it," Naero snarled, refusing to let down her guard.

Jati wore a rather pained expression on her face. "Master Jo has explained matters to me, Ms. Maeris. I quite understand your strong reaction to my…my presence. But please, sit down and let us speak of many things. Will you allow me to pour you a cup? The tea is really quite good."

Naero sat down and nodded, not taking her eyes off the Ejjai.

Om, check that tea for poison.

Already done. No poison. Drink away.

Naero took a sip. They were right. The violet tea was superb.

"So," Naero said, "does this mean that there is an enclave of these hyper-uplifted Ejjai on Oorrii like Jati somewhere? Or is it the regular, vicious, warlike breed that the invasion worlds came to know and love?"

"What would you do if there were?" Master Jo asked.

Naero kept staring at Jati. "Easy. If they are of the latter kind, I would locate and eradicate them."

Jati lowered her face and sighed. "I am the only one of my kind," she said. "I was selected from the frozen specimens that your Intel and Master Jo keep on hand for experimentation. He uplifted me to my current state, and I am thankful to him for that. I'm very sorry that these foes of yours have used less evolved versions of my race and species to attack your worlds and do such great harm."

Naero sneered. "Sorry will never make up for all of the atrocities that were committed by the Ejjai invaders–and that is still going on in some places. There can be no talk of forgiveness."

Jati bowed her head. "No, I suppose not. Yet remember, my people did not ask for this. They did not ask that these things be done to them. Your people are just as warlike. What if the enemy took over Spacers and turned them into their shock troops and weapons?"

Master Jo interrupted Naero. "You're being very rude and hard upon my guest, N. Ease up. Jati had no part in the invasions. And in her current incarnation, she would never do so."

"Master, with respect, I cannot stomach or accept any comparison or parity with the Ejjai. Indeed, Spacers make war when there is no other way, they are a valiant people. Yet they have always been liberators, never conquerors. But I have witnessed firsthand the abomination that the Ejjai call warfare; it is etched and branded forever in my mind for the rest of my days."

"Naero, listen carefully. Jati is going to be sedated, and I want you to shapechange with her."

Naero recoiled in fear and horror. She dropped her tea cup, the cup broke, and her lavender tea spread quickly and stained the table.

Jati moved quickly to clean up the mess.

Master Jo placed a hand on Naero's arm. "We must fully understand our enemies in order to be able to defeat them," he told her.

"No!" Naero insisted. "Become one of them? Are you mad?"

"Quite possibly," Master Jo said with a grin. "This is no jest or joke, Naero. I am quite serious. Just as I have done, you should see for yourself and understand what the enemy actually did to the Ejjai. How they twisted that species for their own ends, making monsters out of them that they were never intended to be–that they never would have become, on their own. That was an abomination as well."

"So, is there a Dakkur habitat on Oorrii as well?" she said in jest.

Master Jo shook his head. "I wish there were, for our sakes, but those creatures are far too advanced and volatile. They were tainted and corrupted long ago. I don't think there is any help for them. But I think the Ejjai can still be saved."

Naero rose and kicked her nanochair behind her, shattering its form. It quickly re-shaped itself at the table according to its presets.

"Saved?" Naero said, nearly in a rage. "We can't save them. They need to be exterminated!"

"Naero," Master Jo said earnestly. "you will change your mind. Certainly the twisted monsters we face can only be put down. But the Ejjai were never that in the beginning. And they were never meant to become what they have been warped into. Trust me. Do this to gain knowledge, insight, and enlightenment. How better to understand our foes? To know them, we must become like them and exist and think like them for a time."

When they went into the med center, Naero still shuddered when she saw Jati sedated on that medbed. She took her place on the one right next to it.

85

Shapechanging into an Ejjai was one of the scariest, and among the weirdest things she had ever done.

Yet right from the beginning, she began to see that Master Jo had been right all along.

The Ejjai evolved from opportunistic pack animals. Their humanoid forms were primal, prehistoric in function and intellect. Statistically, they were no more rapacious than other early sentients at their primordial level of existence. They were pack hunters, pure and simple.

When Naero used her advanced biomancy to study Jati, and then shapechange into her copy, Naero read the genetic history clearly.

What Triax and then the alien enemies mostly did to the Ejjai was monstrous indeed. The pweaking of their genetics was unlike any kind of genetic manipulation she had ever observed.

Everything was done to turn them into hyperviolent monsters and shock troops. All of their increased intellect was bent to shape them that way.

It took Master Jo months of intense labor to undo all that for Jati–just one specimen.

By becoming an Ejjai herself, Naero could see the raw effects of positive and negative life energies of the universe at work. There was indeed good and evil, to every degree and form. The G'lothc were like a Cosmic disease inflicted upon the universe.

They marred and corrupted everything they touched. Yet most things simply existed. They were neither good nor evil, yet each of them had the potential to be shaped into something that was more one than the other, if taken by powers greater than them.

The Ejjai had been enslaved and victimized as badly if not worse than anyone else, and turned into an affliction and a curse upon the galaxy.

After Naero returned to her base form, Master Jo took her and Jati to the storage areas where thousands of frozen, captured Ejjai were held for study and experimentation.

"Do what you think is best," Master Jo told them.

Naero looked to Jati.

Jati nodded and bowed her head.

Naero went among the Ejjai, some of her most hated adversaries, and put forth her advanced, biomancy powers.

She returned them, every one, to their initial forms at the point they had been taken, back to what they had originally evolved to be–just another prehistoric hunting group. Not monsters. Just a stage between animals and sentients.

The task took Naero six entire days of difficult labor.

It was only a few thousand, barely a symbolic gesture, yet it still felt right. They would be kept in their frozen, hibernation sleep for the time being.

Naero took one healthy male and did what Master Jo had done with Jati. She uplifted him to the same level, and gave him the Ejjai name of Baroon, so that Jati would have another of her kind to keep her company. Now they would not be alone.

They could live out their days on Oorrii.

Naero and Master Jo worked out a plan to find a proper world to introduce the Ejjai somewhere, a place where they would not be so invasive, where they wound find challenges, and a place for themselves in an acceptable ecosystem that was right for them.

By that time, Naero had spent nearly an entire year mastering shapechanging. Master Jo met with her very early the next day before dawn.

"The Ejjai matter was your final, official test for shapechanging," Master Jo told her. "And might I add, that you did very well. May you continue to do so. Naero, you now possess a rare gift that few shall ever know. You can understand sentients and other creatures in deep ways that most people never will. That gift will continue to allow you to grow and your personal enlightenment to expand."

Naero bowed. "Thank you, High Master."

"I know this cannot have been easy. I know very well how you felt about the Ejjai. How many still do, and with just cause."

"No, Master. You were right…more than right. Hatred, is a waste of time, effort, emotion, and energy. It often harms the hater, more than the hated. It is better to let go of that, and bring things into greater balance and harmony. I see it all now. We need to fight harder to prevent such things from taking place. No race or species should be enslaved or used in such a fashion. It is the height of wrong, and the mark of evil minds."

"Agreed. You have worked very hard this second year, Naero. And now I have a little reward for you—for all of your tireless work and relentless effort."

Naero grinned. "A reward? What are you talking about?"

Master Jo smiled. "Just take my hand, and trust me. Close your eyes, Naero."

Naero did as he asked. They transported to some place else on Oorrii.

Already she had a strange, heady feeling.

When she opened her eyes, at her first look around in the fading twilight, she thought that she was in the middle of just another patch of thick jungle or forest.

Then she made out the trees. Galu and snoka trees.

She closed her eyes again for a long delicious moment and savored the sweet, cloying aroma of shinga flowers.

As the very first glimmer of dawn flickered on the horizon, joyful voices from Naero's most cherished dreams and memories sang their song of greeting nearby.

The ancient Kexxian words, laden with gentle power, rang out clearly, just as they had for millions of years.

Sha nii hah, ahluu-nii-haa, mah nah-hii, jah ah-loh, ah-dii!

Then came the song of praise and thankfulness.

Yah-duu Ah Shah Lah! Shah hah lah shah-dae! Yah Jhah Vah Shah-Lae. Ae duu vah. Ae duu vah shah lah!

Naero fell to her knees, placed her face in her hands and wept, sobbing beyond all control.

There were Tua still alive, somewhere in the galaxy. How funny. If she had thought about, it might have just occurred to her that if Master Jo had done his Noah's Ark thing, that he would surely have an enclave–a place for the peaceful Tua.

Here she had thought them all dead, and herself to blame, especially after the entire planet of Janosha was lost.

Naero rose up eagerly, smiling and wiping her face.

Master Jo grinned pleasantly on his own. "What do you wish to do, Naero? More than anything else right now? Think and decide carefully. It is your choice."

She did not respond.

Naero did not hesitate.

She was already well-versed in Tua genetics and Biomancy.

Naero changed shape into a Tua approximate with blue-black hair. Her eyes fixed straight ahead, she went forward, to join the Tua as one of them. She wanted nothing less than to be one of them, and share their ways and their love once again.

Deep within her, her heart sang, and she hurried on, waiting for the tribe to take up their next song of wonder.

13

For the next month she became Kali, a young female Tua among that tribe. It was not so rare for individuals from other tribes to wander about looking to find a new place for themselves.

She recalled all that she had known and relearned about the Tua way of life until it all felt natural. Each day was precious to her. She had never known such peace and serenity in all of her life.

Or had she?

Something still troubled her in the back of her mind at times. What had she forgotten? Was it something or someone important? Thinking about the past grew fuzzy and difficult to recall. She was so happy. Why then was her past so troubling to her mind? Why did she continue to suffer from these strange images and dreams?

By then she had proved herself many times over, and she had many handsome suitors.

Why then did that trouble her as well? Love in all its forms was a way of life among the Tua. Why shouldn't she take a mate herself, and know all of the good things in life? After all, she was a Tua now...

Or was she?

Why did she even think like that? What did now mean? How could she have been something or someone different before? People could not change what they were.

Then the very next day the shining Halaena child appeared in the village, like a little star, walking down the main trail, serene, fearless, and determined.

The Tua lined up, males on one side, females on the other, and they bowed to the shining spacechild in great reverence.

Kali saw the child approaching her like some doom, the girl's tiny footfalls thundering across the ground as if in slow motion.

Their eyes locked, and Kali gasped, bringing both of her trembling hands to her trembling lips.

Looking into those impossibly blue eyes suddenly made Kali feel as if some great power had hurled a burning stone straight through her chest and hollowed her out.

As the Halaena drew closer, Kali dropped to her knees.

It felt as if her brain and her mind were suddenly on fire. And a voice in her mind called out to her that she had shut out before.

Shetharra. The child's name was Shetharra. Kali knew that somehow. How did she know that?

Shetharra the little Halaena girl threw her arms Kali, and it was as if a thunderbolt shot through her and drilled her into the very ground.

"Mama, come home to us," Shetharra told her, holding on so tight.

Naero awoke all at once inside of Kali, like one who had just been blasted through a mountain. The barriers were all down now, and in a moment she perceived all that had passed.

Although she still looked like Kali, she had regained the mind of her base form.

She scooped her oldest daughter into her arms and rose up, carrying her into her hut. "I'm sorry I was gone for so long, my little duck."

Shetharra continue to plant soft kisses on her mother's furry face and hold her tight around the neck. "It's all right, momma. Did you have fun playing with the fuzzy mouse people? They look like they would be fun."

"Yes, I did, my sweet one. But you're right, it's time for me to come home now."

She put Shetharra down for a bit. There were things to be put right.

Her daughter looked up at her and grinned, twirling slightly from side to side. "Momma. You could make me into a little fuzzy mouse girl, and we could play with them together if you want?"

Naero laughed aloud. "Maybe some day, little duck. Not today. I've already been away too long."

She made a Tua replicant with the proper appearance and imbued it with Kali's memories and personalities. Naero gave the replicant her Tua clothes and all of her Tua things. Kali would be free to live out her short span of life just like any other Tua, about three decades total.

Naero returned to her base form.

She and her daughter emerged from the hut with Kali. The Tua were very impressed and awed to have two such mighty Halaena among them. Naero explained that her young daughter had wandered into the village, and that they were returning now to the Halaena enclave on Oorrii. They promised friendship and continuing aid and assistance to the Tua. They said that they would visit again soon.

Once the farewells were said, and the proper songs sung, the two Halaena walked into the jungle and got the hell out of there.

Naero met with Khai and Master Jo once back home. She instantly began to apologize, but Master Jo stopped her.

"The fault is not yours, Naero. It was mine for tempting you that way. Both Tess and I felt that it was important for you, as a shapechanger, to experience losing yourself in a form that you found tempting. That will keep you from falling into such trouble again later."

She thought about that and began to feel very angry.

She quickly handed her daughter over to Khai and rounded on Master Jo. "You knew this was going to happen?"

Master Jo held up both hands. "We thought it might, yet nothing is certain. Again, I'm sorry."

"Sorry?" she fumed. "If my daughter wasn't here with me, I'd do my level best to kick you into next week, Master or no Master. How's that for Time Dilation? With both of my feet rammed up your ass! Do you know what you did to me? Do you understand the pain you've caused me and will continue to cause me? On into the future? You don't get it. I wanted to be a Tua. It was wonderful! It was like tearing myself apart coming back out."

Tess rushed in at that moment. "I heard yelling. I thought you'd be pissed off after you came back out of it. That's understandable. But please don't be too hard on Master Jo. We both decided that it would do you good to experience this problem. At least here we could help you get back. What if it happened with you on your own? You'd be lost forever."

Naero clenched her fists. "I'm still not certain that I shouldn't kick both of your assess into mush!"

"We probably couldn't stop you at this point, N. But whether you like it or not, all shifters need to deal with this kind of thing. You have to be able to find a way to bring yourself back out if you get stuck. You won't always be here on Oorrii under controlled conditions, with help standing by."

"Well, get the hell away from me before I change my mind. I need to spend some time with my family and get my head straight after all of this. No more rewards. No more setups."

Naero turned away and stalked off with Khai and Shetharra in tow.

Her recovery took over a week.

Then Master Jo and Den came around, insisting that she take up the last year of her training.

This involved Astral and Interdimensional knowledge, wisdom, and travel.

Master Jo had been her guide into the Astral Plane and other dimensions once before, but that had been a rush job while they were on a mission. They didn't really have the ability to spend much time exploring and learning the finer points about such things.

Having Den Kurtz with them for Astral and dimensional travel was just as natural and logical as having Tess along for shapechanging.

Den could transform himself into any type of energy being at will.

Den explained how transforming into an astral energy being form automatically transported him to the Astral Plane, without having to go to sleep or into an astral trance. "And because I'm completely in an energy being form, there is no vulnerable physical body to leave behind or protect."

"Yes," Master Jo said. "But the increased danger is that if you are attacked and destroyed in the Astral Plane in this form, you are dead and lost forever. Just as a physical being destroyed in the Prime Material Plane can no longer exist in the Astral Plane. Dead is still dead, wherever you are slain."

Naero had to ask. "How important is the Astral Plane to the Spacer Mystics?" she asked. "Just what is it that I need to learn?"

Master Jo tried to explain. "As a Mystic Master, you must be able to enter and leave the Astral Plane safely, by yourself, and with others if need be. While in the Astral Plane, you must be able to navigate it, learn its expanse and how to deal with, overcome, or defeat its many dangers. You must learn to do all of these things to my satisfaction."

Naero grunted slightly. "That sounds like a tall order. Tall, but doable. To a degree, I've managed to do much of that already. Anything else?"

Master Jo popped to the other side of her, his hands on his hips.

"Naero, as usual, I'm glad you asked. You're so great with questions, I love that. Akin to matters at hand, you will also need to be able to work with the Dimensional Council."

"Yeah, I've heard of that. The High Masters keep going off to these vital meetings."

"Naero, you need to know that it changes constantly, and it also constantly gets bigger. It is chaotic and maddening at times, yet there are advanced intelligences out there, some so far away that we will never be able to physically meet with them. They are both from distant galaxies on the other side of the universe, and even from other universes and dimensions entirely."

"What is so vital about these meetings that the Mystics are always risking their lives and leaving themselves vulnerable for our enemies here? What does it matter so much?"

Master Jo just grinned for a moment, hugging his knees to him while he floated up in the air.

"Are you going to tell me, or just giggle to yourself up there, bobbing around?"

Master Jo burst out laughing. "Knowledge, wisdom, and enlightenment, Naero. A myriad of experiences. Sentients who have faced down similar threats to ours. Some failed, and their galaxies and universes are dying or being destroyed while we do what we do here. We cannot help them now. They made too many wrong choices and are doomed. That is just one chance to learn from the folly and mistakes of others, Naero. Just one. That is not enough?"

"I was just asking to learn. I did not say the Dimensional Council was a waste of time and effort."

"No, but you implied some of that, and that's all right. Some skepticism and critical thinking is always helpful. But understand this as well, Naero. In our current situation, from what you have told me and what we now know, the G'lothc are doing everything they can to break out somewhere. They do not care where. And right now it appears that they are finding some success bleeding through the Astral Plane, and then into our own. They are gaining influence, seeking power to use for their ends, and searching for hosts to work their will through, if not house their dark souls."

He looked Naero right in the eye.

"We have no idea exactly how they are managing these temporary, breakouts, or how to stop them. But they are growing more frequent, lasting longer, and getting worse. Therefore, if these attacks are starting in the Astral Plane, we need to find a way to end them or patch things up so that they can't attack us from those directions."

Master Jo and Naero placed themselves into astral trances, while Den felt confident simply going with them in his astral energy form. While in the Astral Plane, they spoke to each other using telepathy. Mindlinks there were super easy, especially if users knew the mind of the person they wished to speak to.

And bonus, it worked across vast distances as well, once you were linked to a person, and in that reality, you could move away or to a sentient you were linked with literally at will–in a flash of thought.

Den took a turn at instruction, not leaving it all to Master Jo.

N, you first need to learn about the numerous dangers in the Astral Plane and others. There are various kinds of what are referred to as feeders, singly or in packs, who directly feed off of the Astral and Cosmic energies of others. Some can be chased off or decoyed easily with attacks or a bit of power shot off into the distance. Others go for the source, and must be fought off or destroyed outright. And some are mindless, while others are actually sentient or partially so.

They went hunting for some of those dangers.

For lures, as in Old Earth fishing, Den and Master Jo used small bundles or pockets of various types of energy in shielded pods to lure in a multitude of feeders.

Some were huge and transparent, like giant, semi-living, gleaming soap bubbles. They could be anywhere from the size of a transport to a city. These energy collectors or feeders ate or gathered energy as they drifted about on the astral currents, either actively hunting or drawn by naturally occurring energy spikes and pockets in the ether.

These are bluugians, Master Jo explained. *They are relatively harmless to us. You would have to stay inside the digestive tract of one of them for days at a time for them to even weaken you.*

Other feeders were not so innocuous, and many feeders fed on each other whenever possible. Some feeders were in shape, similar to lampreys, eels, and huge, bloated gulpers that looked to be bloated blobs with enormous mouths, hence the term, gulper.

Many of these feeders were translucent, and their glowing insides could be seen, as they fed and digested energy.

There were some that looked like combinations between whales and squids.

Then there were the pack feeders, such as sparkling glurim, who looked like sparklers crackling when they fed. They were practically invisible, otherwise. Next came waves of shimmering kreth, who had mouths on both ends and attacked in swarms or shoals similar to Old Earth piranha.

Kreth were vicious, and had to be dispersed and shredded by energy blasts before they drained their victims dry of power and left them behind as empty husks.

Malanches were something in shape between an astral manta ray and a large astral shark, with beautiful glowing, elongated tails and fins. They could hunt in mated pairs, small family pods, or large groups. In the latter, they could be quite formidable.

Next there were zippers, feeders that race in at impossible speeds to spear their prey, gobbling up energy, and then blazing away like comets. They could attack singly, or in coordinated showers of them.

That first week, Naero and Om cataloged over a hundred varieties of weird feeders, with various levels of threat to her.

The following week, they began their cautious pursuit and observation of the two major sentient bands of energy feeders in the Astral Plane: the Khalon, and the Rell. These were astral peoples, humanoid energy forms in shape, but with odd heads.

The Khalon had horns, spikes, and boney ridges growing out of their faces and heads. Some of them also had four arms. The Rell had multiple eyes across their odd-shaped skulls, and sometimes what looked to be two necks. They had what at first Naero thought was long glowing hair, but then at closer inspection, it was comprised of prehensile tentacles which they often used to fight with, or even glowing energy tendrils like those of jellyfish, which were also used in battle.

The two races apparently hated each other with a fanatical vengeance, and made war against one another on a regular basis. Thankfully, they were often kept quite busy doing that.

Khalon and Rell also devoured each other as food sources, and anything else that was Cosmic energy—anything that they could capture or kill. They traveled about in glowing, open boats and greater ships of war, sailing upon the astral winds and energy currents. They made their sails and clothing from the flayed astral hides of whatever or whoever they slew. The way of fixing and curing such astral hides was still a mystery to many.

Naero wondered how they reproduced.

Den said that it was by asexual splitting and dividing, and that many astral creatures did so. That was quite common.

How very odd. Most astral beings did not have gender. Since any of them could reproduce on their own if they had need or felt like it, there was no direct, evolutionary need among those races and creatures for gender or sexuality.

Of course, there were always exceptions, but that seemed to be the general rule overall. Mates, bonding pairs, and different, collective groups of various sizes formed out of need for companionship, cooperative efforts, or self-preservation in a dangerous dimension, if nothing else.

Naero and her instructors kept themselves cloaked and undetectable, as they observed glowing ships of both races exploring and darting about, hunting, sizing each other up and making ferocious attack on one another and anything they came across that could be taken as food.

Few had spoken to either race of astral raiders.

Both Master Jo and Den had made the attempt in many ways, yet it always ended in a battle, where the raiders tried to capture and devour the astral forms of anyone who could provide sustenance.

So much for all of that. And no one had been able to study them close up with biomancy, enough to attempt shapechanging into one or the other. Thus, to a large part, the Khalon and the Rell, the astral raiders, remained a closely protected and dangerous mystery.

As the weeks passed, and Naero's confidence and working knowledge of the Astral Plane grew, she was finally ushered into the Dimensional Council.

At first she was completely overwhelmed.

They were within a great, protected astral structure, looking like a bizarre cathedral. Within there were sweeping, towering swaths of crystalline formations, and waves of multi-color, impossible glass. The astral forms of many sentient beings flitted about, conversing and arguing with each other in a cacophony of confusion.

If this wasn't Babel itself, Naero did not know what was.

Inside, the chamber of deliberation was multiple kilometers in nearly every direction, and it seemed to be constantly expanding at will.

Outside, the insane structure looked like a cocoon, a gigantic chrysalis that was writhing and boiling with creation and energetic madness from within. It defied rational thought in many ways.

Yet inside, as Naero was shown how to tap into various discussions, lectures, arguments, and even musical concerts and various artistic performances and exchanges. The flows of knowledge and enlightenment rang clear.

The desire of all sentients was to know and to share and to seek. And no one wanted to be isolated, only to flare out and fade away without anyone taking note that they had been.

From the least to the greatest, they all felt driven to explore ideas with others, and have their voices heard, before their times ended. And it became very clear that all things came to an eventual end. For general good or ill, species, races, dynasties, and empires ran their courses and then were gone throughout the universe, with astonishing and poignant regularity.

A wider, more expanded view made that fact.

This group in one place was ascending in blazes of glory. While in another, these sentients were in their decline, beginning to fade away, for numerous reasons. Cycles came and went with terrible, inevitable regularity and pattern.

As the wise observed, even entire universes came to various ends, before new universes could erupt in creation and begin all over once more.

And for each universe, there were Cosmic Prophecies, the foreshadow of things to come, based upon both choice and chance. Not all universes survived the threats they naturally faced, and others that were created.

Some universes were cut short before their time and snuffed out, by Great Destroyers and terrible cataclysms.

Here in the Dimensional Council, a host of those experiences could be compared, learned from, experienced, and questioned.

But active, dynamic change in all its beautiful and terrifying forms remained constant. Entire universes and galaxies within them roared forth and were being created each second, just as universes and their galaxies were also collapsing and being destroyed.

These were mind-blowing concepts to encounter, on scales that were beyond staggering, nearly beyond conception and understanding.

It could take many lifetimes to explore even a portion of all of those directions.

For once, Naero beheld something so expansive, that it made even the KDM within her seem small. But she wanted to learn what was going to affect her and her universe and galaxy directly.

Clearly, nothing was ever entirely certain.

How could it be, as everything constantly evolved and changed?

Insights could be gained, but that was probably the best that anyone could ever achieve.

What could be known, Naero wanted to know.

And this was an excellent place to begin.

14

Naero spend alternate weeks exploring the Astral Plane with either Master Vane, Den, or both, and then the next interacting with the Dimensional Council.

Each week was so very different, and that was by design, in order to give her the widest range of possible experience.

One of the fascinating facts about the Astral Plane, was that if people knew where to look, they could locate any access, gateway, or wyrmhole that led to every other dimension possible.

Months went on, they continued to search for an access point to the Dimension of Annihilation, and then the small pocket dimension that the spirits of the G'lothc clung to.

As Master Jo always put it, they knew that they were trying to find a certain grain of sand on an entire beach.

If they could find that access point, they might be able to locate where the enemy was streaming their power and influence through. But so far, they had had no luck in finding it. To make matters worse, the enemy had even pulled back for a time, in fact, keeping a low profile and not showing their hand. Even traces of them and there activities were difficult to pin point.

To Naero, from her past experience, that also usually meant that their foes were concealing their intentions and biding their time, planning something deadly.

Naero surprised both of her instructors by summoning Womi, her friend from among the mercurial and dangerous Kahn-Dar.

When he shot straight at them out of nowhere in his enormous form, Naero had to keep them from attacking him.

The Kahn-Dar were, in fact, very near the top of the food chain of all Cosmic feeders, and not just in the Astral Plane. The immense, dragon like creatures were also among the most accomplished interdimensional travelers. It was too bad that that race as a whole was so volatile, opportunistic, and unpredictable.

Master Jo and Den gasped as she hopped on Womi's back behind his head. They swirled and twisted around in celebration at their re-union. Naero barely held on.

"Naero!" Womi yelled. "How wonderful to see you! Who are these two stiffs you're carousing with? They smell like a bunch of creeps! Why can't I just gobble them down. They'd make a tasty energy snack."

Naero laughed. "Stop being rude. These are my good friends, so don't you dare eat them. We've been exploring, searching for something important, and I need your help."

They came back around, and Naero made the formal introductions.

Once Master Jo and Den were no longer considered food, they could talk in earnest. Naero explained what they were seeking.

"The G'lothc have been slipping out through the Astral Plane and into the Prime Material Plane somehow. We don't know how, and we want to try to find a way to put a stop to it. We need to find the wyrmhole or astral gateway that leads to the Dimension of Annihilation."

Womi shook his head. "Naero, you don't want to go there. It is an extremely dangerous place, for anyone. You want to find that nasty little pocket of the existence that the G'lothc spirits are both clinging to and trying to escape from? That's even worse. No one in their right mind, no matter what their powers are, would actively seek to venture into such a place. It is near one of the vortices into the Beyond, and from that vortex, this is absolutely no return."

"I agree," Naero said. "I have been there once, by accident, pursuing the plots of the enemy. You are more than correct, Womi. It is a place of great dread and abject horror. The lost souls of the G'lothc are terrifying and driven mad with lust to break out and destroy every galaxy they can invade."

"Then why would you possibly want to–"

"Because these foes are threatening to destroy everything I love. We must expose their plots and put an end to them, before they are fully unleashed. Do you know where the access point is in the Astral Plane or not?"

Womi nodded his huge head. "I do, but I am still very loathe to take you there, Naero."

"Please, Womi, you must. I think time grows short for us. You of all sentients know how vile and destructive they are. We must locate them and sniff out their plans."

"Very well, but don't blame me if we are all destroyed in the process. This was definitely not the merry plan that I had in mind when I answered your summons. I had hoped that we could finally have some time to streak around and actually have some fun, not rush right out and find the nastiest possible way to die. That's what you are seeking."

Naero grinned. "Maybe we can still have our fun later, Womi–once we get back, as a celebration."

Womi grunted and puffed out some vapor. "You mean if we get back. I'm serious."

Naero sighed and shuddered slightly, remembering her own grim experiences.

She and her two companions all climbed upon Womi's massive neck and formed riding harnesses and saddles via their imaginations.

Thanks to Womi's dead on reckoning, they flashed into the far off region of the access point within mere instants.

In the Astral Plane, vast distances could be covered extremely quickly, if the traveler knew exactly where they were going.

But as soon as they entered that region, something felt very wrong.

All of them noted it, including Womi.

Naero, I've never felt anything like this. I can't describe it…it's wrong somehow. Something terrible has happen in this place.

I agree.

Proceed with great caution, Master Jo told them. *This entire area has been sucked dry somehow. It has been nullified, completely devoid of any kind of energy whatsoever.* The Astral Plane is never like this.

Den added, *There is nothing in all of the Astral Plane that is capable of doing such a thing.*

There is now, Naero told them.

They studied the devastation and hesitated going straight into the access point.

Around the perimeter, they located shredded, dissolving pieces of slain feeders.

Womi described it all to them through his senses. *Something very powerful beyond measure drew in all of these feeders by the thousands, by the tens of thousands, then destroyed them, in a matter of minutes. The hunters became the hunted, and they were quickly drained and devoured. Whatever fell upon them tore them apart very rapidly from within.*

Master Jo asked, *Can we tell what direction they came from, and in what direction they left?*

Not yet, Womi said. They continued on, gathering information.

In another quadrant they came across shattered fleets of the Khalon and the Rell. Even they had been lured in, most likely to what they thought would be a feast upon a newly exposed astral energy source.

Then they all perished somehow, against foes who struck hard and fast without hesitation, and with ruthless, sudden devastation.

The strange glowing vessels of the astral raiders had been sucked empty, and now their hulks began to dissolve, and disperse into the ether as they broke down.

Naero spotted several hundred Khalon and Rell corpses floating or hiding among the wrecks and the overall destruction.

She checked them, and found most to be dead, mere shells, devoid of energy. Their bodies also, being astral in nature, broke down down and dissolved back into the ether.

She located five on the outskirts that still had flickers of life within them–three Khalon, and two Rell.

Through Biomancy, Naero, Master Jo, and Den studied the raiders and their strange astral bodies. They fed the five survivors enough concentrated astral energy to keep them alive, but not strong enough to regain consciousness and attack them.

Naturally, if they were strong enough, the raiders would latch onto them and try to eat them, by sucking their astral forms empty of their energies, just as something much greater had done to all of them, their fleets, and the other feeders. For the raiders, to attack other astral beings and devour them was as normal as a Spacer breathing air.

Yet cannibalism was rare among the two species of raiders as far as devouring their own kind. And much like humans, they only resorted to that at the last need.

But they actually enjoyed eating their enemies.

It took precious hours, but Naero and her two companions completed a full study of the two races, their languages, and the makeup of their minds and astral bodies as fast as they were able.

They also gleaned vital insights and general concepts from the Khalon and Rell minds about their ways of life and their general histories. The raiders were quite unique and unusual in any number of ways, but they were also very similar to other sentients in many other regards. They preserved knowledge. The strove to better themselves. The wanted to protect and see their kind thrive, even if it was at the expense of others.

They had a blunt and astonishing lack of compassion for any other species but their own. It was almost a total lack thereof.

Utter ruthlessness was the order of the day, for both species of raiders.

Master Jo came up with a plan.

They needed to know what had attacked these raiders. To do that, Naero would shapechange into a Khalon, and Den into a Rell. They would revive the others in two locations far from each other to avoid any further conflict.

Womi and Master Jo would also telepathically monitor both situations from afar through his adepts.

Then Naero and Den would simply question the survivors on what had happened.

Naero revived her three Khalon and gave them time to come around.

"How are we alive?" one said, shaking his head and trying to regain his wits. He blinked at Naero. "Who are you? Where did you come from? Why are you still alive? We should all be dead."

"I am Sheel," she said plainly, choosing a common, personal name. "I was inside one of the other ships when the disaster occurred. Somehow I was spared, and only stunned. When I came to, everything was destroyed. Everyone was dead except for myself and you three. I never saw anything before I blacked out. What was it that killed everyone?

The three of them wept.

Khalon never wept.

The first of the three shook his fists. "We rushed in to attack our foes and seized the advantage as always. Then the destroyers appeared all around us, as if out of nowhere. Like the ancient times that are not spoken of any longer, the Destroyers took many of us over outright, eating into our heads, burning and blasting out our minds. What they did not take over, they blasted and destroyed, siphoning all of our broken energies into themselves in seconds. We could not harm them in any way."

"They were unstoppable," the second Khalon said, hanging his head down in shame and despair.

The third man moaned, nearly sobbing. "They took, slew, or destroyed everything and everyone around them in just a few minutes, with impunity. There was no fighting them. We must get far away from here and try to find others. What if the Destroyers come back?"

Naero scanned the images they had all seen.

They were fell visions of many of the same monstrous things she had witnessed in the G'lothc underworld, clawing to get out.

That was why none of the feeders had a chance.

"All of you are greatly weakened," Naero said. "Go, do your best to get away and spread the warning to our kind. Nothing is happening now. The Destroyers, whatever they were, look to be gone. I'm going to stay behind for a bit and keep searching for anymore survivors and anything else that might help us against further attacks."

"You're a fool, Sheel," the first said, turning away. "Stay in this place of death if you want."

"Go ahead and get yourself killed, you idiot!" the second added. The third said nothing but fled in panic along with the other two. They were traumatized and half out of their minds with terror.

As soon as they were far away, Naero continued on, moving closer and closer to the access point.

When she was close enough to spot it on her own, she returned to her base form.

There were strange power fluctuations and trace flows around the wyrmhole. Very scary.

Naero heard a voice in her head and started slightly. The entire situation had her on edge.

They're not exactly wyrmholes in the same way that you think of such, Den said, taking shape out of the ether miasma. *Travelers call them astral tunnels, and they always lead to a specific place.*

Did you learn anything specific from your two Rell?

Not much more than you, N. I saw the images in their minds. Twisted spirits of the G'lothc? I was horrified at the very sight of them.

Indeed. Unfortunately, I had witness such horrors before, and they have haunted my nightmares ever since.

Master Jo zipped in on Womi to rejoin them.

What bothers me, Master Jo noted, *is the way the Khalon and the Rell described their people as having been taken over, not just killed or destroyed. The G'lothc sought out hosts, and now they have them, perhaps by the thousands.*

Naero had to ask. What are they going to do with such hosts? In the Prime Material Plane, physical hosts burn out within a matter of days under G'lothc spirit possession. Most physical bodies simply can't hold up under all of the stress at those levels of Darkforce power. Master Jo, how much longer will these astral forms stay together?

Master Jo looked very worried. *Perhaps longer that we would like. And you don't see the worst in this. I'm not worried about the raiders and feeders, but if they take over someone's mind in the Astral Plane, they take over the physical body that is left behind in the real world, wherever that might be. Even you and I would both be vulnerable to that, Naero. They would need to weaken us greatly first, but such a thing would be possible.*

Naero studied the access point and turned to Womi. Which way did the possessed horde go, my friend? Did they slip away into the Prime Material Plane, back to their prison realm to free more of their kind, or further off into the Astral Plane to cause who knows what havoc?

Womi studied several directions and even sniffed the ether. The Kahn-Dar, whatever else could be said about them, were marvelous trackers, and could literally sniff out traces of many kinds of energy.

Womi nodded roughly back behind them in the general direction of whence they had come from. *They are still in the Astral Plane with us, and they are bloated with power from their feeding frenzy here. Now they've vanished, concealing themselves in some way. Perhaps they detected me tracking them.*

Oh, no, Master Jo blurted out. *If I'm right, we're in trouble. Let's get back to the Dimensional Council right away. They could already be under heavy attack.*

Naero fumed. We're this close to studying the access point and learning how the enemy is breaking free into the Astral Plane, and then other places from here. Perhaps we can cut them off for good.

Master Jo commanded her. *Naero, we know where it is now. Leave your astral marker if you wish. We can come back in force to deal with it. I order you to return with us. At this time, our friends could need us very badly. We're going. Now!*

She planted a marker just before they raced back to the Dimensional Council.

And it was good that they did so, because the council was indeed under heavy attack, by the enemy in the stolen astral forms of various feeders, enhanced with great quantities of stolen power.

If they were able to take over any of the astral delegates, the G'lothc spirits could easily take over their bodies back in the real universe as well, in whatever galaxies and systems they could go back to.

Naero and her friends charged in on Womi to join the pitch battle already engaged.

15

The delegates of the Dimensional Council were no pushovers, and defended the Chrysalis with powers and skills all their own.

Yet the G'lothc were makers of war from the ancient times. They delighted in their new astral hosts. They kept up a steady barrage of powerful energy blasts, trying to penetrate the defensive screens and rip the chrysalis open, so that they might pour in and swarm to the kill.

Womi assumed his immense battle form, almost a kilometer in length.

He gobbled up energy, ribboning his way through the enemy's packed numbers and feasted on them as only a Kahn-Dar in his prime could, even as the horde turned at bay and attacked them. Womi gave and took damage.

The attacking horde was immense. It filled that entire area around the Chrysalis.

Master Jo blinked into a thousand different places within an instant, like a glowing, golden electron. In his wake, surgical Cosmic energy blasts rocked the enemy and stalled their advance.

Den placed himself between the Chrysalis and the enemy. As pure energy himself, shifting at will, he absorbed and reflected many attacks right back at the enemy, punching into them, taking out the foremost major threats.

Naero chose a position high above the battle where she could make out the enemy forces in total. Then she assumed the astral partial form of her Dark beast.

From that vantage point, she opened her third eye and sprouted four additional arms from her back.

With each hand she directed Cosmic blasts of incredible shock and magnitude, raining down upon the enemy, bent on overwhelming and incinerating great swaths of the large, enemy-possessed horde in a systematic pattern of total devastation.

She was using up her own powers rapidly, but it had to be done.

This battle had to be ended quickly.

She kept tapping freely from the Cosmic flows all about her, even into the energies of the enemy themselves.

In a sudden flash of insight, she noted exactly how the enemy had done the same damn thing against her. Energy absorption. What went around came around. Power was power.

And when enemy forces broke up and tried to assail her vantage point directly, she blasted them and sent them straight to hell in just the same way.

She also had to constantly monitor her friends and their movements and positions, so that she didn't zap them as well by accident.

Her blasts enveloped many kilometers from high up.

Her friends wisely fled the heat she put out, and either helped shield the Chrysalis, or hunted down enemy stragglers attempting to escape on the outskirts.

Womi especially seemed to enjoy doing the latter, and he swelled up after a fine feast of energy.

At last the enemy attack was crushed. If any foes escaped, they were extremely few, and very lucky.

Naero returned to her accustomed astral form, but the extra limbs had been a huge help. She'd remember them for the future.

Perhaps now they could take the time to retrace the enemy's steps back to that astral tunnel leading to the Plane of Annihilation. There was still a great deal they needed to know in order to stem this new tide of terror for good.

They had managed to intercept and fling back one single attack. Yet nothing would stop the enemy from possessing an entirely new group of pawns, in the Prime Material Plane or elsewhere.

Or what if they committed multiple such attacks, in a multitude of places? How would the Alliance stop the enemy then?

Master Jo also cautioned her. *Naero, I noted that some of the G'lothc spirits lost themselves within their voracious hosts and were hardly sentient any longer. All they existed for after that was to feed and continue to feed. When their hosts perished, they perished with them.*

I'm glad for that.

Den was, as it turned out, badly injured. Both Naero and Master Jo regenerated him and Womi, who also took significant damage. The enemy played rough.

A particularly nasty feeder had latched onto Den and it had been a very close confrontation. The Mystic finally used a combination of biomancy and psyonics to fend off the foe and destroy it. He tried to explain further.

You both need to understand, the G'lothc spirit tried everything it could to burn out my mind and take over my form. If they keep this up, they're going to succeed at infiltrating us and our allies at many levels. But I stumbled upon something while I was fighting for my life–a pattern–a weave of flows that protected me and held the thing off.

He showed them the defensive pattern, mostly involving positive energy and the Lifespark.

Naero almost shouted. Den, you're a genius. We need to teach this technique to every Mystic, our allies, and all of the beings on the Dimensional Council capable of using or employing it. Now, at the very least, we can partially shield ourselves and our energies so that our foes cannot feed on them or use them directly against us!

While they were still able, directly after the enemy defeat, they went back to the astral tunnel leading into the area near the Annihilation Dimension, to gather further information.

That plane of existence in itself was similar to a Great Attractor of immense size present in some galaxies, but on an even larger scale. It was a vast, astral singularity the size of an entire dimensions, that drew everything in, and from which, nothing escaped. Within that place, things simply ceased to be, and whatever was left, was spewed into the Beyond– the vast Unknown that existed beyond Naero's universe, and perhaps all universes.

No gentle drifting off into the light, as the souls of the dead went on into the next journey, into the Beyond. Not in that terrible place.

This was a hyper-violent ravaging and tearing asunder that made Naero wonder if anything could withstand something so fearful. After all, it was probably called the Annihilation Dimension for very good reasons.

Even the ether of that placed streamed toward destruction beyond the event horizon. This really was a kind of Great Destroyer.

It took powerful concentration and energy simply to avoid being pulled in, let alone to attempt the insanity of getting in closer.

Then Master Jo spotted something as he meditated on the Destroyer's Cosmic structure. *Naero, there are formations like cracks, like fissures around the approach plane leading in to the event horizon. The stress is so great, that all reality begins to collapse and break down. The Destroyer even damages itself.*

Naero strove to focus and note what he was trying to point out for several long minutes.

I think I see it. You're right, Master. And look there…there is the pocket dimension of the G'lothc. The entire area is rife with such cracks where reality is crumbling and breaking down.

Master Jo groaned. *Within a hundred million years or so, even the enemy and their temporary domain will be torn apart and drawn in, whether they wish it or no.*

Haisha! Naero cried. We sure as hell don't have a hundred million years of so to wait for that happy day. By then our entire universe could be dead and lifeless, if the enemy has their way.

Indeed, Naero. But it is through those very cracks in reality that the enemy is finding a way to break out and spread their influence and evil. At least some of those fissures must lead to the Astral Plane, and through there, they can gather enough strength to attack the minds of others, and then use the hosts to escape into other planes and dimensions.

How do we stop them, Master?

That's the problem, Naero. We can't. We have only one choice, and that is to send a message into the Beyond for aid. There are other powers in the Beyond that the Dimensional Council is just learning about, so vast that we in our dimension cannot comprehend them, and they seem to have the mastery of all things great and small. We know so little about them that they are almost myth and legend. Yet they guard the Beyond jealously, so that nothing that has ever entered within has ever returned.

Perhaps if we make it clear to those powerful forces that these rents in the Plane of Annihilation are allowing the G'lothc and possibly other unwanted things to bleed into all of the planes and dimensions, including, possibly, the Beyond. Then they may take some action to seal the breaches on their own. From what I've seen, these fractures in reality will only grow larger and more dangerous.

How is it possible to send such a message, master?

In the Plane of Light, there are many astral tunnels leading into the beyond. The Dimensional Council must prepare a messenger with the proper information, make contact with the invincible guardians who protect the Beyond at the threshold of the Gates of Light & Dark, and usher the messenger through. Someone must accompany our messenger to help assist the–inevitable transition. It is not without peril.

Naero kept her jaw from dropping. Haisha, master, let me get this straight.

Den finished her thought. *It's true, Naero. A sentient being must surrender their life willingly here, in our reality, to take our message into the Beyond. And for them, there is no coming back. Such a thing can only be accomplished through the planes.*

Master Jo quickly added: *Yet there are many on the council willing to take such a journey. Some of them are immortal here on this side, unless they are destroyed somehow, by force or such. They are either weary or curious or in some way ready to take the next journey of their own free will. N. I would like you to do us the honor of escorting the council's messenger, whoever they choose, to Gates of Light and Dark. We have only learned many of these things recently, in our pursuit of knowledge concerning the Cosmic Prophecies, and what must be accomplished to defeat the coming of the next, Great Destroyer.*

I am honored, master. Tell me what it is that I must do.

Master Jo called to Womi. *Mighty Kahn-Dar. Can you take us to the Gates of Light and Dark? For now, we only need Naero to learn where they are. Then she can return to that place with the messenger.*

Of course I can take us there, you little glowing fool. Any place would be better than this. Let's go!

In a matter of instants, Womi raced through several nearby dimensions as they flashed by, bringing them to the Gates of Light and Dark. This was a border where the two opposite dimensions joined together, and all could feel that it was a place of great energies and hallowed power. Yet another place where sentients crossed over into the next journey of the Beyond.

Light & Dark were neither good nor evil in any conception. They existed here in these dimensions in a purity that was all their own. Only the dead or the dying could pass through the gates and into the Beyond, surrendering their mortal shells on this side as they passed on.

Once Naero marked the place, they returned to the Dimensional Council, where the Chrysalis was still being repaired and strengthened, after the most recent attack. Master Jo explained that there had been others, and that more would probably follow.

The enemy was well aware of the council and found various ways to try to attack it. The most recent attack had simply been yet another.

Naero knew that it was time to say farewell to her friend Womi. It wouldn't be right to ask him to hang around while they went about their business. He'd probably get bored and leave on his own any way.

He sensed her intent, and shrank down to his tiny size and coiled around her arm like a bright blue sparking bracelet. In that form, Naero could nuzzle him fondly against her cheek, the way she had once done.

Thank you, Womi, my amazing friend. You have been so helpful to us and our cause once again. There is no way that we can repay you.

He licked his little chops. *Oh, I don't know. We had some fun. And I did get a tasty meal and an interesting fight. You have grown great in might and wisdom, Change Guardian. Do you still insist to me that you are the counted among the least of your kind?*

They shared laughter together.

My guess is that you will grow greater still. If you wish to repay me, leave these stiffs behind. Let's you and I venture out and have some fun. You want to see the planes? Then there's no one better that a Kahn-Dar to show them to you. While you're at it, bring along this little pulsar that I hear you are raising—this daughter of yours. She fascinates me.

Naero laughed again. How do you know about my daughter Shetharra?

Oh, well, even I hear things regarding the Cosmic Prophecies here and there. And I've checked in on you now and again, without you knowing. I just wanted to see if you were all right.

Thank you, my friend. I promise you, when there is time, I will send for you again, and if I can, I will bring Shetharra along. Then we'll have our fun and adventure.

That is all that I can ask, Naero. Until then, keep safe, and safe journey. It was good to see you.

As always, Womi came and went in a sudden flash.

Once Naero, Master Jo, and Den were back inside, Naero watched as Master Jo went around petitioning and completing the process to have a messenger sent into the Beyond.

The astral form of the being who volunteered to become the messenger was a non-humanoid being known as a Tringlen.

Tringlens were a race of energy beings from a far distant galaxy in their universe. The best way Naero had of describing them or accepting their form was that they looked like the white head of an Old Earth dandelion flower, about to release its seed floaters on the next breath of wind.

Only Tringlens were about sixty millimeters in diameter and moved around by their own volition in the Astral Plane. They had an eighteen millimeter pulsing core of light and energy that held their essence and their mind, or intellect. Then their stalks, or feelers, or whatever people wanted to call them extended out from the surface of the core in all directions. These tendrils also glowed with a soft white-gold light, and ended in feathery nodes that were very sensitive in sensing and manipulating energy around it.

When defending itself, the Tringlens could give off powerful blasts of energy, wave attacks, and Cosmic lightning strikes.

But in their normal friendly modes, Tringlens merely tingled on contact with other beings, and used telepathic links to converse.

I Zuon. How you named?

I am called Naero. Naero Amashin Maeris, of Spacer Clan Maeris.

Zuon greets you, friend. Your energies beautiful. Bright music. You scary too. Sometimes, it good scary. You help take me to Light-Dark Gates?

Yes, Zuon. I will bring you safely to the gates. What you are doing is a noble thing to help our universe, Zuon.

I take message. I glad to go. Much excitement awaits.

It made Naero happy that Zuon felt that way. The Tringlen's mental pattern was simple, but she sensed the highly advanced intellect behind the sentient's disarming, psyonic voice patterns.

Once all of the preparations and agreements were in order with the council, Naero set off with Zuon for the Gates of Light and Dark.

They were not attacked along the way, but a few enemy Vespers tried to slip in and taunt her.

Naero used the new techniques to block them out and avoid such further harassment. The energy shields kept the annoying foes from pinpointing her in the Astral Plane as well.

If they couldn't locate her, they couldn't try to bother her.

As she and Zuon approached the gates, the Tringlen began to fade, weaken, and droop.

Naero carried the brave little creature forward in her open hands, and felt it dying, surrendering its life. That could not help but sadden her. The core pulsed slower and slower. The Tringlen's tendrils drooped and went slack. The entire astral form continued to darken, and lose its ambient light.

She felt Zuon die with each passing instant.

Zuon called weakly to her. *No sad, mighty Naero. My choice. You live good life. Happy. This thing…I do.*

Naero had not expected to be so overcome with emotion, but she was. Tears slipped down her face as they drew closer and closer to one of the astral tunnels leading into the Beyond.

She did not know what else to do. The only thing that seem right to her was to sing the Tua song of love. The words welled up from her heart and soul.

Shae-lah vah hii nah, ellah vii shiinah, jahmii vae sha-noh, Shae-lah vah Yah-vae!

The words and tune of the Kexxian song reverberated throughout the Gates of Light and Dark with out warning, and hurtled back a thousandfold, in rippling waves of power that nearly flung them back like the onset of a sudden maelstrom.

It took all of Naero's strength and force of will to reach the astral tunnel.

And when she did, Zuon's astral form broke down and dissolved completely. The Tringlen's essence passed through the tunnel and carried its message into the Beyond.

Naero had one shining glimpse before the tunnel closed.

She perceived floating, shining orbs of light, as far as could be seen. Was that the Beyond, or just a small bit of it? Naero had witnessed something similar in orbit around lost Janosha years ago, when the bright spirits of the dead Tua had swarmed to her aid.

*

Naero returned to the Dimensional Council, and reported to Master Jo and Den that her mission with Zuon was complete. Brave Zuon of the Tringlens had carried their message into the Beyond. What good it would do, no one yet knew.

Who will receive such a message and what will they do with it, master?

He only smiled at first. *Naero, a while back I would not have had an answer for you. But since that time, many profound things have come to light as we have sought further enlightenment concerning the Cosmic Prophecies. With you on the brink of becoming A Mystic Master yourself, you of all people have the right to know of these new developments.*

He paused for moment. Naero simply stared back at him, waiting for him to divulge more information. She raised one eyebrow.

You will be happy to hear that at last, we have found lost Janosha, Naero. Others on the Dimensional Council know of it. The planet was not destroyed. I don't know if it is even possible for it to be destroyed. You could have never done so.

She cried out and instinctively covered her mouth with both hands. At last she had confirmation that the planet's disappearance had not been her fault in any way.

Where, master? How?

Janosha exists as it always has, but now it does so far away, beyond our reach, on the other side of our universe. It was moved there, just as quickly and as easily as you or I might move a cup from one end of a table to the other, by the unseen hands of beings so great, by comparison, we are but stupid, ignorant children–if that.

Naero blinked, and her eyes went wide. For the moment, she could not find her voice to speak.

Long ago, Naero, the first Spacer Mystics came to Janosha, sensing its great flows of Cosmic Power, even if they did not fully understand them. Such power did not exist there by accident. We met with the gentle Tua and made a pact with them to make use of their world as a training base for future Mystics.

In return, we would adapt their environment slightly and make their lives easier–not perfect–but easier. At first many observed the Tua and thought them fascinating, but once the effects of the Time Dilation were put in place, also first developed on Janosha, interest in such simple natives waned and then fell away completely.

Naero fidgeted and grew impatient. Sure, sure. What does that have to do with the entire planet disappearing and ending up somewhere else?

I'm getting to that Naero. At first we believed that we were the ones observing and testing the Tua. But as it turns out, it was quite the other way around. It was they who were observing and testing us.

I don't understand, Master.

Master Jo sighed. *Naero, the Tua we see in our universe here are simple, serene, and relatively insignificant. But they are mere veils, a small extension of the Tua used to watch, and observe, and test all who they come into contact with. Do you really think that it was an accident that they would encountered both us, and the enemy on Janosha? That was all meant to happen.*

Naero thought on that. "What are the Tua, Master? When I was in trouble and could not help myself, they came to my aid. I saw them as orbs of light. When I had a peek into the Beyond for just an instant when Zuon passed through, I thought I saw such lights again."

Naero, you grew closer to the Tua than anyone ever has. They accepted you as one of their own. You became one of them for a time. They love you as one of their own.

113

And I them, Naero said proudly. And I them. So, can we go to them and speak with them? Will they tell us anything we need to know.

Master Jo chuckled. *No, Naero. The veils of flesh that live in our universe are as children. They collect information through their experiences and interactions with other sentients. We have no idea what they are on the other side. Nor whom they serve. Yet I think them to be among the most mighty of all the beings in the Beyond.*

Naero remembered. The Tua only said that they served the Great Mystery of All Things, and that it was a power so great, that it was beyond all others, and could barely be named, let alone fully understood.

Naero drew her head up high. Master, I will never believe anything evil of the Tua. They are not capable of it, neither here, nor in the Beyond.

I did not say so, Naero. But they wield powers so great, that they can move an entire world half way across an universe, with but a thought.

Not even the ancient Kexx could do such a thing.

And that is not all. We took a survey among the Dimensional Council. There are Tua in all of the current universes that we know of. And to our knowledge and what records are available, Tua have existed in every universe in the past. They are more eternal than any race that has ever been known to exist. There is so much that we will never know about them.

And what do they know about us, Master? Think just how Master Vane treated them. How he and Hashiko abused and neglected them. What must they think of us?

That we are flawed and still growing and learning. Perhaps everything around us is a test of some kind, Naero. A test of many things, to see if we are worthy to survive.

Naero was sure now that it was just so. But if any race deserved to be greater than they were in the Beyond, it was the Tua.

The Tua might indeed be among the mightiest beings in the Beyond, but that does not help us in our here and now. Our Tua cannot solve our problems for us here.

They were never meant to, Master. They are not here to do things for us.

Yes, I agree with that as well. It is up to us. We must find the way. Now the time has come for us to return to Oorrii and our bodies there. We have been gone for a few days, thought it does not seem so to us.

Den returned with them. They centered themselves, and drifted back.

Naero opened her eyes. Her body was being sustained on a medbed in a guarded chamber, next to Master Jo. Den floated around, the same as he always did, without a physical body.

She and Master Jo did not feel weak, just slightly disoriented and stiff. All of that passed quickly, especially with a bit of directed healing and some stretching.

Within the hour, they were back to normal, whatever that was for Naero.

Her third and final year of Change Wisdom training was up in a few weeks, and the Time Dilation would end and kick them back into their universe to continue to defend it.

Master Jo asked her to follow him to the meditation gardens.

Naero focused and went through her thoughts and experiences, while Master Jo did his thing and popped about the way he usually did.

Naero, I want to observe you as you center yourself. Show me the harmony within you.

She did so, without question, without hesitation, quickly and easily, like slipping into her own flight togs. A golden, serene light enveloped her

It was Change Wisdom. Without question, this was clearly her way. Change Wisdom made everything else click together for her. She had almost been so busy trying to survive and thwart the enemy in the Astral Plane that she nearly missed it.

For the first time in her life, she felt secure in what she was, and in what she was going to continue to become. Much of the fear that had held her back and crippled her was now gone.

And if she was a monster, then sobeit–she was mostly a good monster, and only her foes needed to beware of her increasing powers.

She had found her harmony, her center, her true balance point that somehow was insane enough to work for her. Naero Amashin Maeris had finally found her place in the universe, and she was comfortable in that. She knew who and what she was, imperfections and all.

What would come would come, and as always, she would roll with that and do her best. That was all that she or anyone else ever could do with what they had to work with.

She could question herself, and within reason, she could trust herself.

Master Jo laughed. *Can't you see, Naero? Just like Enlightened Change, you still exist, always on the edge of creation and destruction, success and failure.*

Doesn't everyone? You cannot achieve one without risking the other, Master.

How true, Naero. And you are definitely one of those who constantly dares great things, stumbles, falls, gets knocked down, and then rises up to push forward, and keep striving. I have great respect and affection for you, Naero. We still have a several weeks together, but I want you to take time

to celebrate and enjoy yourself with your family, before you must leave here. As far as I am concerned, you have surpassed every test that I have given you, and went well beyond them.

From this moment forward, Naero Amashin Maeris, you will be a Mystic Master of your people, and, as I foresee–much, much more. Congratulations, Master Maeris.

I thought…there would be a ceremony of some kind.

There will be. But first know this.

Ice cold water suddenly exploded all around her as if under pressure.

I've been waiting to do that.

Naero gasped, shivered, and quickly struggled to warm and dry herself.

Then she booted Master Jo a couple of klicks away, as his golden shield orb auto-sealed around him.

Me too, she said through their link, shielding her eyes and watching Jo spin and sail away into the distance. Don't make yourself into a big kickball, master. You're just daring someone to eventually give you a wallop.

An actual ceremony and a banquet were held in her honor that evening, with all of her family and friends and the Mystics present.

Master Maeris made merry. Khai was very proud of her.

Two days later, Master Maeris went looking for Shetharra. Sharrah informed her that Khai had taken their daughter to visit with the High Master on Nezma.

When she transported there, she was directed to the Arena.

Inside, she spotted Khai, Master Jo, and many Mystics standing about observing a contest with great interest.

A contest pitting seven year old Shetharra against a multitude of red, blue, and yellow psyonic construct combatants.

Khai laughed and called out. "Are you ready, sweet girl?"

Shetharra flung her white-hot glowing hair back with a shake and took her offensive stance. She cocked her head and smiled her family's trademark half-smile. Her blazing blue eyes sparkled.

"Bring it!" she cried.

The horde of constructs charged in.

Shetharra passed through them so fast, that few could follow her movements. She became a sweeping wave of white flame and overwhelmed the constructs nearly all at once.

Khai grinned. Everyone else but him and Naero stood aside, utterly astonished.

Master Jo was stammering when he turned to the child's father.

"A prodigy like no other, a Cosmic savant unlike any the Mystics have even seen before. She must be brought to us for training. This is no accident that your child has appeared at this crucial time. Her powers are increasing constantly. She needs guidance."

Naero cut right in. "She has it," Naero said. "And she has the most important thing: love; the love of her family. That's all she needs right now. Maybe when she's ten or eleven, she'll be ready for Mystic Training. I won't have what happened to my Uncle Kean being inflicted on my daughter. She won't be shaped and molded and groomed to be some kind of monster, weapon, or savior. She needs time to have a childhood and be a child."

Khai went right over and stood beside his wife on the right, and crossed his powerful arms. "As the girl's father, I am in complete agreement with my spouse. We have discussed this and made our decision, and it is final. No Mystic training. Not until the age of ten or eleven. Live with that."

"Even if something happened to us," Naero added. "Her guardians and our Clans will respect our wishes, and not allow it."

With nothing left to take down, Shetharra came forward smiling, racing quickly toward her parents, squealing eagerly. "Papa, momma, did you see me? I really like this place. It's fun. Did you see what I did? I beat them–I defeated them all. This place challenges me. I can do this!"

Khai swooped her up into his arms and kissed her on the top of her head. "You did very well, little one. We are very proud of you."

"Papa, Papa. Put me down. Momma, make him stop!"

Naero pulled her away and planted a few kisses of her own on her little duck, before setting her down on her bare feet.

Shetharra had been conceived in the core of a mighty star. Overall, Naero guessed that she was already invulnerable to most hi-tek weapons. Yet she was still gentle of heart, and did not even like to step on bugs.

"Well done," Naero said. "One day you shall return to this place and find your own way, here, Shetharra. Yet today is not that day. We will find other challenges for you before then, my duck."

Shetharra giggled. "I'm not a little duck any more. I am a brave warrior, fearless and bold, just like you and papa."

Naero held out her arms. "Then come, my brave warrior. I have many surprises and adventures for you in the weeks to come. Sometimes you will go with your father or both of us. Today you will come with me. Would you like that?"

"Oh, yes, mama. I love going with you, just the two of us. What are we going to see and do today?"

Naero took her to go see the Tua.

It was slightly bittersweet to see Kali with her new mate, Yavar. They had a litter of three kits.

Shetharra seemed to feel at home among the Tua as well, and soon she was singing the Tua, Kexxian songs right along with Naero and their hosts.

These were among the same songs that Naero sang to her own children and taught to the nursery staff.

Shetharra laughed and giggled, as she stood still with her arms outstretched and the Tua kits climbed all over her, mewing and cooing, until they almost covered her completely.

Then the Tua parents would come by and pluck off their young.

Naero still did not know how the Tua parents could tell the fuzzy little things apart. Perhaps it was by scent, or some other way of knowing.

If Naero had remained Kali, she probably would have learned the trick to it by now. Yet she was glad that she had returned to her own self, her own children, and her own life. She was both complete and needed there.

During her training, she had switched their new son over to Sharrah for safe keeping. But it was Naero's wish to always give natural birth to her children, if it was at all possible.

Sharrah liked sharing their children as Naero's faithful nurse and surrogate. She had even requested the honor of giving birth to some of them at some point. Yet Naero tried to explain that she was still feeling very irrational and selfish about such motherly matters.

She owed that much to Sharrah. At some point she would relent. It was only right.

Naero and Khai were happy having their kids, and doubly happy having them well-cared for and protected, when a mission demanded that they be somewhere else, risking their lives and doing dangerous things that only they could do.

Both of them wanted a large family.

Naero shook herself and came back to being with her oldest daughter in the present, in the glory of a Tua village. The Tua rejoiced at the presence of two such mighty Halaena, and marveled at seeing a rare little one of such dazzling promise, and showered her with gifts and love.

Quite quickly, Naero and Shetharra were clothed in Tua fashion, and Naero felt no shame in being topless like the rest of the Tua women. She felt no shame for her body. She never would.

Adult Tua females had four breasts, two pairs over each other, small but ample and pert during their lives.

The Tua were very sensual, beautiful people, and sex for them was as natural as walking around and breathing.

Shetharra saw pair-bonded couples openly copulating as was the Tua way, and pointed it out to her mother. She thought it was both silly and funny.

Naero always tried to speak truth, and explained that this was just the Tua way of loving each other, but that even among them, such was only for mommies and daddies. Then she explained that among Spacers, their own people, sex was reserved for private times for mommies and daddies.

At her age, Shetharra nodded and seem to accept that. She even repeated words her mother told her. "Different ways for different peoples."

The Tua women and girls in turn, were fascinated with Naero, not only because her breasts were somewhat larger, and very pretty, but mostly because she only had two. And she was not covered in fur, either.

Naero explained that the vast majority of human mothers did not have litters, and usually had one or at most two children at a time. But she did not get into how much longer Spacers lived than Tua, and they did not ask.

Yet even the Tua sensed the veiled greatness and shining love that was within little Shetharra, and they were drawn to her light and beauty like moths to a blazing white flame.

Naero had seldom seen the Tua revere or worship anything but the Great Mystery as they called it. But they came very close to bowing down to the child of light who laughed and danced among them.

Shetharra was indeed a wonder. She loved honestly and openly, with all her heart, and the Tua were akin to love itself.

The leading pair of that village sent runners out to all of the other villages. All of the tribes would come together that evening, and hold a great celebration with the mighty mother and child of the Halaena. There would be feasting, and song, dancing, merriment, and great gladness.

Naero and her daughter moved among the Tua at will that night, and celebrated, feasted, and sang with them.

Wherever she went at night, Shetharra parted the crowds, glowing with a faint aura of white light all about her, and the Tua yearned to reach out and gently touch her as she passed, and the Tua children followed after her in waves, laughing and singing to her.

When it was very late and the celebration was all but winding down, Naero sat speaking with the leaders of all the Tua villages. She held Shetharra sleeping peacefully in her arms while she did so.

Then Khai appeared out of the shadows to retrieve them, glowing with his own faint green energy, and the blazing light of the Cosmic Sword Yii slung over her broad shoulders and back.

The Tua knew who Khai was as the Mystic Enforcer, and now as Naero's mate and Shetharra's father. Yet still, at 2.13 meters tall, to the

119

Tua who were were at most 1.216 to 1.52 meters, Khai was a towering muscled giant with golden, glowing hair.

The female village leaders stared at him in awe and actually looked a bit afraid when they turned aside to Naero with more of their questions.

"He is your mate?"

"Like you, he is very beautiful, but in his own way, as is your fair child."

"Forget that. How does he not kill you when you mate?"

"He would split me in half like firewood!"

"It might be a happy way to leave this life."

Naero laughed along with them. "He is my joy, and my fulfillment. I don't think I could love another but him. It is an honor to share his life, our bed, and make and raise our children together. He is the definition of duty, courage, and honor. And like myself, he loves his family more than his own life."

"Only such a man is fit for you, Naero."

The women hugged and kissed her. "We feel the same way about our mates, yet you are Halaena, and perhaps that is saying enough. We are happy for you all, Naero."

"You know that you and your blood are always welcome in our villages. There will always be a place for you and yours in our families. Do not forget us."

"I won't," Naero said.

Naero handed Khai their daughter, and they began to say their farewells to the Tua.

The next day Naero and Khai spent the day in the compound jungle, with Sharrah and all the nursery staff, including the mantid guardians of the Shai.

The twins, Daeyen and Kathron were now four, almost five. They played with Shetharra, swarming over her, fighting and flying around her. She laughed, deflected their tiny blows and strikes with her hands and feet. They could not harm her in any way.

Yet she gave in and let them win, pretending to fall before them. Then they tumbled together, in explosions of laughter and giggling. Shetharra was the best of big sisters, and loved spending time with her siblings. She was patient and inventive with them, always showing them new things.

They clung to her, and with her great strength, she carried them around without effort.

Daey and Kath did not have Shetha's Cosmic abilities, yet they were Spacer born of champion blood, mighty, strong, and fearless. Their older sister had an abundant nature, and did not lord her incredible abilities over anyone.

Sharrah's belly was big and swollen with Naero and Khai's next son, due in a short while. They would leave Oorrii soon, and if situations warranted, Naero would take over the final few weeks of the gestation process, and then the birth, all with Sharrah's help and that of the medteam they kept on hand.

For the present, they had to wait and see how things were on the outside world.

Just as Naero thought, being on Oorrii and completing her Mystic training was one of the best things she had ever done for herself. She was stronger, wiser, and more stable than she had ever been, and her many powers continued to grow in the directions she wanted and needed them to.

Part of all of that she owed to High Master Jo and the Mystics.

The rest she owed to her Khai, and their family.

Heaven help any being or creature who came after them with the intent to do them harm.

Naero felt more than ready to push forward.

16

Of course the direct call was waiting for them, even as Oorrii emerged from the Time Dilation.

Further problems, threats, and complications from all of the dwindling Gigacorporations awaited them as the Corps continued to topple headlong from favor, power, and history.

The tide of forward human motion was now fully against their stupidity and tyranny. Yet for all their folly and idiocy, the stubborn Corps could still manage to be a threat and a danger–to their own populations.

They knew no other way. How very sad and pathetic.

Out in the remote Hevangian sectors, those fanatical morons were still bent on killing themselves off, rather than join the rest of humanity exploring the galaxy and expanding the Alliance and the pursuit of knowledge and enlightenment.

It would cost billions or more lives to try to stop them from committing cosmicide.

Sadly, the choice was made within the Alliance to simply leave them alone and keep their sectors isolated and embargoed. Naero felt sorry for the children, and the children of the future who were not being given a choice to go on.

How did people stop entire planets whose leaders were hell bent on killing themselves off, rather than embrace new ideas and ways that were clearly proven to be better?

When the worst was over, perhaps some of those fools would survive enough in caves to start over.

Naero and Khai bade farewell to Sharrah and the kids with a sad, apologetic look that the leader of the nursery knew all too well

She merely flicked her hands at them as if they were annoying insects. "Just go. You know we have this. So shut up and return when you can. You'll know where to find us."

On the way past the Hevangian Sectors, on the way to the next confrontation with the Gigacorps powers, Naero and Om took some time to meditate within herself with her new found wisdom and enlightenment.

Naero transformed into Orean, her Kexxian alter-ego, and she and Om explored the vast ocean of wisdom and tek data that was the Kexxian Data Matrix, residing within her.

As always, they began in the repository of Kexxian music and branched out from there. Naero followed in the path of the valiant and powerful Kexxian Dreamers, and could only begin to see all they had known and accomplished.

Compared to them, she was an insect still. Yet their knowledge and the powers and love that had guided them, washed over her and Om in layers of memory, courage, and fierce joy.

For an instant, Naero was pulled out of herself and whisked far away, to a place she had only seen once before.

Surrounding her were a multitude of variations and versions of herself, stretching out as far as she could see.

The chorus of all of her potential selves and possibilities spoke to her using the voice.

YOU HAVE MADE EXCELLENT PERSONAL PROGRESS, YET IT REMAINS TO BE SEEN IF YOU OR THE OTHERS WILL BE READY ENOUGH WHEN THE GREAT DESTROYER APPEARS.

Thanks for the vote of confidence, guys.

YOU HAVE ALSO MADE NO PROGRESS ON LOCATING THE LAST ANCIENT OBELISK STATUE OF ORDER WISDOM AWAITING YOU ON THE SURFACE OF LOST XANATHAR. YOU MUST LOCATE THE OBELISK BEFORE OR SHORTLY AFTER THE FORGING OF THE SECOND COSMIC SWORD. THAT IS VITAL.

Sorry, we've been a little busy.

AS THE TIME OF THE COSMIC PROPHECIES STEP UP, MORE SHALL BE REVEALED. YOU WILL PLAY A CRUCIAL ROLL IN THE FORGING OF THE SECOND COSMIC SWORD, JAA. PREPARE YOURSELF. IT MIGHT PROVE NECESSARY FOR YOU TO SURRENDER YOUR LIFE FOR THE COMPLETION OF THAT TASK. YET NOTHING IS CERTAIN. IF YOU PERISH, IF YOU FAIL, THE TASK OF HELPING THE OTHERS TO CONFRONT THE ADVENT OF THE GREAT DESTROYER MAY VERY WELL FALL TO YOUR OLDEST DAUGHTER. BUT ONLY IF YOU CONTINUE TO GUIDE HER, AND HELP HER TO CONTINUE TO BECOME WORTHY, STRONG, AND WISE ENOUGH TO PREVAIL.

Hey, guys. Is there any way to help me in the here and now–right now?

YOU WILL CONTINUE TO GROW IN POWER, AND BECOME CAPABLE OF USING OUR COLLECTIVE POWERS ON A GREATER BASIS.

Well, I guess that's something to look forward to.

THERE ARE MANY THINGS THAT YOU CANNOT DO ALONE. TRYING TO DO EVERYTHING ALONE CAN BE A WEAKNESS FOR US. ALLY YOURSELF WITH THE RIGHT OTHERS AT THE RIGHT TIME. THE YATTAI, THE ODEN, AND THE LAELOR ARE IN GRAVE DANGER. YOU MUST EITHER SAVE, OR DESTROY THEM BEFORE YOU ALLOW THE ENEMY TO USE THESE RACES IN GREAT NUMBERS AGAINST YOU AND THE OTHERS. THAT WILL SPELL DISASTER FOR ALL.

FAREWELL. WE RETURN YOU NOW TO YOUR VITAL INTERACTIONS WITH THE KDM.

Her Cosmic chorus was so abrupt.

She didn't even have time to thank them, as usual, for next to nothing. Most of what they reminded her about, she already knew. But there was always more to what her potential selves said than what she thought at the time.

But right now, there was nothing more to do than go back to what she had been doing before the little Cosmic interruption.

Rather than continue to search for that single grain of sand on the beach, Naero found that it was usually far better and productive to open herself to the KDM itself, speak openly about the situations and problems that she and her allies were facing, and let the various currents and flows take her where they would.

Once she made her mind clear, and surrendered to the hidden, guiding will of the KDM, she would eventually find things that were useful, if not an outright solution. Although the entire process might still involve many attempts, and much searching.

She was getting used to have to piece things together like an intricate puzzle, and her mind continued to expand and work in those directions.

Stranger than not, singing the Kexxian songs was also often helpful.

But by now, Naero through Orean knew less than fifty songs.

The sum total of songs the Kexx had at their command bordered upon the infinite. And not all of them, by far, were songs of power that could trigger Kexxian miracles.

Many of them were just that–simple songs all on their own, existing only for their own sake.

More grains of sand on the beach.

The Kexx had fought and defeated the ruthless G'lothc at every turn over a very long period, across the sweeping battlefields of several galaxies, some of which had been destroyed or severely damaged in the course of the conflict.

Such terrible loss.

Small insights began to flow into Naero's and Orean's expanding mind which they shared.

Om gained ground as well.

Om, why don't you assume a Kexxian form? It might aid you in filtering through their knowledge.

My way is different from yours, Naero. I am not a shapechanger. I was never a Spacer, a human, or even a Kexx. I am myself. I am Om. I am an advanced AI, designed to protect the secrets of the KDM. It is part of me, and I am a part of it, just as I am now a part of you.

Naero gasped suddenly as all of the pieces of one three dimensional puzzle seemed to rush in and slam together all at once, as if by powerful magnets.

The effect was jarring and bewildering.

That's it, Om. That's at least part of the answers we seek, my friend. We can't do many of these things alone yet. We cannot solve them. Yet together, when we put our abilities and minds together, we might be able to accomplish many further things, together.

Yes, Naero. I think I'm beginning to perceive possibilities we have not fused together before. Let's examine some of my higher level defensive protocols that we have yet been unable to activate and control.

I see them Om. They might be some of the answers we seek, and some few we happen upon, that we weren't even looking for.

They diverted Fleet-1 to the nearest Hevangian world that was threatening to blow itself up with atomics, beneath a planetary shield.

Even spyfixers could not slip in fast enough without the lunatics getting enough advance warning to incinerate themselves and the four billion people on that planet.

"Can this even work?" Khai asked her, after Naero explained the basic theories to him. "It sounds…far-fetched even for you."

"We'll find out. The Alliance pacification fleets and ground forces are standing by?"

"Ready and willing to go in, if there is anything left to save."

"What do we have to lose?" Naero transformed into one of her most powerful Cosmic energy forms and transported out above one of the worlds of her most hated enemies, who now she was attempting to save from themselves.

With me, Om?

Always, N.

Let's do this.

She opened her third eye. Since mastering Enlightened Change Wisdom, when she went into Cosmic mode, her right eye glowed red with Chaos energy, her left eye blue with Order energy, and her third eye glowed with the golden light of Change energy. All over, she glowed with a golden light that penetrated and enveloped her.

Naero startapped, making sure to shield herself as much as possible from the enemy's power to feed upon her and use her energies against her.

She barely heard the whisper of a few, pitiful G'lothc voices, making feeble attempts to confuse her and convince her that she was certain to fail and die horribly.

Om helped her cut off even them.

Together, the two of them focused fully on the great task before them.

Ribbons of flaring, multi-colored energy, mixed with powers both light and dark, shot out from them and enveloped the entire system…in seconds.

The planetary defense shield did not hinder them.

On the surface, the Kexxian defensive protocol sought out and disrupted and negated any kind of atomic or other cosmicide device present, before it could be activated.

There was no warning or alarm.

Next, all docked starships, warships, weaponized vehicles and gunships or platforms had their weapons reduced to inert components.

After that, all military and paramilitary forms of combat armor, meks, and heavy weapons were also reduced to nothing but piles of raw materials. And power cores or fusion cores were completely drained, their energies dispersed. It would be weeks before they could be restarted.

Inert, Cosmic energy pods collected dispersed energies, shut down power stations temporarily, and continued providing emerging power sources to hospitals, medical centers, and aid stations.

Even personal weapons and military arms were rendered inert and unusable, unless the enemy wanted to go back to using rocks and knives, which were messy and highly inefficient.

Anyone committing violent acts was summarily stunned by clouds of patrolling spyfixers immediately after the collapse of the planetary shield.

The astonished lander pacification teams began to drop down en masse to begin their operations, still awed and shaken by the power they had witnessed.

The Allies had made their point, in stunning fashion. Even the other remaining Hevangian worlds finally saw the futility in their own actions. One by one, they began to capitulate, and allow their worlds to begin their transitions into the new age–hopefully an age without so much tyranny, madness, and death.

After their slight detour, Naero and Khai continued on to the next negotiations with the fading Gigacorps.

The talks were being broadcast across the interstellar webnet.

All of the fourteen Gigacorps were being represented by high level Corps officials. Ten of them had submitted to Alliance screening to weed out alien enemy moles and plants.

Four of them still refused, and their participants were being kept isolated in a shielded safe box, just in case.

As soon as Naero and Khai entered, one of the isolated delegates tried setting off a micro atomic in a shield case.

Naero transported the atomic into the core of the nearest star. Then she exposed the alien entity for the horror that it was, and incinerated it and its hollowed out host to dust.

She scanned more of the isolated delegates and exposed and slew two more symbiots.

Next, a full company of second gen enemy phaze troops tried to crash the party.

Khai flashed through two score of them with Yii, leaving them in sparking, disrupting, messy pieces.

Naero took out the rest, opening her third eye and crushing them all to the hyper dense size of heavy marbles, and letting them thump and scatter across the floor.

"The Corps are still clearly riddled with agents of our alien foes. There can be no trusting them or dealing with them until we are certain that they are, in fact, human. I repeat, it is vital that all of the Corps and their officials must be scanned and screened for enemy possession."

"Be that as it may," one of the delegates from Gravlink insisted. "This alien infiltration can be dealt with. But it still does not justify this major power grab of the Alliance to seize Gigacorps property and systems wholesale."

"Completely unacceptable," a Brannock official added.

A Marsten agent stood up next. "You have forced our hands with these extreme actions. The remaining Gigacorps still maintain control over twenty to forty percent of their worlds and their populations. These seizures must end. From this point forward, we will do the only thing that we can to stop these illegal actions. All remaining Corps populations will be held hostage, until all Alliance forces retreat back to the pre-invasion borders. Any attempt to seize further worlds will result in massive casualties among their populations, and the Alliance will bear all responsibility for these losses."

Naero rose up and spoke calmly. "You miserable, pathetic, bloody-handed wretches. Will you stop at nothing to cling to the power and dominion slipping through those hands like sand? Can you not admit that your time in history is ending? One way or another, no matter the price, you will dwindle and fade back into what you were originally meant to be— petty business managers. It was never meant for you to twist people and entire worlds to serve your whims, to exist in your image, to force others to be exactly like you or suffer for it. The economic slavery that you perpetrated, is now over."

The Odyssey Corps delegate fumed and blustered at her. "We aren't bluffing. Attempts to seize our remaining worlds, and their populations will suffer heavy casualties."

"Yes, I believe you bastards would do so. But you are behind the times. Have you not seen the vid footage and reports from Krellok-3 in the Hevangian sectors that are streaming across the Webnet? Take a moment and catch up. And in any case, these worlds are not being seized by the Alliance. Far from it. They are being liberated, and turned over to their peoples. The Alliance is not seizing anything."

"Filthy spack Lies!" the Gelden Corps agent shrieked.

Naero accessed the agent's history through Om in a flash of teknomancy.

"Delegate Harmon Deveroux of Gelden. Were we lying when us filthy spacks bled and died to save your homeworld where you and your family cowered in fear, waiting for the Ejjai to drag you out and fling you into the meatships? No, you will not be allowed to harm your own populations in order to attempt to salvage and sustain even some small portion of your illegal tyranny. Hear the words that I speak now, and heed them.

"Within twenty four standard hours, Shetanna will prove to the Gigacorps cowards that she is indeed the Dark Angel of Death. Your forces cannot stop her. Your leaders cannot escape her wrath. She is about to perform a miracle of justice across nearly thirty-thousand Corps hostage worlds—*at the same time*.

"After the first bell of standard midnight chimes, she and her sisters will begin taking out you and your leaders, systematically eliminating them with impunity, until the Corps give up their murderous threats, and withdraw from the wave of liberation that is taking place across the human sectors. Let me be clear; they are going to kill you all.

"The coming New Age will begin with–or without you to trouble it. All of you check with your staffs, on your ships and back on your worlds. Your links will be broadcast across the Webnet."

Deveroux and dozens of others contacted their hierarchies.

In every one, Shetanna stood at hand, shielded and floating nearby, or even sitting patiently on the top of piles of heavily armed, stunned guards.

"The first bell chimes in less than three standard hours. I suggest you and your fellow managers prepare to take the next journey. For the angels of death have tallied your names, and will begin to mark them off. Within a day, the leadership of the Corps will be gutted from the top down, and you will not be allowed to murder your populations in able to stay in power."

"Y-you're bluffing," a Chikara delegate muttered.

Naero sighed.

A Shetanna appeared floating in the air with her legs crossed behind the delegates, yet she did not take her gleaming violet eyes off the delegates from behind her battle mask.

"Shetanna does not bluff," Naero stated. "Let's hang around until the bell tolls, and see what happens. I have nothing to fear or lose."

The delegates began to look very uncomfortable.

"These talks are over until the Gigacorps have something new to say or bring to the table. And that means capitulation or death. The Alliance is done messing around with you fools, and your commitment to wallowing in denial. And if senseless death begins on any hostage world before it can be suppressed, then all of you Corps lackeys and quislings are forfeit. You will die anyway–with no further negotiations. Do not tempt our resolve."

The Gigacorps capitulated in full, forty standard minutes from midnight.

When the first bell of the nightwatch chimed, the human worlds knew freedom for the first time in centuries.

The first thing the Alliance forces did was sweep in and hunt down Alien infiltrators. As it turned out, they were already legion.

Khai looked at Naero. "I was worried for a while there," he said. "What would you have done if they did not give in? Would your replicants really have killed all of those innocent people, without bringing them to justice and trial?"

Naero smiled slightly and grunted. "Gigacorps leaders are far from innocent, my beloved. And they would face swift and summary justice if they chose to make war on their own helpless populations. Yes. I gave my reps strict orders to gut the leadership of all the Corps in the space of one standard day. They would have carried them out to the letter. Intel has been tracking Corps leaders since before the end of the High Crusade."

Even Khai backed away slightly. "I love you, my heart. But you can be very scary at times."

Naero looked straight ahead. "It was my intent to break their resolve," she said. "If I did not make it terrifying and hopeless for those fools to continue living in blind denial, they would not have surrendered. I always make a point of backing up my threats."

17

In many other vital regions of the Alpha Quadrant, the enemy launched all out attacks on the fringe of the Expansion Zone. They swept across vulnerable, outbound colonial sectors, plunging scores of fringe worlds into all out war and Chaos.

Spacer and Alliance fleets raced to meet this new challenge with courage and swift dispatch.

Admiral Maeris's fleets were no exception and joined the thin lines of defenders at the most vital point. Khai went along with them to engage the enemy directly and lend the support of the Mystic Enforcer.

The main Alliance plan was to strike back quickly, not only there, but across all sectors in a well-coordinated, massive response to hammer the enemy hard and throw them back.

The enemy fleets facing Naero's forces massed behind new huge dreadnaughts of alien design, sporting massive firepower. Such vessels did appear to be very formidable, in response to some of the big ships of the Spacer fleets.

Naero orchestrated her arm of the attack from her command platform, her adept hands and fingers flashing from holopanel to holopanel, flying back and forth.

Waves of starfighters from both sides clashed, attempting to penetrate each other's outer defensive screens.

Then the enemy sent in their bigs to blast a way through the Spacer battle formations.

Naero sent in her juggernauts to counter and engage, on optimal attack vectors.

The bigs wheeled and maneuvered about, slugging it out face to face, taking and causing damage.

Massive energy weapons of blinding power shot out wide beams of various colors, punching and carving into one another as the complex naval battle flared full on.

A knot of fresh enemy bigs jumped in very close on the starboard flank and tried to roll up the Alliance formations there.

Naero countered and shifted the formations of her forces to compensate, but it wasn't going to be enough.

"Khai, our fleets could use a little Cosmic support out there on our furthest right. I think we should both go."

He nodded. "Ready when you are. Let's back each other up."

Naero turned command over to her waiting strategic and tactical replicant. Nariine jumped up from where she watched and waited, took over without hesitation, and continued to flex and adapt with the changing flows and patterns of battle.

Naero and Khai transported directly among the enemy flanking bigs, hurtling at them, big guns blazing.

The vast warships dwarfed them in their human-sized energy forms.

"Take on the ones to the left," Naero told him, "while I deal with those on our right. Reverse direction to disrupt anything you miss on the first pass, and meet back here. I'll do the same."

Khai formed his indestructible green glowing energy sphere around himself and accelerated to high attack speed. He proceeded to blast blazing, exploding holes straight through the enemy dreadnaughts, tearing out vital systems, slicing through fire control, drives, and power cores.

Naero assumed her partial Dark beast form and phazed through big after big, leaving behind orbs of concentrated Cosmic energy, forty meters in diameter.

When they began to cook off half a minute after her first pass, the enemy bigs charging in detonated from within, scattering burning wreckage across the battle grid.

Khai reversed direction and came back through the line of crippled ships, causing many of them to list and float, completely disrupted and disabled. Over half of them exploded at random.

Hundreds of lesser warships kept coming, blazing away.

Naero and Khai were still so small in size by comparison that it was very difficult for the enemy to target them properly. And the pair used cloaking and phazing to confuse matters further, striking again from unseen vectors.

Fleet after enemy fleet stalled or floated helpless, completely drained of energy.

Naero and Khai took that stolen power and reflected it back at other enemy formations, slicing through many vessels at a time.

The devastating pair regrouped, allowing the Alliance forces to race in and overtake the fleeing remnants of the enemy assault.

But while the two Cosmic Champions were busy in those areas, they could not be in other places.

A dark, vaguely serpentine form, three kilometers in length with a massive head, wreathed in Darkfire, phazed in and out among the Alliance rear formations. Without any warning, hundreds of Alliance ships were vaporized and many more severely damaged.

The entire Alliance rear had been shattered, almost instantly.

"The Dakkur king!" Nero shouted across her link to Khai.

They transported that way to engage the monster, yet it phazed and warped away as quickly as it came.

The attacks they launched struck nothing and passed out into empty space.

The Black King's laughter blared and echoed through their minds. The creature's Cosmic and psyonic might were extremely formidable.

The beast cleverly concealed his true powers.

JUST A TASTE OF WHAT IS COMING, SPACK WEAKLINGS. YOU DARE TO AROUSE OUR GREAT WROTH? WHEN THE END COMES UPON YOU, WE SHALL SWEEP ACROSS QUADRANT AFTER QUADRANT. YOU THINK TO STAND BEFORE US? WE WILL BE UNSTOPPABLE!

It was already too late, but Naero called in reinforcements through Om.

The running battle with the enemy invasion forces continued for two standard weeks before it was all over.

The enemy fought to the death, as usual.

After the high casualties of the initial engagements, further losses were kept surprisingly low.

But Naero gave full warning to Intel and Spacer Naval Command.

Even this large attack was just a feint, a probe meant to test the metal of the Alliance and their resolve.

The enemy was toying with them, most likely in preparation for the arrival of the looming, enemy armada waiting to find a way to flood into the Alliance galaxy.

The Alliance had barely a handful of Cosmic Champions.

That also included her seven-year-old daughter, Shetharra, who her mother was loathe to send to war at her young age.

As a mother, that would only be a last resort, before all was lost.

How many Dakkur Dark Kings were there? How many White Queens? If the enemy unleashed them and their Armada all at once, they could roll over entire quadrants at a time. Was that the enemy's plan then?

There was only one other Cosmic Guardian such as herself.

Naero needed to locate and take counsel with Her Uncle Baeven.

18

Naero and her outcast uncle met on Zorin-2, one of his safeworlds. They caught up and discussed matters while sparring together in their partial Dark beast forms, across a vast, desolate volcanic plain.

Three live volcanoes alone were active within eighty kilometers of their isolated practice zone. The planet's vulcanism was very dynamic.

The two Cosmic Guardians crashed and clashed together, blinding combinations hurtling back and forth. They battled on an elite level that few in the galaxy could match.

They unleashed Cosmic attacks at will, blasting each other through rock formations, and ramming each other into the ground.

Their nearly indestructible energy forms endured damage that would have wiped out entire naval fleets, and armies of hi-tek military forces.

They recovered and regenerated almost at will and kept battling.

"Congratulations upon completing your Mystic Training, Master Maeris. I thought doing so would serve you well."

They locked and strove to throw each other off balance.

To Naero's delight, they were now equally matched in speed, strength, technique, and cunning. But her uncle still held a slight edge over her in experience.

Yet even there, Naero was rapidly closing the gap with him.

As it was, they were virtually equals as combatants.

"No, I must say, Naero. Well done. You've really improved. You've perfected your own style, and you have skills that I have never known. If we really went at it, it would be a toss up. Half of the time you would win, and the other half for me. It would be a draw in the end."

Naero bowed to him slightly and pulled back. "Thank you again, uncle. Let's take a breather, shall we? There's so much I want to show and discuss with you."

"All right. There's a very nice waterfall a hundred klicks away. Follow me."

The area of the waterfall was exceptionally lovely, and Naero marveled at the double rainbows in the sprays of water about it, and the many tropical bees, humming birds, and other rare birds of paradise of shocking and vibrant, colorful variety.

They assumed their base forms once again and sat on some rocks, drinking fresh, clean, cold water that their fixers brought them in crystal goblets.

"You know, Baeven. With my quickening talent, I can teach you any of my skills that you would like to learn, and show you how to master them."

"That's sounds like an excellent idea, Naero. Let's work on them one at a time as we go along. There are several that I would like to master on my own."

"There's one new defensive psyonic and Cosmic measure in particular that I think you'll find very useful these days. I already shared it with Khai and Jan. I'll teach it to Shalaen when we meet next. The Mystics are now training all adepts to learn it."

She went on to describe how the enemy was using her powerful energies against her and others."

Naero passed that knowledge on to him via her mindlink and then with her her quickening ability. From there they practiced the shielding effect until Baeven had it down.

She also shared other kinds of more subtle knowledge and experience through their link. These were things that she had learned in general, that might prove useful to him as well. Baeven might never learn or experience them on his own in his line of work.

Naero went on to describe some of the bizarre encounters she had survived, and some of the enemy's new tricks.

Baeven shook his fists in the air. "We can't trust those slippery bastards, Naero. That's for damn sure. They're going to keep trying to find ways to come at us from different vectors and take us down. We must remain vigilant."

"I'm afraid it only gets worse," she said. Next she told him about the weakening of the actual pocket dimension that contained the G'lothc spirits. How the dimension's fractures and fissures were allowing those highly dangerous, lost souls to escape, and send their dark will and their vile influence streaming into the Astral Plane. And from there foes attacked into the Prime Material Plane and their universe and galaxy.

"That is a terrible new development," Baeven said. "We can discuss it with Jia, but I don't see what we could possibly do to seal such breaches."

"Not even if we gather together all of the Cosmic players that we know? What if we concentrated all of our powers in an attempt to fuse just one of the fissures at–"

"We still couldn't begin to even touch one of them, and have any hope to affect such structures in any way, Naero. It would take powers and energies far greater than a million of us or more combined, beyond anything we could ever hope to muster. We cannot operate on that kind of scale. Don't you see? We might even make the situation worse."

Naero frowned and looked down at her feet with a sigh. There weren't a million of them. "I guess I didn't fully comprehend what it was we were up against. I hoped that we could find a way to do something."

"Yes, well it was a nice thought, and it would make things easier for us. Our problems only seem to stack up against us. If the enemy can slip out through the Astral Plane and then from there into any part of our universe at will, they can come at us from anywhere. It gives them a huge advantage against us."

They discussed the brief appearance of the Dakkur Dark King.

"He is mocking us, clearly," Baeven said. "He's making a challenge, pure and simple. When the time is right, he might even begin hunting us, trying to take us down one at a time if he can. We can't let that happen. Just as with the White Queens, we must take on any Black Kings at least two at a time. Double team them. I'll contact Ra."

"You defeated a Dark King on your own," Naero said. "And I killed a White Queen of the Dakkur on my own, in single combat. Although I did use kind of a nasty trick to polish her off."

"If they die and we live, take the win. But Naero, in all honesty, I still think it was a fluke that I vanquished the Dark King that I fought. I got lucky, that's all. By rights he should have digested me and shit out my dust. Gaviok did help me soften him up a bit before he went back down. The point is that both of us barely survived the damage done to us. I still

137

wouldn't relish the odds of just one of us taking on one of those damn monsters alone."

"That raises another important question," Naero said. "If there are more Dakkur kings, how many could there be at one time? What if they and their queens came at us in a group, all at once?"

Baeven laughed heartily. "Well then, I guess we'd have to pucker up and kiss or sorry asses goodbye."

Naero felt the blood drain from her face.

She didn't quite relish the dark humor in such statements.

"Don't worry, Naero. Such a thing as you envision is never going to happen. Due to the instinctive, territorial nature of Dakkur Kings and their White Queens, they would never cooperate in such a fashion. First, these beings are, thankfully, exceedingly rare.

"Second, as I said, if they even sensed each other within the same quadrant, they would be overcome with the desire to pit themselves against each other until one of them, and all of their queens, were slain. They are mental about competition and about any of their own kind threatening their dominion, and their territory."

"But, hypothetically by that logic, the enemy could have a Dakkur King and a nest of queens causing trouble in each of our four quadrants?"

Baeven halted. "I suppose it could be possible, in a technical sense, but it still would be highly unlikely. It would not occur naturally."

Since when was anything about the enemy natural, in any way, shape, or form?

Next, they discussed the eventual arrival of the enemy's massive Armada, lurking in the next galaxy closest to them.

"That is a major concern as well," Baeven said. "Eventually, the enemy will cobble together enough tek and energy to find another way to send them through. If we can detect it soon enough, we might be able to fight them to a standstill and shut down their access point once again. Then we wear down the remnants of anything that came through.

"That is precisely why I have been expending much time and effort on expanding our fixer net of detection throughout the four quadrants of our galaxy."

Naero shifted her weight and stretched her back, sipping some more cold water. It was surprisingly refreshing.

"How soon will it be complete?" she asked.

"Only a hundred and forty standard years, and that's if the expansion continues at optimal rates of replication."

Naero rolled her eyes. "Great...after we're all long dead."

"Ahh...but I'm concentrating on the two quadrants closest to our neighboring galaxy."

"But they could come through anywhere," Naero protested.

Baeven frowned at her. "Must you find fault with all of my allusions and suppositions? At least I'm doing something. I don't see the Alliance tackling the matter."

Naero sucked air in through her teeth. "I'm sorry. But that's another thing entirely. The Alliance is getting spread too thin. Spacers and our other allies can't shoulder all of this alone. As soon as the landers get done kicking out the Corps, they're going to need to modify their fleets and shoulder a big part of the load with us.

"At the very least, they'll need to defend much of the Alpha Quadrant while we hunt down the enemy strongholds hiding in the Gamma Quadrant. Spacers can't be everywhere, and we can't be expected to do it all–not with everything we're up against."

"I'm not arguing with you there. But I must say. You've really come into your own, Naero. You parents would be proud. You're quickly becoming one of the great leaders of your generation. I'm nowhere near as good with people as you are."

The Shadow Fox whispered in above them and opened a hatch. Baeven and then Naero floated up through it and it sealed behind them.

They went onto the bridge, and Naero embraced and greeted Jia, Danjen, and S'krin.

They exchanged their usual jibes and good-natured ribbing and quips.

She observed that Danjen was off his mystery kick, and back to dressing up like a wild west gunslinger, except for the blaster pistols in his custom made holsters.

He actually looked amazingly stupid with his furry ass hide, his brown and white cowhide chaps without pants, and his prehensile tail bobbing around out the back of his loin cloth.

The goofy ten gallon hat only completed the idiotic look for the fuzzy moron. What an imbecile.

The Spacer and human descendants of Old Earth where the actual cowboy originated probably didn't even know what the heck a cowboy or a gunslinger was any longer in any case.

"Howdy!" Danjen exclaimed with manic glee.

Naero just shook her head and looked away. She hugged the fuzzy goofball anyway.

"Hey Naero. Maybe you can help me. I've been doing some more wild west research…"

Oh, no. Not again.

"I want to get some spurs, but I can't figure out what they exactly were and what they were for."

"Danjen, what the hell do you need spurs for in any case? If I recall, they were worn on the ankles and heels of boots so that riders could jab them into horses and other such mounts to encourage them to run faster on command. You don't have a horse, and you wouldn't know what to do with one if you did. You aren't going to wear leather boots on you hairy legs any more than you wear pants, which just makes you wearing chaps and a loin cloth both obscene and silly."

"Hmmm…guess I'll pass on the spurs, then. But I still like the chaps. They're nice and breezy, and they protect against rattlers in the low country."

She slapped her hand over her eyes, and dragged it down over her nose and mouth. "Haisha, Danjen; you're on a starship. There are no rattlers, and no low country. Now get the hell away from me, just in case your brand of madness is somehow catching."

He laughed. "Good to see you too, N."

Naero still had a week before she would rendezvous with her fleets and Khai. She had other places to go, and she hoped that Baeven and Company would join her.

First they caught up Jia and the crew on what they had been discussing.

"I need to touch base with Shalaen and Tarim," Naero said. "They're out this way overseeing part of the expansion for the Mining Consortium. Did you hear? Their wedding is scheduled to take place in less than a year, about ten months away."

"I'll plot it in," Jia said. "If it's not too much trouble, Bae and I will make an appearance. But we don't want to ruin anything by any of the authorities trying to arrest us."

Naero grinned. "That does make social appearances a bit of a hassle. It almost happened at mine and Khai's wedding, but I told Klyne that I would never forgive him if he tried anything."

"We were all very thankful for that, N." Jia noted.

"So," Baeven said. "Where will this meeting with Shalaen and Tarim take place?"

"Oh, it's close by on Rieger-8. Jia, did you confirm my requests, under my naval codes?"

"Affirmative. Under way as we speak," Jia said. They went into jump. "Arrival in fourteen minutes plus. Have a cold drink and we'll be on the ground and docking."

Yet when they arrived in system, Baeven insisted that they came in under stealth mode, simply out of old habit on his part.

The small, frontier starport on Rieger-8 did not transmit or respond in any way.

That was both odd and alarming. Someone should be on duty to answer.

"Check the assigned Alliance fleets nearby, protecting this system," Naero said, out of curiosity.

Jia and Om replied almost at once.

Every one of those fleets had been drawn off to neighboring sectors because of increased enemy activity.

Rieger-8 was barely a dust speck on the fringe, on the very rim of the expansion. As boom settlements went, it was just beginning, with a starting population of less than a hundred thousand.

But that was about to change, because the Mining Consortium knew full well that one of the next threads of the exploration expansion out into the unknown was going to explode into dozens of new earthlikes just discovered, and rich mining worlds ripe for the picking.

Rieger-8 was going to be the staging point for another big push. The expansion was turning out to be the lifeblood of the growing Alliance. It fueled exploration and the dreams of trillions of former Gigacorps slaves yearning to be free and wishing to carve out something for themselves in the bold new future during their lifetimes.

They kept coming and pushing out further into the unknown in all directions, despite the risks and uncertainties, despite all of the dangers.

Naero shook herself back to the problem at hand.

Something was very wrong on Rieger-8.

They scanned the system and its lone starport and colonial settlement, on the western edge of an oceanic continent just above the tropics. The place was a paradise, except for an occasional major earthquake and or tsunami every century or so.

There were forty-one starships of various types docked at the small, pop-up modular starport of Joshua Tech design. It was almost at the full capacity of fifty ships that it was designed for.

Not a single ship was moving in or out of the system or even preparing to do so. Again, highly unusual.

They could scan the area more closely after they entered the atmosphere. They kept fixers and stealth probes deployed and active as they went in.

"I'm close enough, now," Naero said, "and I'm worried about Shalaen and Tarim. I'm going in with my fixers. They'll pump everything I see and find back to you. Follow on as you—"

"I'm going in with you," Baeven said. "Like we said, we need to pair up and stick together more."

"Copy that," Naero said with a nod. "Let's ride, and go in in phazed stealth mode."

"Sound good, N. Ready to pop."

"He we go."

In a flash they were on surface, just a few meters outside of the starport.

Om reported immediately, at the same time that Naero and Baeven read the same thing.

Naero, high levels of psyonic activity. Be careful.

Fixers spread wide, maximum gathering dispersal, Om. Where is everyone and what are they doing?

Of the eighty-six thousand, three hundred and twenty people in the colony, most of them appear to have been stunned, N. They're scattered more or less everywhere, concentrated in dwellings, work areas, and public zones and on the starships, just as you might expect.

Sounds like one of the enemy's mass stunning ships, Om. They could nail an entire, small, tight colony like this in four our five hits and take out everyone. But why would they stun them? Why would they want everybody alive? The enemy doesn't usually work this way at all. Normally they murder everyone first thing, and ask questions later.

It wasn't a mass stunner ship, N. The signatures are all wrong. Take a look at them with teknomancy for a moment. I'm having trouble making the details out.

All right.

"What's going on?" Baeven stopped and asked her. "You got something?"

Naero held up one finger. "Everyone's been stunned. I'm trying to figure out who did it and how. Give me a moment to analyze. Info flooding in."

Whatever this was, it was very powerful, acted quickly, and operates on a very wide scale, N.

Naero gasped. We've faced this threat before. I'd recognize these signs anywhere, but our foes are doing their level best to cover their tracks better. The trace energies are Cosmic, and from stepped up, Darkforce powers. The patterns are messed up and off the scales, but it's a mental pattern of a demented mind.

"Baeven. Be on your guard. Danner's on scene somewhere and I'm guessing he's brought plenty of friends with him. He's trying to remain hidden and avoid detection."

"Got it. Until we waltz right into his trap.

"What the heck is a waltz, any way?"

"An old fashioned dance from ancient times. You see it in old vids sometimes. It's actually very pleasant. Is Khai a good dancer?"

Naero snorted. "Only if you like your feet stomped on. So, no. But the man has many other endearing qualities that more than compensate. We simply won't be entering any dance contests anytime soon."

"So, who gets to waltz in and spring the trap?"

"Let's shoot for it, uncle–one, two, shoot."

Naero went with blade, which beat kick, but lost out to blaster.

Baeven chose blaster and won.

Haisha, she should have trusted her gut and went with kick, which would have disarmed and beaten blaster.

"All right," Baeven said eagerly, "I'll slip in quietly and make it look good when they expose me. You and the others back me up. Jia and the rest should be here soon. Tell them to keep watching the sector for any new enemy forces jumping in."

"Will do. Good luck."

"Thanks." Baeven transported into the main Mining Consortium stronghold bored into the mountain rock nearby.

Naero continued to monitor his progress and send instructions to Jia.

"Some kind of jamming already, Naero. My fixers can't penetrate ahead of us and down into the bunker compound. Are you still getting this?"

"Baeven, your feeds are breaking up, but I still read you."

"It's going to cut off at some point. Perhaps you should–"

And as if on cue, Baeven's feeds cut off at that point exactly.

An alert from Jia. "Bae and Naero, enemy attack fleets pouring in from several jump points. Lot's of company your way within one hour or less."

"Alliance response fleets?"

"Already here, cloaked and waiting. Called in on your naval codes hours ago, just as you requested, before we jumped. Fireworks should start up in seconds."

It was good to be an admiral at times. And it wasn't even a hunch.

Naero had come under every type of attack imaginable, so many times that she just naturally started planning for them as if they were routine.

If she went somewhere and wasn't attacked, now that would be a surprise.

"Come down and stay out of sight while I go in after Baeven. I think you'll know when we need help."

"When things start exploding, we'll be ready."

Naero grinned. "You know my family too well."

When she transported to the point of Baeven's last transmission, it led her to a series of wide, underground mining access shafts.

143

It was miner policy to first bore out a defensive stronghold for any colony on the fringe. Vulnerability in the Unknown Sectors demanded it.

Too many colonies could simply be wiped out otherwise. And by the time help arrived from the Alliance fleets, the attackers could be long gone, leaving only death and devastation behind them.

The miners learned early on that if they dug themselves a deep enough hole first thing and supplied it, that they could hold out for a few days up to a few weeks. By then, hopefully some kind of help would swoop in to relieve them.

Naero sent fixers in all directions to scan the system.

It extended four kilometers down and spread out in an expanding radius of twenty kilometers.

Clearly, Rieger-8 had been slotted to become a major expansion hub from the get go, with an emergency bunker that size.

But she couldn't locate Baeven, or get a link back up with him. Definitely some kind of major jamming going on, and it was psyonic in nature, too.

By now the Darkforce signatures were so intense and powerful that they all bled together and became meaningless.

Then Naero came across the stunned bodies of colonists of many different ages, including older children between seven and the upper teens. A few here and there at first, and then piles of them, even some choking the corridors.

Many of these people had been stunned with powerful psyonics.

Shalaen.

Others had been shot with stun needles and stun bolts.

Tarim.

Finally her fixers made relay contact with one of Baeven's. He was proceeding down further into the main underground compound. The various blast doors cut off the strongpoints where the colonists would hold out in bunkers in case of attack.

Baeven ran into thousands of people who seemed to be under some kind of mind control.

Naero instantly checked the Cosmic flows. Yes, most definitely. The energy control signatures were feeding off of Shalaen's Cosmic energies, the more she channeled. And they used that power to take over the minds of the colonists, and turn them against Shalaen and Tarim.

That's why all of these people had been stunned. Her friends clearly had no wish to kill or harm their own people.

But they couldn't allow themselves to be taken by these pawns either.

A garbled transmission from Jia tried to punch through. But it was cut off.

Naero guessed that they would see Danner or some other such enemies arrive shortly to collect whoever they could capture. And the enemy wasn't picky. They'd gladly take her and Baeven as well as Shalaen.

Naero had a few surprises ready for them.

Like Baeven, she would need to get past the thousands of colonists further within, who were still under enemy control.

For the time being, she went back to being cloaked and phazed.

The controlled colonists were massed around one of the blast doors, pounding on it in futility with their bloody hands and fists.

An enemy vesper tried to slip in and whisper crap to her about defeat and how she had no chance.

Naero cut the thing off psyonically and then crushed it.

Then she turned to the colonists massed before the blast doors and shielded them all, encasing them in a huge hollow pod of specialized Cosmic force.

Cut off from the alien assholes pulling their strings, the puppets all crumpled to the ground.

Naero sent agonizing, Lifespark jolts of feedback shooting through those strings and connections. Any kind of positive energy was like antimatter to the foul G'lothc. She hoped that it zapped their asses good, and roasted their chestnuts, if they had any.

She shielded that entire chamber, so that the bastards could not return and pick up where they left off.

Naero then used telekinesis as gently as she could to scoop and move the stunned colonists away from the outer blast doors. She was certain that Baeven had already phazed his way through, and was probably with Shalaen and Tarim by now.

She attempted to do the same thing, and passed through the shelter's heavy defensive barriers with phazing.

At last, there was Shalaen and Tarim with Baeven as expected, talking things over in a meeting chamber. Her two good friends rushed to her when she popped in on them. It was a huge relief to find them safe.

The enemy most likely could care less about anyone but Shalaen. Individuals who could wield Cosmic powers were rare and valuable commodities.

She could sense that Shalaen had healed Tarim very recently of several superficial wounds, probably gained from defending Shalaen from the mindless mob on their way down there.

The hugging and catching up took a few moments.

145

"We're still sitting ducks down here," Baeven warned them. "No doubt the enemy knows where we are and they'll be coming for us soon, I'm thinking. Naero, can you transport us out of here? Up to the surface or onboard *The Shadow Fox?*"

Naero checked. "Negative. Not through twenty kilometers of rock."

"Hmm…I was afraid of that. Then I guess we'd better hike back the way we came, and fast. Can we all fly?"

"I can't," Tarim said. "Leave me behind. The enemy doesn't want me. It's Shalaen they're after."

"Beloved, I won't leave you behind!" Shalaen insisted.

"Screw that," Naero said. She teknomanced her gravwing onto Tarim and sprouted her psyonic wings at will, opening her third eye all at once.

Next she popped out her four extra arms, each one wielding an advanced weapon that she summoned. "Let's fly. Stay between me and Baeven. Uncle, you've got our six."

"Copy that."

They streaked ahead, while Om used stealth fixers to cloak, phaze, and shield Tarim and Shalaen.

Naero linked with Shalaen's mind and revealed to her how to block the enemy methods to feed off of her own Cosmic energies and take control of people around her.

They made it to the upper access shafts, the stone chambers opening up into huge ventilation domes and stalled movers.

With out warning they passed through what seemed to be some kind of energized, Darkforce net that activated only as they passed through it, blazing bright red and orange.

It nailed them all with heavy, Darkforce shock charges and disrupted their stealth modes and phazing.

All of them crashed to the ground and struggled to rise.

An enormous wyrmhole opened up, and a gigantic, segmented Darkforce dynamo mek stepped through and rose up, towering fifteen meters high. He almost reached the top of the dome.

Naero's insane brother Danner fueled the monstrosity, contained within the round, shielded facemask, wreathed in Darkforce energy and bolts of Darkforce lightning. He used the voice to chortle and echo his booming words.

"AHH…EVEN BETTER. SISTER, UNCLE. WELCOME TO THE PARTY. NOW WE'LL MAKE USE OF ALL OF YOU AND YOUR ENERGIES TO BEGIN THE DESTRUCTION OF YOUR GALAXY!"

Clouds of Darkforce generators of many sizes poured through the wyrmhole and waited to pour through. There wasn't enough room for them all.

Danner blasted his way up to the surface, through the dome and hundreds of feet of earth and rock.

Naero acted quickly, encasing Tarim in an energy pod and transporting him back to the starport.

The next instant, she, Baeven, and Shalaen were swarmed upon by the Darkforce generators.

Together they destroyed almost two dozen of the vile, living machines in the intense, brief fight that followed.

Most of the generators contained Yattai, energy beings related to Shalaen, and her mother. Once free of the ruined generators, the Yattai quickly escaped back into the planes they came from.

The other hosts looked to be a few Oden, and other partial energy beings of a type never seen before.

Perhaps the latter were the Laelor, that Naero had heard mention of.

The enemy quickly gathered them up, before the weakened hosts could attempt to escape.

Naero and Baeven had transformed into their partial Dark beast modes, but it did them little good. The three Cosmic defenders were now encased and trapped in Darkforce globes that the Darkforce generators formed around them.

The properties of these globes constantly drained their energies at a sickening rate.

They continued to startap, struggle, and resist, but the enemy only collected their energies faster.

19

Danner brought them and the Wyrmhole up to the surface. He floated his captives high up into the sky toward the yawning gateway.

The Shadow Fox attempted to intercept them, guns blazing, blasting many of the Darkforce generators.

But too late, Danner and the rest escaped within the wyrmhole, dragging their captives along with them.

Once they passed through it, the wyrmhole closed behind them, cutting off any further chance of rescue.

Naero clearly spotted the Plane of Annihilation speeding ever closer, and the glowing cracks surrounding the G'lothc pocket dimension, pulsating with destructive energies.

Globules of unstable Darkforce energy swelled up from the cracks.

She began to have a very bad feeling.

Naero sensed what was going on and the fear of it ripped through her. Om, has the enemy gone completely insane?

I'm sure of it, Naero! They've somehow used psyonics, biomancy, and teknomancy to link trickle feeds to the Plane of Annihilation itself. They're attempting to trigger a massive cataclysmic feedback blast across the dimensions and into the Prime Material Plane. All of reality could be shattered, rents and tears ripping the universe wide open!

Shalaen linked with Naero's and then Baeven's mind. *The enemy means to destroy us all! Look at what they are planning.*

Baeven assessed the situation with them. *They'll still need a catalyst for the chain reaction, like setting off an atomic, but on a dimensional scale. A concentrated blast of Cosmic energy to trigger the far greater detonation. Where are they going to–*

Danner suddenly loomed over them all, he and his horde of bloated, Darkforce energy collectors sweeping them toward their rendezvous with oblivion. *That's where all of us come in. The explosion I set off using all of our Cosmic energies will blast a gaping wound across the universe!* Danner laughed with genuine maniacal glee. Only he would agree to such a mad plan.

Danner, this is beyond cosmicide; even your masters will be killed. They'll be destroyed along with us.

Hee hee! As if I ever truly had any who could be my masters. That's the glorious risk they take, and oops–they're already dead! It's just as probable that they'll be set free of their prison, and scattered across several shattered dimensions, weakened and ripe for conquest. They'll have their pick of hosts then.

But Danner, you'll die as well. You will cease to be.

I know. Isn't it spectacular? Everything dies; why not us? Wahoo!

Shalaen cried out, *A massive energy wave is fast approaching us from the Astral Plane, I've never seen anything like it!*

Baeven noted it as well. *What the hell is that?*

A building wave of shining white fire rushed toward them at miraculous speed.

No, no, not here, Naero muttered in terror.

Danner panicked. *Get to the cracks. Detonate. Detonate!*

By then the blinding wave swept through them all.

Shetharra was at the core of the wave, blazing like a star.

She severed Danner's massive head from his mek neck with one blow.

When the gigantic body fell upon and attempted to enveloped her, she exploded it into melting pieces that shot in many directions.

By that time, Naero and Baeven burst free from their energy prisons and helped free Shalaen.

The horde of Darkforce generators swarmed at Shetharra, almost covering her shield sphere completely, struggling to drain her of her powers.

An expanding wave of impossible force flung them all away from her at high speed, destroy some outright, and damaging others.

The horde quickly regroup around Danner, regenerating constantly, maneuvering and preparing for another attack.

Naero rushed to her daughter's side, with Baeven on their right and Shalaen on their left.

Shetharra, you should not have come here, my girl.

Her daughter spoke with the voice without even thinking. I COULDN'T LET THEM DESTROY YOU, MAMA. I HAD TO COME. I COULD FEEL IT, AND IT MADE ME HURT INSIDE. THEY WERE GOING TO DO A VERY BAD THING. I COULDN'T LET THAT HAPPEN. WE MUST STOP THEM!

Ahh... Danner said, *My little meddling niece, come to crash the party. Far too late fools! You are still outnumbered and outmatched. Drive them into the fissures and finish them. We can still do this. Glory is our destiny!*

There upon the edge of Oblivion, the four Cosmic champions fought to decide the fate of their universe.

Yet even with Shetharra's mighty aid, the power of the enemy was still very great, and slowly drove them back by force toward the volatile, destabilizing fissures surrounding the prison dimension of the vile G'lothc.

Shetharra blasted Danner out of the mek head, but he was still wreathed in the Darkforce, his body contained in Darkforce armor.

Danner had merged with the Darkforce almost completely.

Naero went on the attack with everything she had. Her third eye open wide, she summoned her extra limbs and all of her most powerful Cosmic weapons. Beams shot out from her eyes, and sonic blasts from her open mouth. Still more attacks blazed from her hands.

All of her attacks hammered Danner without let up, punching and driving him burning and spinning ever closer to the event horizon of the Annihilation Plane's own, Great Destroyer.

Then Danner countered, with tentacles of Darkforce energy rippling out from his body and enveloping his older sister, drawing him in with him.

Is this the fate you planned for me, sister? No, no, no! I think I'll fling you in instead, and you shall die alone and be torn asunder for all time, screaming in torment until the end the universe! How delicious will that be?

Shetharra slammed into Danner and tore her mother free, nailing her mad uncle with shocking punches and kicks in blazing fury.

SHE IS NOT ALONE. WE ARE NOT ALONE. YOU EVIL ONES HAVE ENRAGED MANY OTHERS WITH YOUR ACTIONS. NOW THEY COME FOR YOU!

Thousands of shining, humanoid energy beings appeared in a cloud all about the enemy, and closed in on the servants and living machine abominations of the Darkforce.

The Yattai! My kind have at last come in force to deal with this scourge. Shalaen wept with joy and wrath, and rose up to fight beside her mother's people against the foes that strove to enslave and obliterate them all.

The rage of the Yattai could be felt all around them.

Get to the cracks! Danner commanded his remaining force of slaves. *Detonate. Detonate anyway!*

The enemy forces struggled to reach the unstable fissures, even as the Yattai fell upon them, seeking their revenge.

Danner exploded the Darkforce protective suit around him and all of his tentacles at once, stunning even Shetharra for a time.

He was revealed in his true form, riddled with Darkforce disease, a broken, twisted, misshapen freak.

But he wrapped his weird deformed limbs around his glowing niece and hurtled toward the event horizon of doom laughing.

Well, if I can't drag you in with me, sib. I guess I'll have to settle for your little brat!

Naero slammed into the insane fiend with all of her might. She shattered one of his arms, nearly tore one of his twisted legs off.

Finally Shetharra was free.

Naero shielded her and sent her hurtling back away from certain destruction. The Great Destroyer was tugging hard at both of them now.

Danner tried to spit bloody Darkforce into her face. Naero blocked it with one hand.

Ahh...yes. Back to what I planned in the–

Naero screamed, "Eye of Annihilation!"

The combined beams from all three of her eyes drove into Danner and shot him forward. He continued shrieking and laughing, until he tipped over the event horizon and was taken.

At last his sick laughter was silenced.

Naero snarled, "Farewell, brother."

From there it was all that she could do to claw and fight her way back herself.

A knot of Yattai protected Shetharra as she came around.

Yet at that moment, some of the Darkforce generators managed to reach the Cosmic cracks before Baeven, Shalaen and the Yattai could cut them down.

Naero tried to scream psyonically to all present. Protect yourselves!

She barely had time to throw up shields around her daughter and then herself.

Then the detonation struck.

The enemy did not succeed in tearing a hole across the dimensions. Yet many Yattai close in to the zero point were vaporized, along with the rest of the enemy generators.

As a result, the prison dimension of the G'lothc was blasted wide open, and their Darkforce spirits began to boil out by the multitudes.

They immediately assailed the Yattai and tried to burn out their minds to take them over as hosts.

Get back. Regroup. Don't let those things touch you! Shalaen warned. For some it was already too late. Their Yattai comrades combined powers to destroy the possessed, rather than let the enemy use their energy forms.

Even Naero was horrified. How could they stop something this big?

A group of G'lothc spirits swept forward, enveloping an entire swarm of Yattai, quickly melding into an enormous Darkforce behemoth. It roared at them in fury. WE ARE FREE! NOW WE TAKE YOU ALL!

Baeven sliced through the monster in his partial Dark beast form, with all of his glowing green Cosmic blades spinning.

Shut the fuck up, you gutless assholes!

The Guardian of Chaos energy also controlled the Darkforce.

For good measure, Baeven detonated an orb of Darkforce energy inside the thing, and it ceased to exist.

But that only bought them a short respite. The defenders still fell back, before the expanding wave of horror that continued to flood out at them.

Shetharra took her mother's hand. *The Song of Summoning, Mama. Sing it with me. The shining lights love us. They will come if we sing for them.*

Naero took her daughter in her arms, closed her eyes, and together they sang at the top of their voices, against all powers of destruction and evil that loomed and roared before them.

Then all things went still. The roaring babble of the G'lothc legions was cut off and silenced.

When Naero opened her eyes, Shetharra broke into laughter, the sound like the ringing of clear bells.

All around them, large glowing spheres of bright energy filled the air, and even the celestial Yattai were amazed and moved to awe.

As insane as it felt, Naero was overwhelmed with the strong impression that she should know who and what these things were. How could she?

A mighty voice boomed from out of midst of one of the glowing orbs into their minds.

WE ARE, AND WE HAVE COME FROM THE BEYOND TO PREVENT REALITY ITSELF FROM BEING ALTERED. WHO HATH DONE THESE THINGS? THESE

THINGS SHOULD NOT BE AT THIS TIME. THE TIME OF THE COSMIC PROPHECIES IS NOT YET AT HAND.

IT IS TOO SOON FOR THE DARK SOULS OF THE STUBBORN AND MISGUIDED G'LOTHC TO BE UNLEASHED FROM THEIR SELF-MADE PRISON, TO FINALLY DECIDE THEIR FATE FOR ALL TIME. THERE IS A TIME SET FOR ALL THINGS. THESE THINGS WILL BE AMENDED AND PROPERLY RESTORED. NEVER AGAIN SHALL ANY BE ALLOWED TO INTERFERE WITH DESTINY AND THE COSMIC PROPHECY IN THESE WAYS. THAT IS ALL.

After a bright flash, the G'lothc prison dimension stood not only restored, but reinforced, with them howling back inside it. There were no more glowing cracks or fissures.

Apparently, destiny was back on track after the enemy tried to cheat and rig the game in their favor. There were forces keeping watch that weren't going to allow that. Yet it appeared that all things would have their day.

The glowing orbs began to shrink down and fade away.

Naero covered her mouth and gasped.

She finally recognized them in their smaller forms.

Two of them drifted near Shetharra, and the spacechild caught them in her hands like fire flies and giggled. *They know you, Mama, I feel their great love for us. Can you hear their voices?*

I was Bahan, beloved friend Naero.

And I was Iika. We did not expect to meet with you again in this life. Your daughter is as beautiful as you are Halaena.

Alas, we cannot stay long. We must return to the Beyond and our stations there.

We serve the Great Mystery here, and in the Beyond as the Tua always have. We help test and guard all of the universes against reckless madness and folly such as this. Such things cannot be allowed.

The destiny of each universe is meant to play out as it will, and all things will be tested and decided at the proper time, directed by the choices of all involved. That destiny cannot be circumvented or destroyed.

In extremely rare cases such as this, we are sometimes forced to act.

Their voices blurred together for a bit, but that did not matter. Naero did have a question she wished to ask, whether they would answer it or not.

What is the Beyond like?

Iika laughed, as she did before while she had lived. *Sister, you know we cannot say.*

You will take your next journey when it is your time to do so, Naero. Not before. What do you think it will be like?

Naero grinned and touched the soul orbs pulsing in the palms of her little daughter's glowing hands with overpowering affection.

I think…I think everything is a test.

Now it was Bahan's turn to laugh. *Well answered. Master Vane and Lady Hashiko are with us in the Beyond. Now we are testing them.*

I'd sure like to see some of that.

They still have so much to learn, Iika said. *Master Vane is learning powerful lessons of humility and endurance in his current new form of a helpless young Tua girl, who faces many challenges at the hands of difficult and demanding masters. A lesson he was incapable of even perceiving before. But I think now, he is beginning to have some valuable insights into the hearts of others, and his own.*

Vane? Naero could hardly imagine any of that.

And what of Hashi, Bahan? Naero asked.

She is learning to truly love herself and others. A vital lesson that is as difficult for her in the Beyond, as it was for her here in this life. But we have not given up on her yet. There is hope for both of them still. You know how patient the Tua can be.

Naero chuckled. Well, good luck to them.

Suddenly she had a sobering thought about what tests and lessons might be awaiting her. But that was far off in the future…she hoped.

All too soon, Iika and Bahan were the last of the Beyonders to fade away. They spoke as one.

Our task is done. We must go. Farewell brave Naero. Bright Shetharra.

Naero was already crying. Goodbye, again, my beloved friends.

Shetharra leaned in and kissed them even as they faded. *Goodbye pretty ones!*

They were gone the next instant. Shetharra turn around in her mother's arms. *Don't worry, Mama. They'll be waiting for us. We'll meet them again, someday. But I have so many questions. The head bad one. Was he really my uncle?*

Naero sighed deeply, but the best answer was always the truth. At least as much truth as a very wise seven year old needed to hear.

Yes, Shetharra. He was Uncle Jan's twin brother, and my little brother as well. Unknown to our family, the enemy captured him long ago when he was a baby, and hurt him very badly for many years. That forced him to choose to become as bad as them. Possibly even worse in some ways.

That was a very bad thing, Mama. Maybe that's why he was so sad and messed up inside. I wish we could have helped him somehow. He's gone now, right Mama?

Yes, sweet girl. He's gone forever. He had to be stopped. I couldn't let him harm us any longer.

Can we go home now, Mama? I'm tired and hungry and I want to see Papa and everyone else. And then I might want to nap for a bit. I'm tired. Will you sing to me?

Naero closed her eyes. I will always sing to you, my little duck.

Baeven came up to them and put his arms around them both protectively. *I think we're done here. Your friend's going to stay behind with her people for a bit. They have a lot more catching up to do, she said. And they want to join the Alliance to help protect their people. You two all right?*

Naero nodded. Sure we are, uncle. Let's go home.

20

There would be other battles to come. Their list of foes still seemed endless. But for the present, the enemy had been thrown back once again, and disaster averted. Remnants of their broken plots were still on the loose here and there. They still needed to be hunted down and taken out; but that was all for another day.

However brief the respite was, triumph needed to be savored and fully enjoyed.

Naero and Khai celebrated by summoning Womi and taking a two day tour sweeping throughout the wonders of the Astral Plane. They took Shetharra, Daeyen, and Kathron with them. The kids loved it all.

Where else could they get to zip around on the back of a kilometer long dragon creature and see sights that would amaze anyone with a heart and soul?

At one point another remnant group of enemy-possessed feeders attempted to swoop in and attack them.

Before anyone else could respond, a blinding white wave of Cosmic force raced forward at impossible speed, overwhelmed and obliterated the enemy forces with astounding speed and fury.

After the devastation cleared, Shetharra floated before them defiantly, both of her open hands outstretched. Waves of Cosmic energy coruscated around her advanced, astral energy form. Her long white hair whipped around her, fully aflame like a young star.

She turned to back to them, her third eye wide open, blazing with white fire. Orbs of the same white fire encased both of her tiny hands without harming her.

Naero gasped. That fire wasn't just ignited from the Lifespark. No, it was the Flame Eternal itself, and Shetharra wielded it naturally, without hesitation.

The greatest force in the universe.

Only the Seven Dreamers of the Kexx had been capable of summoning the Flame Eternal, and in the end, that pure flame had destroyed both them, and the Six Champions of the G'lothc.

"They meant to harm my family," she explained. "I saw into their minds the terrible things they intended to do. I could not allow that. I will never allow such. They will need to get past me first, and I will fight them with all that I am."

The white fire fades and flickered away. Shetharra returned to her regular astral form, and floated back into the waiting arms of her parents.

"You are our blood. We're proud of you for protecting those you love," Khai told her.

Naero wept and kissed her brave little duck. "This is the blood you come from and you are of the flame eternal. But in the future, sweet girl, let your father and I be the first line of defense. If any of the enemy ever break through past us, then you can deal with them, Shetharra. Do you understand?"

She nodded. A great weariness came over their spacechild, no doubt from her exertions for one so young, and Naero held her close, monitoring her and regenerating her energies for a long while.

The rest of their holiday in the Astral plane went without incident. Womi showed them wonder after wonder. They all learned of many things that only the Kahn-Dar understood and knew about. Naero's children interacted with Womi as if he were their friend as well, and soon they were. A great fondness between them developed–especially between Womi and Shetharra.

Naero had guessed that might happen.

Upon their return, it was soon time for the next member of the family to join Clans William and Maeris.

157

Naero re-considered and granted the honor to Sharrah, who was incredibly moved and thankful for the kind gesture.

It was Sharrah's wish, and easy to grant, for all that she did.

Khai and Naero were present at the birthing. Naero did all that she could with biomancy to help the process go smoothly and quickly, with a minimum of time and the associated pain.

Allantar Thaeved Williams was born at three bells, strong and healthy–if not a little squished looking, and took his names from his mighty fathers of old.

Khai cut the cord very carefully with Yii.

Sharrah held the new little scion first, and then Naero and Khai.

Naero felt the overpowering love that all Spacer mothers felt for all of their children, and quietly vowed to herself to embrace every moment of life, no matter what came their way.

That was the way to live, to defy all of the odds and the dangers and rocket straight ahead. Naero wasn't going to slow down. She wasn't going to stop as long as the breath of life still coursed in her breast.

For the first time in her life, she felt in control of herself and her own destiny. She was free to live her life the way she chose–in freedom.

Naero Amashin Maeris held up her beautiful new son Allantar and looked forward through his eyes. That was one of the big secrets in life, in everything. Nothing ever stopped.

Everything around Naero kept going, changing, and evolving.

And so would she and all that she held dear.

Joy always mixed with sorrow, and everything in between.

Naero curled one corner of her mouth into a sly smile and took in a deep breath.

More threats and challenges would certainly continue to hurtle their way at top speed.

By all the Powers…let them come.

THE END

Follow the continuing adventures of Naero and her Allies in:

THE GAMMA QUADRANT

Please Post A Book Review Right Now

Please post a review of this book where you purchased it, if you enjoyed it.

Just twenty little words are all that is required. Twenty words that say what you liked about this book while it is still fresh in your heart, mind, and soul. Please do so now before something else makes you forget.

Here is the link for *Naero's Mastery* if you purchased it on Amazon:

smarturl.it/NaerosMastery

Please click on the link and post your review now.
Done? The author would personally like to thank you very much.

In this busy world, everyone is pressed for time. Our time is so important, no doubt. It has reached the point now where authors of nearly every stripe compete not only for sales, but to garner reviews from their readers. Some authors even stoop to "purchasing" reviews in social media that some services now offer in bulk.

In the publish or perish work of competitive fiction, book reviews from readers are golden, they have now become a commodity even.

Many in the business even consider book reviews as important, or even more important than book sales in some ways. As crazy as that sounds.

So therefore, trust us in this. If you have authors whom you adore, and you want to read more of their books in the future, please post as many reviews for them as you can in all of the forms of social media that you use.

Doing so will help your favorite authors in numerous ways that you cannot even possibly imagine. Never forget that fact. Book reviews matter a great deal.

Please don't be a troll.

Amazon Kindle Review Link for *Naero's Mastery*:

smarturl.it/NaerosMastery

Barnes & Noble Review Link

<u>Good Reads Review Link</u>

Please post one or more reviews for Mason and each of his books, everywhere that you can.

Thank you once again.

Cheers,

Mason Elliott

Please enjoy this teaser for The Citation Series, Book 4:

THE GAMMA QUADRANT

Amazon Link: smarturl.it/TheGammaQuadrant

THE CITATION SERIES, BOOK 4
*NAERO'S
WAR:*

THE GAMMA QUADRANT

Amazon link: smarturl.it/TheGammaQuadrant

by Mason Elliott

1

The night before the mission into the Interdimensions, Naero had a dream where the stars fell.

If they did not actually fall out in space, then their light was being extinguished, one at a time and then in whole bunches. What did it all mean?

It was as if the darkness itself had come to life, like some predatory thing, and was penetrating and devouring them from within.

Then a very bright star appeared, placing itself before all the rest as if defending them. It came against the darkness, but in the end, it too was finally overwhelmed and it was consumed. All of the rest quickly perished, until there was only silence, darkness, and death.

The last thing Naero recalled before she started up out of her nightmare was the weeping and tormented cries of children, all suddenly silenced.

After all that, she found it very hard to get back to sleep.

For her, such dreams were almost always a warning of some kind.

Despite bad dreams, on the morrow, Naero and her strike force slipped into the Interdimensions for only the second time.

Shalaen and several more cautious, even frightened Yattai stayed close together.

The energized aether of the various folds and pocket dimensions they zipped through were all brightly colored, each in their own way, with varied, fractal patterns and bursts and splashes of Cosmic energies.

Yet with their third eyes, and all of their heightened senses from being in their energy forms, all of the joined realms they passed through pulsed and reeked with Chaos, destruction, slaughter, and subjugation of the resident sentient beings within.

Something was very wrong.

Thank goodness not all of the Interdimensions were linked.

Many might yet have survived the sweeping tide of violence that had struck hard in these places.

From the information that they had gathered thus far, these regions of Interdimensions adjacent to the Gamma Quadrant were being ravaged and torn apart by waves of deadly, invading forces.

Unknown until just very recently, the escaped hordes of vile, G'lothc spirits, shades, wraiths, or whatever it was appropriate to name the evil things, had waged a horrifying war. This was clearly a campaign of attrition, enslavement, and destruction that if left unchecked, could spread outward against the energy being races far beyond.

SpaceTime operated with much greater variation in the Interdimensions. Vast distances were traversed much easier by beings in energized, Cosmic forms. Much like the Astral Plane, in many cases such enormous distances could be leaped with the speed and power of thought.

It usually helped to have the conceptual reference of a starting and ending point.

This new enemy war, however, struck hard and without warning among most of the energy being races close to the Gamma quadrant.

Most of the known species of energy beings were being ruthlessly and systematically farmed and enslaved with impunity, to the point of extinction. Who knew how many other energy being races, yet to be encountered were also being attacked in this grave fashion as well?

Now that the majority of the great enemies were once more contained in their prison of near annihilation, a full assessment of the terrible losses suffered among those other, many and elusive interdimensional beings needed to be made, or at the very least attempted.

The Alliance could not simply hang back and cede the newly discovered and vital Interdimensions to the Great Adversary.

Naero's friend Shalaen and her valiant people, the energy beings known collectively as the Yattai, proved to be invaluable new comrades, and offered to assist the sentient, Prime Material races and allies in the known galaxy and beyond.

The Interdimensions were nearly as strange and beyond as one could find, save for the actual Beyond itself.

Naero and Shalaen remarked to each other about what amazing times of terror, wonder, and enlightenment they lived within.

How odd that the Yattai energy beings had once stood firm and stubborn as the staunchest isolationists.

All of that had changed and been swept away by their near destruction at the hands of the great enemy.

Near genocide quickly convinced them that they could no longer ignore the greater threats at hand, to them and others.

Not even near ascended energy beings were safe any longer. In fact, the enemy and its slaves hunted all such beings down now on a wide and regular basis, in order to use them as power sources for Darkforce generators…or for things far worse.

In the uncertainty of the Interdimensions, especially now, they stuck together and maintained their telepathic links to each other. That was the most efficient form of communication.

We have heard grim rumors from among the surviving remnants of the other energy being races, Shalaen informed Naero and her people. *It is said that Nahaxrathrax, the most ancient and most powerful of all the Dakkur Dark Emperors, has taken to devouring energy beings whole, by the hundreds as if they were grapes. He does this horrid thing, not only to increase his vaunted power, but because he enjoys devouring souls. We know of nothing that can stop this monster. And he has also willingly joined with legions of the fell spirits of the G'lothc housed within himself, and added their power, knowledge, and influence to his own malignant force of will.*

Even worse, another Yattai known as Jaeyar added. *He has sworn to somehow bring back The Six G'lothc Champions of the Darkforce!*

Shalaen gasped. *That would be a great evil and disadvantage to us.*

Jaeyar shook his head. *Indeed. It would mean the end.*

Now just wait a moment, Naero said. The Seven Kexxian Dreamers destroyed the Six in their final battle together, millions of years ago. How could such fiends be brought back into existence?

Indeed, Jaeyar told them. *Their mighty physical forms were obliterated, but their dark souls–their evil spirits–still lurk among the G'lothc within their Cosmic prison realm. They wait only for their release at the end times of the Cosmic Prophecies. Even the G'lothc themselves feared the Six– whom they mistakenly created after many millennia of evolution and genetic and Cosmic manipulation.*

For until they stood before the Seven Kexxian Dreamers, the Six knew no equals. They were unstoppable, unmatched in ruthless villainy and depraved atrocities splattered all across several galaxies. Sentients took their own lives in wholesale panic before letting themselves or their children fall under the hands of one or more of the Six. Time and time again, entire populations were tormented and finally wiped out, according to their whims. What monsters they were.

Shalaen wept into her hands, seeing those age old memories in the hearts and minds of her people for the first time. *What mad folly is this? Such horrors cannot be unleashed on the universe again.*

Naero sighed heavily. Alas, I have both seen and sensed the hideous power of the Dark Emperor of the Dakkur. Nahaxrathrax will dare much, and stop at nothing. The enemy has the same insane plan that it has always pursued: destroy all life in the universe. They seek to somehow create or summon the Great Destroyer to accomplish this. That is a great part of what drives the ancient, Cosmic Prophecies.

We and all free sentients must band together and stop him. Like all of our greater foes, the Dark Emperor must be hunted down and utterly destroyed, before he does the same thing to us.

They passed into another realm, and the terror and death that filled it for light years and parsecs at a time sickened them almost instantly, even in their energy forms.

Naero had not thought that possible.

What is this dread place? Naero asked her Yattai friends.

Jaeyar frowned. *This was one of the wide realms of the Laelor, a race of energy beings slightly younger than the Yattai.*

What has happened here? Shalaen cried. *I sense torture and death all around us on a scale that is nearly unimaginable. Countless energy beings perished within this dimension. The aether itself is thick with the after effects of suffering and violence beyond reckoning.*

Even Naero could sense in part what was overpowering the Yattai. Terrible things had taken place here, and the psyonic memory and screams of the fallen still hung in the aether and echoed in the minds of all who passed that way. Spirit beings left horrific scars behind them in their passing.

This entire realm was scarred, scorched, and stained with horror.

It was a place haunted now by destruction and terror.

She also sensed in every way, the passing of the Dark Emperor and his fell servants, as well as something else that she could not yet define.

Where they had passed, the enemy left death and oblivion in their wake.

Now there were only what seemed to be flakes and bits of glowing, energized cinder and ash scattered upon the aether winds. Cosmic bits, shades, and shadows. All that remained of many Laelor energy beings and whatever constructs they had made.

A vibrant, advanced society and culture now forever ravaged and lost.

It was almost as if everything had been disintegrated, but how?

Naero asked. Shalaen, can you tell how many Laelor perished in this realm?

Shalaen glanced at Jaeyar and a few other Yattai, confirming first with them. *By our reckoning, some four hundred and sixteen thousand, three hundred and eighty nine...and counting, Naero. From the energy readings and shadow images left behind, the Laelor made a brave stand, and did their best to hold back the enemy. But the Dark Emperor and his hosts were still far too powerful for them to withstand. Many were taken away as energy slaves. The rest were merely slaughtered, in some terrible way that even we cannot yet comprehend.*

Naero gathered data and readings from Om, the Kexxian AI defensive protocol merged with her mind. As always, his essence came along with her. Their findings together were even more frightening and ominous.

Shalaen, I don't want to alarm you and the other Yattai, but something else was at work here. Even the Dark Emperor and his servants could not have wiped out so many powerful Laelor on their own, so quickly.

Shalaen turned to her. *Then what could it have been?*

I'm sensing some kind of low level, Darkforce energy residue in the aether. That's part of what's making us so sick and uneasy. I fear that this was some new super weapon of the enemy, designed especially to work within the Interdimensions, on an immense scale. Something we haven't seen before. And perhaps more than one kind of it."

What was it? Jaeyar asked.

Naero shook her head. I don't know yet, but by my calculations, these new threats tore the Laelor defenders apart as if they were paper. And they just didn't simply consume the Laelor–these new threats converted them somehow, and made them part of the attacking swarm, or whatever it was that the Dark Emperor unleashed against them. I have never sensed such malignant powers before. They defy definition, but the results are clear for all of us to detect.

Ahh! Shalaen cried out, rubbing her arm suddenly.

Naero rushed over to her to see. What is it?

Shalaen continued to wince painfully. *It's nothing. One of those bits of Cosmic ash. It really burned when it-*

Naero asked, How can it possibly harm your energy form?

She was screaming in pain an instant later, by the time Naero studied the arm wound with a mix of biomancy and teknomancy.

The mote of Cosmic ash flared with modified Darkforce and in another second, had burned through and consumed most of Shalaen's spirit form arm from the elbow down.

Even as it consumed Shalaen's hand, Naero quickly ensnared the particles and froze them solid within a concentrated sphere of countering Cosmic energy. She tucked the sample away for further study and turned back to Shalaen.

Her good friend struggled with the pain.

This was rapidly becoming very frightening.

The clouds of energy infused ash floating nearby suddenly came to life and swept toward them, rushing at them all with menacing focus and intent.

Naero cried out psyonically in warning.

Withdraw! Don't let those particles touch you. It's part of an attack!

Naero instantly vaporized the concentrated particle clouds directly around them in a bright flare of Lifespark energy. Such positive energies passed through them all and did no harm. Yet it consumed the attacking, microscopic Darkforce particles, and purified any residual portion of Shalaen's virulent, spreading wound.

Naero's longtime friend clutched her own damaged arm, struggling to regenerate it. *You stopped it! Thank you. The pain was agonizing, N.*

I imagine it was. It appears to be some kind of malignant, Darkforce phage that converts other energy forms into more of itself. That is one major way that the Laelor were crushed so easily.

Jaeyar raised the alarm. *There is another entire nebula of those Cosmic phage particles sweeping straight at us, half a parsec in diameter.*

Even Naero could not take on a swarm that enormous.

Order everyone out of this sector, she shouted telepathically. Flee! If that nebula overtakes us, we'll be completely devoured and converted, just like the Laelor. This is another new super weapon of the G'lothc.

Together they sped out of that region, but it was touch and go for many moments.

The phage storm continued to gather speed and pursue them closely, reaching out with long tendrils of Darkforce particles stabbing forward at them with great, deliberate speed.

The phage operated as if it were a living, ravenous collective organism with intent, purpose, and force of will.

At the last instant, Naero and her allies escaped that diseased realm, sealed off the access to it, and then destroyed the portal in that region behind them.

Until they had a way to counter this new threat, no energy beings could ever enter such a place safely again. The phage swarm had to be cut off and kept from infecting and attacking any other Interdimensional realm or separate pocket dimensions.

A large scale cure or defense against the enemy Darkforce phage would need to be developed. If the enemy used this new weapon successfully once, they would clearly press their advantage again.

The Yattai sent the warning out to all of the other known energy being sentients in the Gamma Quadrant and beyond.

Naero brought out and studied the frozen sample of the phage she possessed, with the necessary Cosmic mix and Om's help. The phage was yet another relentless threat that their ruthless and resourceful enemies inflicted upon them.

She and her allies had also sensed other threats yet to be revealed.

Amazon Link: smarturl.it/TheGammaQuadrant

If you have not read Book One of *Mergeworld*, however unlikely that might be, please enjoy this teaser by Mason Elliott and Garan R. R. Faraday. Here is the Amazon purchase link:

smarturl.it/Mergeworld

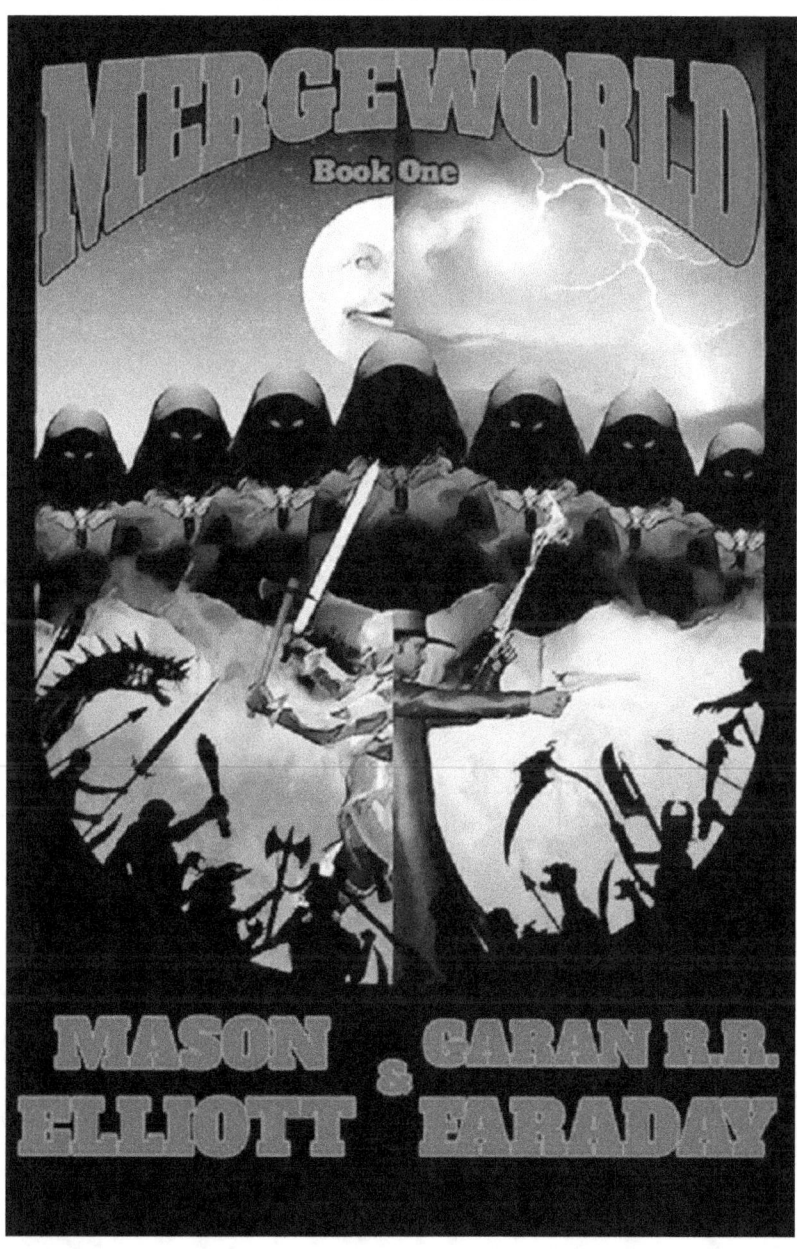

Mergeworld

Book One

by Mason Elliott and Garan R. R Faraday

1

David Pritchard woke up gasping from one nightmare and went straight into another. A terrible agony tore through him as if the universe twisted him inside out.

Then he snapped back again.

What in damnation had just happened? Something…was very wrong.

Startled, groggy, it only took an instant for his bleary mind to figure out.

Flames engulfed the front of his college apartment building. The stench of smoke, screams, and breaking glass outside only confirmed it.

He was dazed and blinked his scratchy eyes. The first thing he instinctively reached out for was the framed picture of his dead parents.

That was the last picture he had of them from a few years back, right after he started college in South Bend.

They hugged and smiled at each other in medieval garb at the Bristol Renaissance Fair up in Wisconsin. The picture froze both of them happily in time, retired in their forties. Unlike many parents that age, they weren't divorced and they still loved one another. One of their ren-fair pals took that picture for them on their digital camera.

The same camera retrieved from the car accident on the Illinois highways on their way back home from Bristol. A tractor-trailer jackknifed in the heavy rain and took them away.

The same weekend David begged off going with them.

He blew that picture up in Photoshop, printed out an 8 x 10, and bought a nice oak frame for it. He kept it with him wherever he went. He'd die before he'd part with it, fire or no.

All that history and pain flashed through David as he clutched their picture close to him in the dark. He didn't even have to see it, just cling to it in his hands. That picture always sat prominently behind his small alarm clock on his night stand with his smart phone and wallet while he slept. That was how he found it, even in the semi-dark. He also grabbed his phone and wallet.

His clock normally flashed bright green. Power outage, probably from the fire. And the back-up battery must have gone dead. Light switches? Nothing, of course, do to the fire.

The growing reek of smoke triggered his desire for self-preservation. Once he got out, he could call his friend Mason Tyler, who lived in a duplex over on Allen Street. His buddy Mace would help him.

Somewhat more awake now, David struggled not to panic. He staggered out of his room like a robot. His lanky, five-eleven frame stumbled down the hall toward his front door. He stubbed his little toe hard in the darkness. A second later he grunted and cursed the sudden blinding spread of pain, but kept moving.

Oh, hell. No way out the front.

Dangerous ribbons of smoke curled violently through the metal front door frame and snaked up across the ceiling like an upside down waterfall. The paint of the metal fire door already bubbled and blistered. David choked and swallowed hard.

If that door had been wood, his entire apartment might have already been completely engulfed. He might not have even come to. He saw no sense in touching the steaming door knob.

The apartment building stairs acted like a natural chimney, funneling the fire and heat straight up.

A window–climb out a window. He was only on the second floor.

His three richer roomies were already off on spring break for the next week, to the Bahamas or some such. Their parents could afford such junkets. David could not.

He suddenly realized two very important things. The fire hadn't spread to the back part of the apartment building yet.

Next, he was only wearing navy boxers and a gray T-shirt over his shaking frame.

Early April in South Bend, Indiana could be any weather from sun and sixties to a flippin' blizzard.

Clothes. Only seconds to throw some on. Even in the dim, flickering orange light spilling out of the thick curtains, he spotted his laundry basket on the couch.

The smoke in the living room grew thicker. He put his precious picture, smartphone, and wallet down for only a few moments.

Jeans. On. Socks. On. He snatched up his thick blue, gold, and green hoody from the back of the old couch where he usually left it, and pulled into its soft, warm, comfort. Stocking cap. Popped on his head. Wool scarf.

Around the neck. He sat down and jammed on his old gray Nike running shoes, feeling a pair of thin gloves and keys in his hoody pockets still, when he bent over.

Ready to ride, or, at least climb out the back window to escape burning to death.

He stuffed his folks' picture, wallet, and smartphone into his dark green Jansport backpack with his pad, gel pens, and a few books. He zipped it all up.

To the back window. He pulled the curtains aside and yanked the big panel open.

He jumped slightly, at some guy who already climbed down the back of the building from the third floor. Their eyes locked, only a window screen between them in the dim, pre-dawn light and the cold morning air.

The guy looked utterly terrified.

"Watch out!" he warned, trying to keep his voice low. "Those things are killing people. They're everywhere!"

"What things?" What was this guy freaking out about?

The guy jolted wide-eyed and then choked.

A bloody iron arrowhead jutted out the front of his throat. In the time it took them both to blink, another arrow punched through the front of his chest, out of his T-shirt. The poor guy's mouth gaped and worked. Then his eyes rolled up white. He fell backwards, head down.

David grabbed for him, but missed, his hands blocked by the barrier of the screen. He tore it away and stuck his head out the window.

He spotted strange movement down in the darkness.

Two dark, twisted, hunched-over figures loped in on bandy legs and clawed feet wrapped in fur and rags. They were smaller than humans, about four to five feet tall and very skinny and wiry.

Whatever they were, they were definitely not human.

One of them slit the dead guy's throat from ear to ear with a long, wicked-looking rusty knife.

Blood spurted bright black in the night.

The other creature sniffed the air and snarled up at David with a greenish-black, twisted, inhuman face. Long pointed ears stuck out of holes in its ragged hood. It had a big warty nose, and gleaming green eyes. It gave full draw to the same kind of short, black bow of jagged horn that the other one carried.

The creature took dead aim at David.

And fired.

Please enjoy this teaser for Mergeworld, Book 2:
Amazon Link: smarturl.it/Mergeworld2

Mergeworld

Book Two

Amazon Link: smarturl.it/Mergeworld2

by Mason Elliott and Garan R. R Faraday

"Several of the enemy mage prisoners have escaped," a runner came to warn them. The young trooper looked terrified.

Mason drew his Spillers. They would have to be enough. After the bath, he didn't have all of his other guns. And there wasn't time to go after them.

It also worried him that he still felt–off his game, somehow. Something was still very wrong with him, but he couldn't figure out what. Perhaps that was merely what sorrow and depression felt like.

Blondie shook the terrified runner. "Calm down. Tell me what you know. Which prisoners? How many of them?"

"S-six, six, I think. They tried to free the rest, but the guards on the scene shot two down. Then the enemy mages fled this way, and started killing everyone they could find with magic."

Troops screamed, and close by to the west, magic blasts went off, and the sounds of battle and further bursts of magical rapidly sped their way.

The runner continued to stammer, "The tall n-n-necromancer is leading them. Five others. I don't know their names. As soon as they broke out, the duty officer sent me after you two and the Thul woman."

Blondie let the runner go. "Try to find the Thul. Go. Keep spreading the alarm."

"Yes, s-sir!" The young runner looked only too happy to keep running.

"They're coming for us, aren't they, Blondie?" Mason asked, hefting his Spillers.

Blondie clenched both fists, and violet magefire flared up to his elbows. "Yep. Just like I said they would. How do you want to do this, Mace?"

"Hmmm…too many to hit them head on. Let's go at them from the flanks. I'll hit them on the left."

His blond friend nodded. "Then I'll take them on the right. The necromancer's going to be the toughest of the lot. Let's peel off the other five, if we can, and then take him on together."

"Sounds good, Blondie. Let's ride."

They skirted around to either side, trying to stick to cover and stay out of sight. Mason quickly lost sight of his friend.

It did briefly occur to him that this would be an excellent time for Blondie to turn on them all, and help the mages make good their escape. But at this point, Mason had no choice but to keep trusting his good friend.

Blondie said that his abilities were returning.

He could tell them anything he wanted. How would they know if it was the truth or not?

From the sounds of things, the militia troops were putting up a pretty good fight and delaying the enemy at least somewhat. Each precious second they could hold them back, more troops would pour in.

Yet even as Mason got into position to attack, the enemy mages continued to push through, causing death and destruction all around them, and leaving many casualties in their wake.

Startled troops could slow the enemy down, but they would be hard pressed to stop six enemy mages bent on a rampage of devastation.

They were lucky that it wasn't all thirteen of the mage captives on the loose.

At Blondie's urging, Major Bill had spread several of the captive mages out to other nearby, secret locations–beyond the limited range of their prisoners' telepathy.

Mason spotted the enemy. The necromancer strode out in front with another sorcerer. A pair of enemy wizards marched slightly behind them on either side, guarding their flanks and watching the rear.

Blondie stepped up and raked the enemy left and the middle with violet lightning that knocked four of the six off their feet, and stunned the two flankers.

The first flanker on the other side turned to attack Blondie. The second one raised his hands and his eyes got big when he saw the Pistolero step out and aim both of his pistols.

Click! Click!

Nothing. Mason's guns wouldn't fire. He cocked and pulled the triggers again.

Nothing.

By then the one mage was charging Blondie, exploding anything that was made of wood around him. He sent the shards and splinters and whirling debris at Blondie, while the necromancer and the other sorcerer still looked dazed and tried to regain their feet. And the mage facing Mason shot greenish-yellow flames out of his hands at all before him.

Mason dove out of the way, tucked and rolled out of sight, and then crouched and ran. The enemy wizard would be on him in seconds.

Finally he came to a building and ducked inside. He scrambled out of sight into an adjoining back storage room and ducked down. He tried his guns again. Still nothing. Why was this happening,? Now of all times?

Blondie needed him out there.

Maybe if he reloaded. Yeah, that would do it.

Slowing his breathing, doing his best to stay calm, he broke out his spare cylinders for his guns and swapped them out. He was fast at it, but every second counted.

He went back out into the fight. As he expected, the fighting quickly turned Blondie's way, and blasts of magic nearby showed where the foes were pursuing Blondie hard and blasting everything around him. Blondie fought back as best he could, but from what Mason could tell, his friend was outnumbered four to one.

He raced that way, not even trying to stay under cover this time. He had to catch up quickly, and take them from behind, if possible.

Mason sped around a building and almost slammed into the same enemy mage as before. This one seemed to be holding back and protecting the rear of the other three while they stalked Blondie.

Mason had intended to shoot them on sight, but he clobbered the mage from behind now that he was right on top of him. The mage grunted and dropped, unconscious.

Pistol-whipping worked better in this instance. Mason dragged the mage back out of sight and quickly gagged him, and bound his hands and ankles behind him.

At this distance, Mason would not have any trouble taking out the other three with one or two shots, once he spotted them again. And their spells gave them away when they fired. Hopefully, Blondie was staying ahead of them.

Mason rushed forward once more, spotted several troops closing in with bows and crossbows, and motioned for them to go around and close in from one side or the other.

Finally he spotted the necromancer and the one wizard, crouched down and making plans of some kind.

Mason took aim at them with both barrels.

Click. Click.

Crap, not again. What the hell was going on?

Even worse, the necromancer turned and locked eyes with him.

"There's the other one. Let's get him!" All of their hands glowed with magefire.

Mason turned and ran for it. Dark lightning and exploding ice covered the area he had just been in.

His foes were right after him. Archers tried to fire upon the mages, but they swept the troops away from their positions with blasts of power.

A stone or outcropping of brick caught the toe of Mason's boot. He hurtled down upon his face, and tried to roll back up to his feet.

The third enemy mage stepped out right in front of Mason.

Now, the three of them had him fairly trapped.

"Kill him!" the necromancer roared.

The wizard still hesitated an instant. Then he prepared a spell, his hands beginning to glow brighter and brighter.

They were only a dozen or so feet away. Mason hurled his useless pistols at the wizard.

One missed as the fellow dodged to one side.

The other smacked him squarely in the face and dazed and bloodied him.

Mason expected to be cut down from behind by the other two enemies any second.

He glanced back just as the two stood ready to unleash their spells.

Amazon Link to *Mergeworld, Book Two*: smarturl.it/Mergeworld2

Enjoy this teaser from **Mergeworld,** Book Three
Amazon Link. smarturl.it/Mergeworld3

Mergeworld

Book Three

by Mason Elliott and Garan R. R Faraday

Amazon Link. smarturl.it/Mergeworld3

DAVID

Ten days after the Elkhart battle, the Allies of Michiana declared a victory celebration to be held on August first, in honor of the defeat of the Dark Khabal, the Kolugtathuloth colossus, and the Dragon Cult in Elkhart. The names of the victorious dead would be read aloud and their families honored. General Dirk Blackwood always tried to assess needs in private, make sure that the families of the fallen were taken care of, and not just left to fend for themselves.

This was yet another reason why Dirk was universally loved and respected by those who followed him. They knew that even if they went down in battle, as long as Michiana survived, those they were fighting for were going to be all right. Many of the militia leaders noticed that as well, and applied similar practices to their forces with a similar degree of success.

David and Jerriel attended the party nearest to their home, one of many such celebrations held across town in smaller groups. Most of their friends were there. Dirk and Belinda spoke briefly about the construction progress on several forts and strong points, and the massive fortresses taking shape in the center of town. Tens of thousands of people volunteered to work on constructing these safe points. The progress of so much concentrated effort by so many became staggering. Everyone wanted a fortification nearby. If the monsters overran the town again, everyone wanted a safe place to go to.

Dirk, Jerriel, and many others spoke about the rapidly expanding war with the Dark Khabal. Not just in Michiana, but most likely across both worlds of the Merge and on every continent.

David's heart always sank at the prospect of such talk. It made his efforts and the sacrifices of his friends and neighbors all seem so small and insignificant. When would such a war possibly end? How would he and Jerriel ever have a normal life together? Would they all eventually be killed?

David and Jerriel had inspected several of the new fortified safe sites. He brought up his misgivings about an endless war at the celebration.

"I hope we never need to fall back on all of those hard points," Dirk said in response. "But it's also good to be prepared. They'll be there if we need them. I won't leave us without such defenses for our civilians ever again. This could be a long war for all we know. Modern home and business structures–Pre-Merge–are now worthless for defensive purposes, against the types of foes and threats we now face. We've barely managed to survive. Now we have to think long term, into the future about so many things."

"Many other important local buildings are being hardened and fortified as well," Belinda added. "People will have any number of safe places close by to retreat to, if the town is ever cut off and attacked in the same ways."

They looked over the posted maps nearby and noted all of the coordinated locations spaced throughout town. People were assigned to hard points in their area. If that was where the people would go for protection, no wonder they worked on them with such fervor.

There were numerous artist renderings as to what the finished designs would look like. A generic, medieval castle or eighteenth century fortress look prevailed.

On a lighter, more enjoyable note, there was still sufficient food and even drink at the parties. Some of the fresh food and drink was shipped in from Elkhart and the surrounding area, so as not to waste it. Freshly slaughtered livestock of any kind: beef, pork, goats, sheep, geese, ducks, chickens was now a luxury that would need to be rationed, even at festivals. Much of it was used to feed the army and the population in general so that nothing went to waste.

Thul-Kazar and Thulkara did not complain one bit about more food to eat. They dove into the feast like the champion eaters they were. Thulls loved barbecue, all of the sauces, all of the spices and flavors.

That included the side dishes and desserts and the beer and wine that flowed freely as well. As a special thanks to their pair of valiant barbarians, Dirk made sure they had plenty to chow on, even for them.

David sat contentedly in a circle of his friends while their troops danced and made merry all around just after sunset. They utilized a hodge-podge of lawn chairs, camp chairs, and folding chairs around a bonfire in the middle of their part of camp.

Every time he glanced at Jerriel, David's heart pounded. He could barely take his eyes off her. His love and desire for her seemed only to increase with each passing second. For the time being he smiled at his own happiness and good fortune.

"What do you miss the most about the world before the Merge?" Robert Billings suddenly asked aloud.

"My smart phone, my computer," Steven Hayward blurted out almost instantly. "Video games, Wi-Fi, and the Internet, all the friends I had online. I hope they're all okay, wherever they are."

Steven was barely sixteen. He'd seen death and war up close, and still he sounded busted up more about missing his online life that he had once enjoyed so much.

The heartbreak in his voice affected everyone.

"Running water. Especially hot water," Belinda Blackwood said.

"I'm really going to miss air conditioning, after this summer," Pete Steiner added.

Lots of agreement there.

"Cell phones for sure," Carrie Daniels noted. "Talking to my mom whenever I wanted. My sister in St. Louis. Now I don't know where they are or if they're even alive."

There were a great many worries about the fate of distant relatives.

"The Tharanorians call St. Louis Kavendo. They're all probably doing the same thing there that we're trying to do here," Dirk said. "Survive and look ahead."

No one mentioned the vile Dragon Cult model for towns. Everyone hoped that atrocity was just a fluke.

"Restaurants," Tim Carroll said. "Fast Food. Junk food. Sit down places. It's funny how much of the past we took for granted, like it would always be there. Then one day, it was all gone…forever."

Several people wept.

Everyone grew quiet for a time.

Other voices spoke up from out of the shadows. "Cars. Roads. Motorcycles. Trucks. The freedom and ability go anywhere you wanted, whenever you wanted."

"It's not the same," Zack Lancaster said. "It just isn't the same."

Again, lots of agreement on that note.

"You don't see planes or jets in the sky anymore," someone else spoke up. "Except for those few hot air balloons we've been seeing, we don't fly anymore as a people."

Carrie Daniels sighed heavily and wiped her eyes, half sobbing. "I miss all of the stores and going shopping. We used to have so much fun. I remember going to the mall with my parents and my brothers and sisters. Then my friends. You just can't do that any more. All you see now is the same, tired open street markets with the same old used junk to barter and trade that they had a few months ago. Ugh!"

"Well, I still miss electricity more than anything else," Owen Sanders said. "Think about how much stuff required electricity. That's the thing we miss the most. Electricity made all of this other stuff possible."

"Movies, Blue Ray, DVD's," Jacob Meyer noted. Lots of nods and agreement there. "I was a film buff. I saw two movies a week on the big screen, usually a matinee of a new release or a dollar show. Then there were video downloads, movie rentals. None of that works anymore."

"Not without electricity," Owen persisted.

"I'm so glad to be working with the development teams," Robert Billings said. "Big things are on the way, I assure you. Just going to work is something to do each day. But doesn't anyone miss their job before the Merge, or the people they worked with?"

Several boos there.

"Hey," someone shouted. "Screw that! I hated going to work."

"Yeah, my boss was a dick!"

Lots of people laughed and chimed in.

"My friend, you gotta be kidding me," David said to Rob. "There were a lot of crummy jobs."

His friend persisted. "There still are. That doesn't change that much. Not to mention all of this survival crap. But don't we all have friends and acquaintances that we just don't see anymore? They might still be safe, or on the other side, we hope."

"You can try to find out," Jerriel said. "We're trying to reconnect people and find out which side everyone is on. And who survived, and who did not."

"Get this," Mason cut in, with a wink at Tori. "The weird thing is, some people went and started completely new lives and relationships on the other side already–within a matter of months–and now they don't want to be found by some of those people they knew before. It can be a caution."

People continued to be strange and foolish. Yet everyone had friends and family on the other side, as well as out of town. Those points kept coming up again and again.

"I miss television, TV news, World, National, local," Nick Denardi said. "I was a news junkie. Now we're cut off from everyone else. We don't know what's happening in other places, or on the other side."

"Some day we will," Belinda said, "we'll branch out and make contact with all of the other civilized areas, here in the New World, and the Old World across the pond–on both sides."

"That could take years," Ellis Newcombe said. "Maybe decades and maybe never. We could all be dead a month from now."

Someone else chipped in. "There are rumors going around that there are cities where the Urth people are at war with the people from Tharanor."

"That was bound to happen," another added. "People don't always see eye to eye, and one group often tries to dominate another. The side that has more magic than Urth people do might be tempted to remain dominant. That's the only way they know."

"We've heard those rumors as well," Belinda said. "Along with all kinds of crazy reports, everything from ghosts in many places, to bodies of giant crabs washed up on the east coast beaches."

Jerriel pointed a finger at David, her eyes wide. "I warned you about Shochi. I warned you. They do exist, and they are a major threat."

Everyone began to babble at once, going out of control until Rabbi Bergman banged on the big gong set up to call people to dinner.

"Let's try not to be so pessimistic," Bergman noted. "Or let the worst of our imaginations run away with us. We don't know the truth of any of these wild fears yet. We might be able to re-connect with other survivors more quickly if we can locate and train more travelers and other mages in general."

"We need more Champions of all kinds. Magic is the real new power. For better or worse," Dirk Blackwood said. "This is the world we live in now. The world we must fight and struggle to survive in–for the sake of each other and humanity from this point on. And we face enough threats as it is. This is our new reality. This is what matters…not what was. Not what we have lost, what is gone, either for now or forever. What we face now and what we cling to now is what matters most."

No one said anything more for a long while.

An hour later, David and Jerriel and some of their friends visited the camp of the Marrandorians.

Prince Valandin and Prince Alendel looked as if they were feeling no pain, celebrating and drinking heartily with their wizards, knights, and other troops.

They spotted Jerriel right off.

"Cousin! Noble allies. Welcome. Welcome! Join us. Please sit!

"Toast. A toast!

"A toast!" many voices took up the cry.

Thul-Kazar did not hesitate to have his massive drinking horn filled.

David took a sip from his goblet after it was topped off with golden, sweet-smelling liquid.

Mead. They drank mead, tart and delicious, tasting of honeyed blackberries. He didn't want to drink much more, his head already a bit tipsy. Getting really drunk always made him sleepy or sick and then sleepy.

David lifted his glass to the princes.

"Your Highnesses. Much honor and thanks to you and your people, especially your wizards." He saluted Pharrio, Maelen, and Urnessan again. "Without your aid, the battle in Elkhart would have been lost."

"Here here!" Thul-Kazar said. "I will drink to that. But then," he chuckled. "I will drink to most anything."

They joined him in laughter.

"The day would have been lost," Prince Valandin noted, "had you and your friends not taken out those transport gates. Not to mention your crucial alliance with the green dragon."

"Shavalkathar goes where and does what he will," David said. "I can take no credit for that. He is a force of nature. But I admit, it was a great help that he showed up and took out the red dragon for us when he did so."

"Indeed," Pharrio said, "to Shavalkathar!"

"To our ally, the green dragon!" others shouted.

Only the Thulls did not drink; they had no great love for dragons.

David wondered. 'Ally' was perhaps a bit of a stretch just yet.

Valandin took Jerriel's hand. "Dear cousin, it is so good to see you alive and well. And your radiant smile." He glanced at David and smirked.

"And to see you happy, when you aren't battling demons, monsters, dragons, or otherwise fighting for your life."

"That's the truth," David said. It was good to have a break from being at war.

"I'm so glad you and dear Alendel and your people came to our aid," Jerriel said graciously. "You couldn't have arrived at a better time." She hugged them both.

Valandin looked at David for the first time and appraised him. "You have done well, Captain," he said. "Did you know that she is a princess of my royal line? Her standing is distant, yes, but a princess all the same."

"She is the queen of my stars," David said. "Jerriel is simply amazing. I could not think more highly of her than I do, or love her more. She is my world."

Jerriel looked at him and sobbed, reaching out to touch his face.

"I know your worth, my friend, on the field and as a man, from the short time that I have been with you. You have my blessing. As Prince of the Realm, I will not oppose your union with my cousin in any way."

David considered that rather odd. He had never even thought to ask for this fellow's blessing on anything, let alone his love for Jerriel. Perhaps he would have done so if Jerriel's father, had he been alive and present, but not some distant prince or cousin, ally or no.

Valandin persisted, but in his defense, he was quite tipsy. "I do so Even though you are an Urther and a commoner. And even though she was once my own betrothed, from when we were children."

David felt more than slightly uncomfortable and did not quite know what to say. "Thank you, Your Highness."

"She has told you about us, am I correct?"

"Yes?" was all that David would offer in return. This was getting rude.

Valandin breathed a sigh of relief. "Good. I did not want there to be any misunderstandings that could mar our friendship. My cousin's heart has been free for years. She has no obligation to me. I myself am betrothed, if my beloved can still make the voyage across the sea to join us here in the New World. The Merge has upset so many of our private plans."

"Congratulations," Jerriel said. "I am so happy for you, Valan."

"What does the future hold for the two of you?" Prince Alendel finally asked. "Surely two so in love must have a wedding planned?"

David took Jerriel's hand as she tried to motion him to silence. "There has scarcely been any time. If not for all of the troubles, I would marry her this instant. But we've been so busy trying to help our people survive that we've barely spoken together about our personal future."

"It has been incredibly hectic," Jerriel agreed. "The day will come when it will, when the time is right. I too would wed David this instant. So sure is my heart of him, and his place in my life."

"Well, I wouldn't put it off too much longer if I were you," Valandin warned. He took another drink which he probably shouldn't have. His speech already slurred slightly. "After all, you don't want your children to end up landless bastards."

Jerriel looked down slightly.

David tried very hard not to be angry.

He wasn't used to being around any kind of royalty, and Tharanorian royalty not at all. Perhaps princes in their world felt free to say anything they wanted, however unkind. Not surprising, since they had a more medieval mentality. Valandin was a leader from a completely different culture, age, and mindset.

David struggled to understand that. He tried very hard not to take offense.

He rose from where he sat and went to fill his goblet again with sweet scarlet wine this time.

Rowdy troops hooted and hollered nearby, carousing and rough housing.

A football sailed in out of nowhere and smashed David in the side of the head just as he was walking back.

As buzzed as he was, David toppled forward, crashed right into Valandin, and dumped the cold red wine all over the prince. The collision tumbled them both the ground.

Everyone gasped.

"Get off me, you drunken, bloody oaf!" Valandin roared out loud, assuming he was being attacked. He lashed out on the ground and backhanded David in the face.

David deflected further blows and tried to roll away.

"How dare you attack me!" Valandin raged, obviously drunk himself. "After I befriended you and paid you honor!"

Prince Alendel pulled his brother back.

Thul-Kazar wrapped a huge, hairy arm around David and pulled him away.

Jerriel stepped in between them all.

"Cousin, please. There must be some mistake. I'm certain that David was not trying to attack or offend you. It must have been an accident. Both of you have been celebrating far too much."

David rubbed his head and his eye. His head swirled even woozier than before.

"It's true," he said. "I meant no disrespect. I was just terribly clumsy. That was all. I admit, I've had too much."

The crown prince would not relent. "So, you were drunk and dumped your wine on me and knocked me down merely out of clumsiness? What kind of fool do you take me for?"

Jerriel looked at him confused. "David, what happened?"

"It was an accident, I swear Your Highness."

"Yes, of course it was," the prince sneered.

"It was. I went over to fill my cup, and on the way back a football came in out of the darkness and whacked me in the head! I lost my balance." He pointed at the ground in the dark, but the ball had either bounced away somewhere or been retrieved.

Valandin looked around. "And did anyone see this 'football' or whatever it was strike him?"

No one else had noticed, apparently. But they had all been talking and their heads were down. They weren't watching him.

"I was dizzy already and lost my balance when it struck me. I'm sorry!" David went down on one knee. "I truly, truly apologize my lord. The fault was entirely mine, but it was not in any way intentional."

"I must insist upon satisfaction," Valandin said proudly, wine still dripping down him and staining his clothes. "On the morrow, two hours past mid-morning."

Jerriel paled. "Cousin. Please. Do not do this."

"Not a word from you, Jerriel. You chose your man, not I. He will face me this next day and know my displeasure, or be branded a coward." He glared at David. "Your choice of weapons, bumpkin! Good night and rest well." He pulled away from Alendel violently and stalked off, his stunned guards clustered about him.

Prince Alendel looked embarrassed and turned back to them. "I guess the evening's merriment is now ended. I will speak to him. We've all had too much to drink. Things will be better in the morning."

"I hope so," Jerriel said. "David, we'd better go."

David felt at a loss for words. It was all so stupid, and yet it was still his fault. "Jerriel, I'm sorry. I didn't mean for any of this to…"

"Please. Let's just leave," she said wearily.

No one else knew what to say.

"I don't want to fight him," David said. "We're allies. We should be friends."

"If he challenges you, you must accept," Thul-Kazar said. "You are no coward. This is now a matter of honor."

"Screw that," David said. "We're allies. We can't be quarreling with each other."

"Oh, please," Jerriel said, sounding more than slightly irritated. "You were all drunk from the celebration. That makes all of you fools in this affair."

"I am not drunk, milady" Thul-Kazar said. He belched like a foghorn.

"Not yet," Alejandro said, "and not for want of trying."

"The night is still young," the big Thull said.

Jerriel shook her head. "This is ridiculous. Hopefully it will all blow over tomorrow after everyone sobers up. Alendel will talk some sense into him. Valandin usually listens to him."

"We can only hope," David said. "Any kind of duel would be a disaster. We need to inform Dirk and the Council about this incident."

"We'll send word. If a duel does take place, you cannot harm him," Jerriel said. "I mean, if he insists on fighting you."

"I'm supposed to just to stand around and let him beat on me?"

"He's the Crown Prince of Kellendra. He's family. He's an ally. You cannot harm him in any way."

"Jerriel, I have no intention of doing so. I hate this sort of thing. This is all a terrible misunderstanding!"

The next day promised to be interesting.

Prince Alendel came to them the next morning, his face somber and grim.

"You've got to be kidding me," David said, rising to his feet.

Jerriel groaned, "Oh, no."

"I'm afraid so, my friends. My brother is still angry about the incident. A bad hangover has done nothing to improve his mood, nor his judgement, I'm afraid. We must meet on the field of honor within the hour. I must take back your choice of weapons, Captain."

"Can we at least speak to him, Your Highness?" David said.

"I'm afraid that time is past. Please, your choice of weapons, my lord?"

"Boffers then," David said.

Alendel looked at a loss. "What? What in the devil are…?"

David showed him one. "Boffers. A practice weapon. Flexible plastic, covered with foam, harmless for sparring."

The prince reddened visibly. "Seriously, my lord?"

Thul-Kazar looked up from his hangover long enough to curse in disgust.

Prince Alendel frowned. "I'm afraid that will not do, Captain. They must be real weapons. No practice weapons. This is a real duel."

In that case, David came up with the best possible option. "Fists then."

Alendel raised an eyebrow.

"What, fists aren't allowed?" David asked. In most duels fisticuffs were a valid option.

"No, that is quite acceptable. Just…unusual for knights."

"I am not a knight. I'll face him open handed and settle the matter that way."

"Very well, fists it is, then. I will inform my brother. We shall await you at the appointed place."

He bowed and left them.

Thul-Kazar cheered. "Excellent. How good are you at brawling, my boy?"

David shook his head. "So-so. I'm better with swords and weapons. I had a little boxing training, and a little wrestling in High School. Three years of Karate as a kid. I earned a brown belt."

"Good, good," Thul-Kazar said. "I don't know what you are talking about, but I hope it all helps you in the brawl. I can't wait to watch."

"Thanks," David said. "I'd better stretch out. Jerriel, how good is Valandin hand-to-hand?"

"I think Alendel's a little better at it, thank goodness," she said. "I don't know. They've both had combat training since they were boys, but I never watched much of it."

"They're warriors," Jason Inada said. "You can tell just by looking at the two of them. And we've seen them on the battlefield. We know they can handle themselves. I would expect the worst."

"Excellent. A fine contest then," Thul-Kazar said.

Mason and Tori rushed in together. "We just heard," Mason said. "Is there any way to call it off?"

David shook his head. "I wish this all hadn't happened. I don't want to do this. I fight beside my friends, not against them."

"I'll be your second. What weapons did you choose?" Mason asked.

"Fists."

Tori sighed. "At least it wasn't swords, or pistols," she said, tapping one of her holsters.

"I could fight him for you," Thul-Kazar suddenly offered. "I enjoy a good brawl."

Jerriel's eyes widened in complete fear.

"No!" almost everyone said, startling even the Thull.

"No. Thank you," David told the Barbarian giant. "I appreciate your brave offer, my friend. But this is my dilemma. I will face him on my own terms."

Amazon Link. smarturl.it/Mergeworld3

If you have not read the original Naero Books by Mason Elliott, please enjoy the following teaser from the first Spacer Clans Adventure, Book 1: smarturl.it/NaerosRun

NAERO'S
RUN

NAERO'S RUN

Amazon Link to Naero's Run: smarturl.it/NaerosRun

by Mason Elliott

"We've got more than enough to consider here," Aunt Sleak said. "We'll post our final decisions on the Spacer ClanNet. All crew, take a breather. We're out of jump in less than two standard hours. Everyone on duty needs to be at their ready stations. Dismissed."

Naero went back to her quarters to do some laundry and a little more reading before they emerged. With regular effort, her quarters were less of a disaster than usual. She'd kept her bunk and her floor more or less cleared off, and slept in her bunk regularly now, instead of on the floor or in zero-G or a float bag.

And definitely not in her flex chair, as she had for years because she either couldn't get her bunk panel out or it was too piled up with crap.

Being small had its advantages. She could curl up like a cat and get comfortable almost anywhere for a snooze.

But keeping her quarters in better shape was a promise she made and kept–to herself–and her parents.

They emerged from jump with the customary shuddering of the ship. The fleet spread out into is standard formation, emerging back into real Space-Time.

Naero punched up their positions on one of her screens, even though she didn't have bridge duty for several hours.

The Shinai flanked *The Dromon* on the port side, with *The Slipper* posted starboard. Their two smaller ships, *The Nevada* and *The Ardala*, brought up the rear this time.

A red hot scarlet particle beam, 60mm in diameter, lanced through Naero's walls like they were paper, disrupting her wallscreens.

A direct hit from a big gun.

At the very least, from a heavy destroyer.

Warning lights flashed immediately.

The rupture in the hull led to an immediate explosive decompression.

Naero held on tight to her bunk and went flat on the floor as the hull sealed itself.

All ships were vulnerable coming out of jump. They couldn't activate their shields until right after they emerged.

Someone had been waiting for them.

The Dromon continued getting rocked by multiple hits from what felt like several spinal guns and secondary batteries.

But the big planetoid could take it and give back plenty, her quad main guns humming and whining to life, coming online.

Naero hit her wristcom. All her screens down.

"Bridge. Status?"

"We stepped into it. They were waiting for us. We're under heavy fire. Multiple bogeys."

The general alert sounded.

"Battle Stations. Battle Stations."

Aunt Sleak cut over the com. "All hands. All hands, to your stations. Prepare for battle. All ships, all batteries, return fire. Launch all fighters."

Naero suited up and raced to the drop bay of her fighter. She met Jan along the way.

More intense fire. *Dromon* reeled and fired back.

She and Jan almost got rocked off their feet again.

A security team intercepted them at the launching bays.

Their fighters had already dropped with their backup pilots.

"The fleet captain wants you two at your secondary defense stations, not out in the mix."

Jan started to protest.

"Orders are orders. Get to your stations."

They ran to their remote gunnery stations, small secured cubicles with a chair and a console, operating triple pulse turrets on the hardpoints above them.

Naero brought up her autotargeting displays, weapons already powered up and humming.

The secondary battery gunnery stations operated independently and were well-protected. They were also fully automated, but they still functioned more effectively with a human interface.

Coordinated targeting profiles came online as she watched.

Jan operated a torp turret nearby.

Directly ahead of the fleet. Twelve elite Matayan destroyers, each with a dozen escort fighters.

Half of their number pursued and attacked a convoy of two dozen independent mining freighters.

Aunt Sleak's fleet scrambled, launched, and deployed a total of threescore fighters in a standard Alpha-Charlie-1 defensive screen.

They were outnumbered two to one.

"All batteries make ready. Incoming torps," the bridge com sounded.

Countermeasures took out half of the blips heading their way.

Spacer fighters and the forward defensive batteries blasted the rest.

"That attack's a diversion," Naero muttered.

Shinai's fire control and com computers fixed on and monitored all channels–including those between the hapless freighters and the corsairs.

"Mayday, mayday, we are under intense corsair attack. All ships. Assistance, assistance. Heavy damage and casualties."

"What do you want?" another panic-stricken voice cried out. "We'll surrender. You can board us. We have no goods and few supplies. Please, stop firing. Our ships are full of workers–full of people. You're killing civilians. We're on fire!"

Scanners displayed an awful, one-sided battle among the transports.

Most of the old bulk freighters didn't even have weapons.

Each of the heavily armed Matayan destroyers was more than a match for them or most of the ships in Aunt Sleak's fleet.

Except for the 6m quad spinal guns of *The Dromon*.

One crippled freighter broke apart and exploded under concentrated fire from three destroyers. It didn't have any shields, and only minimal armor. Its two turrets either didn't work or had been taken out already.

Static and Matayan battle language rang out in triumph.

Dromon's four primary guns cut loose, lighting up the entire sector. Its blue-white blasts ripped into the lead corsair flagship and its wingships, disrupting their shields.

The starboard wingship took two hits and listed to one side. Its aft section exploded.

"This is Captain Sleak Maeris of Clan Maeris. Enemy vessels, be advised: Cease hostilities and vacate this system or be destroyed."

Matayan curses and laughter her only reply.

"Clan Maeris," one of the freighter captains cut in. "This is Captain Philsen of *The Botaru*. Help us! Our situation is desperate. The corsairs are trying to destroy us. We don't know why."

"Acknowledged. We're coming in. Disperse if you can. You're still too bunched up. Scatter and concentrate on defensive actions. Jump if you're able. We'll try to draw them off. We're boosting your distress call."

Three more corsairs turned on the fleet, with all twelve dozen fighters full front on intercept.

The other trio of Matayan attackers kept after the freighters.

Naero heard the pleading and the screams on the open channel, just before another freighter got blasted to oblivion.

Naero realized she had tears on her face.

Was that how her parents went? Blasted to death by Matayan guns?

The rage she felt nearly overwhelmed her reason.

She checked her systems, gripped the controls of her gunnery station, and forced her emotions to go cold.

Against superior numbers, Naero and her Clan Fleet closed for battle.

Amazon Link to Naero's Run: smarturl.it/NaerosRun

Please enjoy the following teaser from **a** spinoff series that we call**:** The Citation Series, Book 1, smarturl.it/TheAnnexationWar Naero's War:

The Annexation War

NAERO'S WAR:
THE ANNEXATION WAR

Annexation War Amazon Link: smarturl.it/TheAnnexationWar

by Mason Elliott

Naero's flagship, *The Hippolyta,* was one of the latest, Dromon Class dreadnaughts. These warships were fashioned out of dense, iron-nickel planetoids, not less than half a kilometer in diameter. Incredibly tough and rugged on their own.

It took the most powerful mining plasma-borers–working in precise conjunction with construction fixers and an army of teks–months to hollow out armored crew quarters, lift and transport tubes, launching and loading bays. Next came space for power cores, sublight engines, jump drives, backups, gravitics, life support, sensor arrays, communications, navigation, weapons, main bridge and backup bridge.

Set in the exact heart of *The Hippolyta* were its signature big guns. A quad of the largest production guns ever constructed on any ship of war: Four, *16 meter*, rapid-fire, particle beam cannons.

Cannons any larger than that exploded, melted, or otherwise were not feasible within the limits of current tek and materials. Thirty-six secondary batteries, assorted specialized weapons and gun emplacements, and forty-five advanced fighters.

Seven hundred and forty able crew, including a full Rifle Company of two hundred and forty Spacer Marines, and all of their equipment, vehicles, and gear for ship's security and rapid response deployment. Strike Fleet Six's Marines came from the 3rd Spacer Marine Division–known as *The Death Eyes*–because of their superb snipers and their overall, excellent marksmanship ratings. Marines made up a third of the warship's complement.

Their motto: *If We Can See It...We Can Kill It!*

The main bridge was a massive armored dome constructed on top of the dreadnaught's big metal, rough-hewn orb, protected by heavy blast doors, and the latest, most advanced shielding in the fleet. Within, the circular bridge was laid out in four levels under the huge dome, a dome sixty meters high.

Each bridge tier was separated by the height of a few steps from one to the next. The inner three levels could rotate in any direction, independent of the others.

The fleet captain's command nanochair and station occupied the highest tier. Each bridge station had its own secondary shielding, in case enemy fire penetrated the shields, the blast screens, and the hull.

In combat, bridges were routinely targeted, for obvious reasons.

From that primary vantage point, the strike fleet captain could direct battles in three hundred and sixty degrees, through an advanced, battleholo display surrounding her, full zoom data-feeds, constantly updated by battle AIs. Naero could manipulate the displays by nanosensors programmed into the fingertips of her nanosuit gloves.

The battle display system also recognized her voice pattern, and would respond to voice commands, or commands punched in manually through pads on her command chair, or via other backups.

The next bridge level down from hers held the secondary bridge stations: Helm, Weapons, Communications, Navigation, and Scanning, spaced out equally along their ring.

The third ring held all of the twelve tertiary bridge stations, that monitored, controlled, and coordinated all of the ship's other important functions:

Engineering
Gravitics
Life Support
Power Supply
Security
Shields
Medical
Jump and Sub-light Drives
Damage Control
Alliance Fleet and Intel Communications
Main Computer
Launching Bays

The fourth ring went to the two powerlifts, leading from the bridge to the other movers, decks, and levels of the ship. All lift and access points throughout the ship were constantly guarded by two battle-ready Marines, stationed on either side.

If a warship was boarded by enemy assault craft during a battle, invaders could be cut off and eliminated between decks, before they could reach a vital area.

Today, Strike Fleet Six had a mission–a simple one.

Captain Naero Maeris and her fifty warships proceeded to probe the next system on the outer, port arcwall of the Alliance advance at Beleron-4.

A routine run. Current intel assured them to expect little or no Triaxian presence or resistance.

By any stretch of the imagination, Beleron-4 was a nothing world, in the middle of nowhere, with zero, nacha–absolutely no strategic or tactical value whatsoever.

Checking it off the list on the pacified worlds of the Alliance system-hopping schedule was more-or-less just a formality.

But it still had to be done. And Naero and her lot drew the duty at random.

So why did Naero's sense of warning go bonkers?

After they jumped in, simple three-stack, Delta-India-3 formation, the reasons for alarm grew perfectly clear.

They came in right on top of twenty Triaxian fleets of the enemy's latest warships.

And a gigantic new flagship–as huge as *The Hippolyta*–the advanced design of which did not even register as existing.

It had never been seen before.

Naero shot to her feet, kicked her command nanochair back out the way and sent it down into the nanofloor of her top-tier bridge control station.

She instantly called her battle display holos up in spinning, horizontal glowing ribbons and rings all around her.

Data relays went wild. Her fingers flashed among the highlighted screen arcs, taking control of them and their parameters.

Multiple warnings sounded, and with excellent reason.

Nothing about this was good in any way.

Haisha! Twenty enemy fleets could chop them into confetti–well before any other Alliance forces could even jump in to help.

No strategy, no formation could possibly save them against superior numbers such as these.

"All ships, full withdraw. Emergency retreat on this vector, in Charlie-Romeo-7, cone-ring formation. Shields and all weapons full front and hot. Maximize all targeting profiles on the lead attacking enemy elements–they'll be on us in seconds. Whatever happens–we fight until our carriers and some of our ships can break free and jump out behind us. Get the carriers out first!"

For a split second, everyone braced for the sheets of flame that would quickly overtake and overwhelm them.

Annexation War Amazon Link: smarturl.it/TheAnnexationWar

NAERO'S GAMBIT

smarturl.it/NaerosGambit

NAERO'S GAMBIT

Naero's Gambit Amazon Link: smarturl.it/NaerosGambit

by Mason Elliott

Klyne set the huge Mystic testing room on board *The Kathmandu* to muted gray. Smartwalls, floor, and ceiling, Naero saw no equipment, no padding.

The lights were set low.

From experience, Naero knew that in a training room, just about anything could pop up out of anywhere.

She wore nothing but her black Nytex flight togs.

To her surprise, Klyne and his two adepts wore dark gray Nytex togs also, but with hoods and masks pulled up over their heads. Only their keen eyes showed.

All three of the Mystics appeared to be in top physical condition, including Klyne.

One of the adepts was female, with huge green eyes and light freckles across her nose. The other was male, with the black slanted eyes of the Lii-Kim Clans.

If black was the color of Spacers, the Mystics traditionally wore gray.

They all sat with their legs crossed in lotus fashion, focusing their abilities through meditation, and mental discipline. They formed a triangle, each side about three meters apart, with them at the points.

"Follow our instructions," Klyne said. "Take your place among us. Sit in the center; sit as we do. Face the instructor."

A circle of white light appeared at the center of the triangle. Naero walked over and sat down in it, facing Klyne. Her skin barely began to tingle.

A wider ring of similar light appeared, including the instructor and his two adepts.

Every hair on Naero's body went stiff with electric force.

"You have chosen to come before the circle of Spacer Mystics to be tested for Mystic training. Speak your name."

"Naero Amashin Maeris."

"You agree to be tested?"

"I do."

"I am Klyne, the instructor. My assistants are Adept Iselle, and Adept Makita. We shall refer to you as Adept Candidate Naero. Follow our instructions. Respond only if asked to respond. If you require any medical attention, it will be administered at the end of the testing. Until then, you are expected to endure and continue to do your best. If you understand, say yes."

"Yes."

"The training will begin. Defend yourself."

Without warning, Makita's attack smashed into her.

She blocked one or two out every four or five blows.

A snapwheel kick sent her flying twenty meters, nearly winding her.

The only things that saved her at all, once again, were the experience and knowledge she gained from her training sessions with Baeven.

Makita proved stronger and faster than her, but he still paled in comparison to the outcast's terrifying prowess.

Makita charged her.

Naero met him part way.

She took several punishing strikes, but flipped him hard to the ground.

He swept her legs.

They tangled on the ground, wrestling, slipping out of holds, twisting like snakes. They pummeled each other all the while.

They broke, crouched low, and launched themselves at each other again, like Thellurian fighting blue cranes.

Naero landed a whipkick on the side of Makita's head.

He clipped her under the chin, grabbed her leg and ankle and swung her hard into the floor, stunning her.

She struggled to get up.

For a few dizzy moments, she couldn't.

She rose up and staggered back into her fighting stance.

She half-smiled.

"Come on."

Makita bowed his head, just slightly, and drew back.

"Defend yourself, "Klyne said again.

Naero whirled to face Iselle.

Too late.

An invisible force slammed into her arms and torso, flinging her back.

She rolled with the strike and came back up into her stance.

Iselle fought her from a distance, punching and striking with her hands in rapid combinations.

Naero struggled to advance, to close the distance between them, while heavy, unseen blows rained down on her from every direction, knocking her one way, and then the other.

"Telekinetic combat," Klyne called out. "Try to sense and block the blows. You cannot see them. Reach out with your battle senses, with your mind. Feel them coming. Counter and deflect them. True masters can fight thus, without even moving, simply by concentrating."

At least Iselle still had to physically move in order to project her attacks. That was some help.

Closer. Get closer.

Iselle thrust both hands forward violently.

A wall of force drove Naero slowly back. She pushed against it, slowing it even more.

"Resist. Focus on the energy before you," Klyne told her, "before it smashes you into the far wall. Fight back. Defeat it."

She rolled to one side and then the other. The barrier felt solid.

Naero leaped up four meters, felt the top, and flipped herself over it.

Iselle withdrew a step, cupping both hands loosely on the sides of her face.

Spinning orbs of pure telekinetic force shot out, rapid-fire.

Naero barely perceived them where they warped through the air; they made explosive popping sounds.

She tried to dodge them. One whirred past her head like an invisible ball at high speed.

The next clipped her left shoulder, spinning her aside.

Another knocked one leg out from under her.

She kept her feet and ducked, weaving to either side in turns.

Iselle directed her attack at Naero's feet.

Naero lost her footing, slipping and sliding on what felt like a bunch of invisible ball bearings cast beneath her.

She tried to roll back to her feet, but panes of force battered her from all sides, keeping her off balance.

It felt like being a rubber ball, bouncing around in a box that someone shook.

The sides of the box rapidly closed in.

They tightened all around her, threatening to crush her.

She couldn't breathe.

Iselle released her without warning.

Naero sprawled, gasping, face down on the floor.

"I'm somewhat surprised," Klyne noted. "Preliminary tests demonstrate no psyonic aptitude or innate talent to my trained senses whatsoever. That in itself is very rare. After your battle with the former Danner entity, we simply assumed that you would exhibit some kind of psyonic ability."

"I burned myself out dealing with the entity. I burned both of us out. I'm a nud once more." She admitted it openly. "None of my former abilities have returned."

So she wasn't psyonic anymore. Not even a teknomancer. Disappointing, but not the end of the universe.

"Yet I sense something incredibly strange within you," Klyne said. "What could it be?"

Was it Om? He was still inside her somewhere. He had not emerged again either.

"Take your place at the center of us once more. Face me again."

Naero did so, resisting an urge to massage several bruises.

Klyne positioned himself directly in front of her, sitting lotus fashion just like her and the others.

"I'm going to attempt to merge directly with your mind telepathically, one of my gifts. I'm also an Auralcognitor. Once I link with your mind, I can sense any type of psyonic energy field you might have, active, passive, or latent. I might even be able to trigger or bring them out to the surface. There might be some discomfort. Shall we proceed?"

"Sure."

"Do as I do. I will show you how to place your hands to effect the mind merge."

Klyne cupped his left hand firmly behind the base of her skull.

Naero followed his lead.

He placed the fingers of his right hand on precise spots on her face.

Thumb on her forehead, directly between her eyes.

Index finger on her left temple.

The next two fingers curled slightly in front of her left ear. His smallest finger hooked at the point of her ear and jaw.

As soon as Naero placed her right hand the same way, she gasped slightly.

Thin hairs of what felt like burning hot energy threaded their way slowly through the layers of her awareness.

She could feel Klyne connecting with her thoughts, joining their two minds.

The dull ache continued to grow.

"You should be feeling the initial discomfort. Hold still. Keep focusing. Almost there. Almost…"

A spike of pure agony exploded within her skull.

Naero screamed, transfixed as if by lightning.

Through the torment, a voice awoke in her mind full-force.

Protocols unlocked and engaged. We...are.

Interface...partial.

Om awoke, reacting instinctively with fear and vast power.

Threat detected...Protect all access.

Neural net...INTRUSION. UNWARRANTED.

LEVEL 1.359 DEFENSIVE RESPONSE.

An intense blast wave of white-hot psyonic energy fanned out rapidly from the epicenter of her immolated mind.

Naero continued to scream.

As if far away in the distance, Klyne and his two adepts also shrieked.

*

Naero blinked, her eyes and mouth frozen open.

She lay with her head to one side, in a puddle of her own mixed blood and spittle.

More pain struck her when she attempted to move.

Blood continued to stream from her eyes, ears, nose, and mouth–a bloody mess.

It felt as if a fusion grenade had blown her head open.

She reached up with her hands, to make sure her skull was still intact.

Some kind of noise.

Warning alarms sounded.

A ship. Yes, they were on a ship. The Spacer Intel Ship *The Kathmandu*. She was...being tested, for the Mystics.

Something had gone terribly wrong.

Naero focused, getting to her hands and knees.

She heard other voices, groaning and whimpering.

Makita lay sprawled in a broken tangle, blasted across the room. His gray clothing had been shredded and scorched into tatters. He choked and coughed.

To the other side, Iselle fared little better. She lay convulsing, blasted, scorched, a yellow-white bone of her forearm sticking out of her wrenched flesh. One side of her face was blistered, her red hair burned, some of it still smoking. She trembled and shuddered in pain and terror.

Naero looked around for Klyne, and found the instructor in a burned, bloody heap, lying beneath a dark red smear on the far wall. His hands were charred black, and he was missing fingers.

Naero could not walk. She couldn't even stand. She crawled to Klyne as quickly as she could.

He still lived, just barely.

Then she noticed the intense effects of the blast, all around the room, less than a meter up.

A massive expanding ring of Cosmic force had sliced into the duranadium hull of the smartwalls, punching a deep crease right through them where they buckled, all along its full diameter.

The force of the strike disrupted all systems. The entire training room was compacted, crushed, and heavily damaged.

Rescuers struggled to force their way through the various ruined doors and access panels.

Naero's Gambit Amazon Link: smarturl.it/NaerosGambit

Please enjoy the following teaser from the next book in the Citation Series, Book Two:

NAERO'S
WAR:

THE
HIGH
CRUSADE

smarturl.it/TheHighCrusade

THE CITATION SERIES, BOOK TWO

NAERO'S WAR:

THE HIGH CRUSADE

by Mason Elliott

Amazon Link for the *The High Crusade:* smarturl.it/TheHighCrusade

General Walker's Marines from Bravo Command maneuvered into position under the cover of darkness using their stealth gear.

Naero agreed to slip in ahead and bait the trap, in her battlefield role as Shetanna–*The Dark Angel of Death.*

Get ready, Om. The show's about to start.

I will need some time to prepare, concentrate, and focus enough of our energies in reserve, before you deplete them all again.

Just get ready and keep us ready. I'm going to set our game plan in motion.

I will do all that I can to assist. Call upon me when you require me. Good hunting, Naero.

Thanks, Om.

The invaders would do anything to have a chance to destroy or capture her.

She was, in fact, the actual, literal bait, and the trap was being set for an entire invasion force of Ejjai elite that ravaged the Corps border world of Tholos-4.

No local planetary army, military, or militia had been able to stand before the horrific onslaught of the alien invaders.

The Ejjai hammered the local landers into submission with advanced artillery, orbital bombardment from Ejjai fleets, and close assault gunships and gravtanks.

Then the terrifying collection process began, and all the living, wounded, and dead were hurled into the shrieking, whining processing blades of the robotic meatships.

The horrible sounds of the meatships warred with the screams of their countless victims.

Given time, Ejjai mass cloning factories and robotic ship- and weapon-building factories would also be established onworld.

The murdering bastards had already wiped three major cities and their mixed populations off the surface of the hapless planet, before Naero and the Marines could even deploy onworld.

The enemy left those lost cities little more than red, blackened, burning scars and stains that could be viewed from orbit.

Nothing left alive.

Ejjai hyaenanoids loved carrion.

Every man, woman, and child of any kind, species, or age that the enemy captured was routinely tortured, killed, and processed into rotting ration blocks in the horrific, robotic meatships of the invading aliens. That included any sentients, pets, livestock–anything and everything that was meat.

The meatblock rations were frozen only to keep them from breaking down and decaying completely.

Hatred was too gentle a word for what most humans felt for the Ejjai invaders and their extreme methods. Spacers, landers, and each of the other known races that encountered the Ejjai quickly learned to feel the same way.

This vile, uplifted, intrusive, and opportunistic species needed to be completely exterminated wherever it was encountered.

The invaders proved that they were incapable of coexisting with any other living things.

The Ejjai could only dominate, torture, and destroy all life that they encountered, anything they could sink their teeth and claws into. Uplifting them, and giving them advanced weapons and starships had only turned them into a galactic abomination, an interstellar menace, a virulent plague.

An utter nightmare.

One that needed to end for the poor people of Tholos-4.

Naero and her Marine allies were there to see to that.

It was amusing that the Ejjai always saw themselves as invincible, the supreme warriors.

Shetanna and Bravo Command quickly intended to disavow the foe of such jaded notions, time and time again.

The Marines of Bravo Command were the textbook picture of professional warriors. A legend among all the known systems.

Naero loved serving with the elite of the elite. Together they made a fantastic team.

Even the Ejjai had learned grudgingly to fear them from their initial engagements, and the proof was there.

Every invader force that came up against Bravo Command had been completely wiped out–in record time. And then Bravo quietly packed up and headed on to the next world, ready to do it all over again.

The enemy struggled to halt the Spacer advance and throw it back.

They tried everything they could think of.

Increased enemy numbers.

Different tactics.

New weapons–traps and tricks of many different kinds.

The Ejjai generals turned themselves inside out trying to find a solution–a way to achieve victory against the Spacer advance.

Bravo Command slipped in and ruined the invader's sick, twisted party every single time.

And Shetanna, The Dark Angel of Death, continued to use all of her amazing, Mystic powers and abilities to help the Marines keep up the pressure and drive the enemy to terror, madness, and distraction.

General Walker worked closely with Spacer Intel, always making sure his leathernecks had the latest hi-tek toys, weapons, and armor that came online.

As a result, they landed an entire Marine division on Tholos-4 and slipped into position, without the enemy even knowing they were there yet.

By the time the Spacer Fleets swept in to destroy the enemy naval forces, Bravo Command would already be implementing their plan to put the foe down hard and fast on the ground.

Three Marine infantry regiments, one artillery regiment, plus specialized units of meks, armor, and air-to-ground support.

The ghosts of Bravo Command spread the impending Shadow of Vengeance and Death over their foes like an unseen net, without any knowledge or awareness among the invaders themselves.

Bravo and Shetanna prepared for another stunning series of lightning attacks.

All became poised and ready, while the heedless enemy celebrated their vile victories and atrocities.

Naero struggled to remain silent as she slipped in among the foe. Death and damnation to any invader who thought they could invade the human sectors with impunity, death, and cosmicide.

On every world, the invader needed to be taught that bloody lesson.

Naero strode right into the belly of the beast.

Alone.

Defiant.

By now she was supremely confident in her skills and abilities and all of her comrades depending on her and backing her up.

Her cloaked combat armor made her virtually invisible. The Ejjai could not even smell her.

She used her gravwing to slip into the most heavily guarded command and control bunker the enemy possessed. With her skill and her tek, she could crawl upside down on the ceilings like an unseen insect.

Her miniature vidcams and audio collectors fed data to Intel in real time, covering everything she saw.

Naero's small contingent of cloaked Intel fixers and microdrones stayed close, ready to disrupt key enemy systems and communications, planting microbombs and detonation devices as they went.

The Invader High Command celebrated their latest triumph with what one might expect from them—a huge, decadent, disgusting feast—held within a shielded bunker.

They set up their victory celebration within a huge underground arena, probably used by the Tholosians for some kind of urban or regional sporting events.

Ejjai got drunk on stinking, fermented grog made from human blood. They shipped it in from the meatships by the tankerful.

Under the bright lights of the hi-tek arena, tens of thousands of Ejjai feasted and celebrated their latest victories. The enemy generals praised their troops and used the huge arena vidscreens to plot out their next attacks on the three nearest Tholosian cities.

On the center of the playing field, Ejjai transports and appropriated trucks had also hauled in and dumped huge piles of human corpses from the local population for their undefeated troops to feed on.

Piles of fresh and not-so-fresh meat, diverted from the enemy meatships to help sate the troops in large numbers.

One of the piles was all dead children and infants.

Even worse, to Naero's horror, some of the bodies in the various meat piles were somehow still alive. They twitched or cried out in pain and terror. Some weakly attempted to crawl away despite broken or missing limbs.

The Ejjai quickly seized them and began tormenting them even further, laughing hysterically at the sport. They stabbed, cut, and skinned them alive–or otherwise got creative.

As Ejjai were wont to do.

Ejjai were among the vilest, most disgusting creatures Naero had even encountered.

She resisted the very strong impulse to cut loose on them right then and there.

But she couldn't–not yet.

These monsters needed to die. Every single one of them.

And very soon, she would have a direct hand in launching the attack that would accomplish just that.

The timing had to be just right, so she steeled herself.

The generals. Reach the generals and stay ready.

Six Ejjai generals held court like warlords at huge tables overflowing with comconsoles, sensor stations, map screens, and piles of loot. And the bloody remains of horrific, eviscerated meals.

The bulk of all Ejjai clone troops remained predominantly female. Smaller male Ejjai concubines were kept around on leashes for fun, for the leaders. They even dressed them in human clothing and poorly fitting human lingerie.

As an oddity, one of the generals even had a human male dressed up as a concubine. But the poor guy apparently had to be kept in a heavily guarded pen off to one side–to keep all of the other Ejjai from devouring and murdering him, most likely in that order.

Naero circled around the generals and studied the arena, trying to devise the best way to take them all down.

She listened intently to the plans the enemy generals were making, feeding it all to Intel.

"So, are all of the atomics and genocide devices in place yet?"

Another general pulled up a mapscreen displaying all of their installation of such devices planetwide.

Naero instantly transmitted all of that data directly to Spacer Intel as well–priority alert.

Intel and Bravo Command were most likely already neutralizing the most vital elements of the enemy plot. These genocide devices could be scanned and located from orbit. But it was always good to be sure, and to know their exact locations.

The Ejjai generals scoffed. "We will be ready for anything the enemy can throw at us in less than a day," one of the other Ejjai generals boasted.

"They won't know what's going to hit them until it's too late."

"Good, very good. Speed things up if you can. Get it all up and ready."

"Don't worry, sir. We will be more than ready to deal with their so-called Bravo Command—and their spack witch."

All of the Ejjai generals had a good laugh and congratulated each other.

The lead general stepped up to a waiting podium and addressed the crowd.

"Great news, sisters! We have it on good authority that the spacks are sending their precious Bravo Command and their spack witch Shetanna against us."

Lots of cursing and booing about that roared up.

Their lead general continued. "This time, we are more than ready for them!"

Huge rounds of applause to that.

"Let me just say that we have some heavy duty surprises of our own ready and waiting and in store for our enemies. We can't wait for them to get here—and have them all for dinner!"

That brought an even bigger round of cheering, cursing, and applause.

"We will engage the spacks in a matter of days, and with our increased numbers and new weapons—I say we're going to kick their asses and stomp them bloody. We will gut them! I want all my girls out there to feast on spack Marine flesh until you puke!"

Further rounds of cheering and vile responses.

"We will ferment their blood in our huge vats and get drunk on it!"

More horrendous rounds of cheering and applause.

"And once we have captured their filthy spack witch, all of you will watch as I personally cut her up and rape her with red-hot knives, and torture her to death over the course of an entire week. She'll sing to all of us with her screams. Then I myself will feast upon her guts, and eat her heart while the light in her eyes fades. I'll crack her skull open and eat her brains!"

The Ejjai went crazy.

"Wait until we post *that* on the webnets for the spacks and the skinners to watch! I promise you victory. We cannot be defeated. And we will sweep the human skinners and all the other inferior races into our meatships and out of all existence. They are our prey! Yet another galaxy that shall fall to us and our mighty masters!"

More about their mysterious masters. Interesting.

Furious cheering continued in waves.

"So, my warriors. Feast on meat until you vomit, and then feast some more. Then prepare for battle as we crush our foes and ravage the rest of this world. We shall drown it all in blood and swim in it! Prepare for our ultimate victory! Our time has come. None can stand against us!"

They erupted in an orgy of celebration and vile gluttony.

Fights broke out among the meat piles, and the Ejjai fought with and murdered each other in their frenzy.

The lead general returned to the others, rubbing her claws together eagerly in the midst of the chaos.

"My sisters, I have a special treat that I've saved just for us, at this exact moment. Please, enjoy my precious gifts to you all." She motioned to a large knot of troops off to one side among some gravtanks.

A full squad of Ejjai in heavy battle armor led out six terrified human women, all of them naked and extremely pregnant.

None of them had a mark on them. Yet.

But from the looks on their pale faces, they all knew very well what the enemy generals intended to do with them. Each of them was heavy with child, in the later stages of pregnancy.

That they had remained unspoiled and unharmed up until now would quickly change for the worse–the worst fate imaginable.

Although they were unbound, there was no chance for any of these captives to break free or escape on their own against so many foes.

The generals each glared at them and gloated. The Ejjai generals slavered and drooled, snapping jaws and smacking lips.

Each general had a set of rusty, bloodstained butchering tools that they began to place out in front of them in heady, eager anticipation of their coming feast.

Then the squad of Ejjai troops guarding the six women suddenly staggered a few feet away as if drunk.

Some melted into slag where they stood.

Other Ejjai troops exploded.

The six human captives looked around in confusion.

The next instant, they all vanished.

The six Ejjai generals shot to their feet in stunned surprise.

They couldn't even speak, but a few flung cleavers and knives at the spot where the captives had stood.

Their weapons fell harmlessly to the ground.

All of this was captured and displayed on the big arena screens, and slowly attracted the attention of the astonished crowds.

Then Shetanna appeared as if by magic, right before the lead Ejjai general, resplendent in her full Angel of Death mode. She was all dressed in black, shining black hair flowing in the wind, violet eyes burning above her mask.

Twin bloodred katanas crackled and hissed in the damp air, at the ready in either hand.

Every eye fixed on her—while the mini-gravpods from her fixers whisked the six cloaked, female captives away to safety.

Naero only had to buy few more seconds for them to make it out. Fierce Marines waited nearby to take charge of them and keep them safe.

With the six captives out of the way, at last Shetanna could go to work.

"I have come for you, filthy Ejjai cowards. I am Shetanna!" she cried.

She rammed both of her swords through the lead general's eyes and out the back of the Ejjai's scorched skull.

Two of the generals tried to run.

The other three tried to attack her.

It did not matter.

Bolts of scarlet lighting tore forth from both her blades, ripping and blasting the other five into charred pieces of meat and bone.

Naero cloaked and shot away as the area around the tables was engulfed in torrents of enemy weapon fire the very next instant.

Then the gravtanks, gunships, transports, and other vehicles lined up nearby began to explode.

Naero projected multiple holos of herself all over the arena and in the in the air, drawing fire in all directions.

She used *the voice*, her words booming and echoing from several directions.

"EJJAI FILTH. PREPARE TO MEET DEATH. FOR SHETANNA IS THE DARK ANGEL OF DEATH, AND HAS NO FEAR OF MURDERING COWARDS."

The Ejjai fired in panic from so many angles that they cut down each other by the hundreds—just as Naero planned.

Fear began to infect them.

Gouts of red lightning lashed into the arena stands from several directions like gigantic whips of destruction. The devastation flung dead and dying Ejjai everywhere in a cyclone of slaughter, adding to the total chaos and confusion.

"NO MERCY, EJJAI SCUM. NO ESCAPE. FEAR IS MY MOTHER, DEATH MY SIRE, AND I THEIR DAUGHTER! YOU CANNOT HARM ME. THERE IS NO ESCAPE FOR YOU!"

Just as the enemy started to figure out they were shooting at holos and murdering each other wholesale, Naero merged with one of her mirror images in the midst of hundreds of Ejjai in the arena stands.

Multiple thin rods of red Chaos energy shot from her, fanning out in a diameter of thirty meters.

First she impaled hundreds of the shocked invaders.

When she spun, the red blades chopped them all into smaller gory chunks and pieces.

Torrents of unleashed Ejjai blood suddenly gathered and swept down the arena, carrying others away in a sudden red, rushing tide of gore.

Naero cloaked and flashed away again.

More enemy fire stormed and tore at her former position.

She took the place of another holo, and sent forth a sweeping hurricane of of Chaos bubbles and orbs of every shape and size into another section of the stands.

The explosions collapsed that entire section. Wreckage toppled inward.

Next she appeared on the field before the horrendous meat piles, in the midst of hundreds of more frantic enemies.

Half of them flung their weapons away and ran in terror before her as she raced toward them. So much for the valiant Ejjai.

"STAND AND FIGHT, SCUM!"

Naero surged and fought with the mob of foes, sweeping one way and then the other, cutting them down by dozens, by scores.

She moved among them so fast they could not focus their attacks.

Then she would abruptly change direction and sweep another way before they could hem her in.

She unleashed more scarlet lightning strikes.

She sent random Chaos blasts into packed pockets of foes.

At times she just whirled and passed through them with her swords fully extended, mowing them down in lines and bunches.

Once she had shattered them completely, she merely turned her back on them and began walking away quickly and with determination, toward the nearest exit.

Naero set her shield pod full-on.

Three enemy tanks roared at her, cannons blazing.

Naero dodged and deflected their blasts into the stands.

Two gravtanks she exploded with Chaos bombs.

The last she sliced the last in half with her swords and kept walking calmly, straight through the burning wreckage as the gravtank exploded directly behind her to either side.

She ignored all enemy fire directed at her, kept walking, and cut down anything stupid enough to attempt to stand before her.

She crackled with destroying red lightning as she passed into one of the exit tunnels, laying waste to anything before her.

The enemy regrouped and poured into the tunnel in hot pursuit.

Just as Naero hoped they would.

Another kill zone. How convenient of them to all bunch up for her.

She turned at bay, just before exiting, and focused all of her energies in an intense Chaos blast cone.

The massive detonation tore the tunnel apart and blasted shredded pieces of the packed invaders out the other end, right before a massive fireball that followed hard thereafter.

Naero cloaked, and called out over her secure link.

"You guys ready? I've got them primed, but I'm also almost out of juice."

"We're in place and ready to join the show, Shetanna. You okay? Do you need us to extract you?"

"Negative. I can finish my part. It just takes a lot of energy to sustain attacks at this level. You guys know that. Did Intel take care of those genocide devices?"

"Almost all accounted for."

"All right, I'm setting up for my final show. They'll take the bait, all right. You guys hit them hard when they do."

"Hard as we can, Shetanna. You know us."

"I sure do, and I can't wait to watch it all go down–right from the front row. Copy that. Make the legends proud, Bravo."

She took up her position in the center of the fallen city nearby, just outside of the shattered arena.

She formed a Chaos construct around her that duplicated her and her every move.

Her construct became a scarlet, gigantic version of herself, semi-transparent and fifteen meters tall, red and glowing with huge blazing swords.

She stomped on a mea ship and slashed at it until it exploded.

Then she attacked the cloneship factory next to it.

"FACE ME, COWARDS. SHETANNA SHOWS YOU HER MIGHT. SHOW ME YOURS. FACE ME AND PERISH!"

Yet in actuality, her energies waned with each passing second.

It wasn't like being back on Janosha where there was limitless Cosmic energy to tap into. Away from the Mystic Homeworlds, Naero's energy levels and her abilities were not infinite or limitless.

She made a good show of it, but even she could not sustain these levels of attack for very long.

The entire enemy invasion roared to life and locked on, bunching and sweeping her way, to engage her from all directions.

The Ejjai went insane with fury.

Up in the skies above and beyond Tholos-4, the Spacer navy sent the invader fleets spinning down in flames.

Thousands of Spacer Marines suddenly materialized out of the black at key points and positions.

Phantoms who owned the night.

The black was their domain, their element, and they surrendered it to no one.

Bravo Command unleashed a torrent of concentrated, interlocking fire against the bunched-up invaders. Veils of destroying fire, artillery, and ordnance rained down–a deluge of precisely timed destruction that no living thing could possibly survive.

Within a matter of minutes, a quarter of a million Ejjai invaders flashed and flared into a sweeping typhoon of white-hot death that overtook them.

Shetanna had done her job all too well.

Completely drained of all her Mystic energies for the moment, she could barely stand.

Even as she staggered away, a full platoon of gigantic Ejjai Sterodans in phaze armor appeared all around her.

They piled on and overwhelmed her with their greater mass and several shock charges that hit and rippled through both them and her. The shock charges rattled Naero's teeth in her skull.

The Ejjai and their mysterious masters still wanted her and the KDM alive and intact, apparently.

Naero grinned.

Yet another trap, and she had stumbled right into it.

This time, the enemy thought they had her at last.

Yet Naero knew something they did not, and called out into her own mind.

Om–you're up. They've got me.

Take these bastards down hard and fast!

Amazon Link for the *The High Crusade:* smarturl.it/TheHighCrusade

Please enjoy the following teaser from the next Spacer Clans Adventure, Book 3:

NAERO'S FURY

smarturl.it/NaerosFury

NAERO'S FURY

Amazon Link to Naero's Fury: smarturl.it/NaerosFury

by Mason Elliott

Naero still hadn't done it much, but going into a direct trance to enter the Astral Plane shouldn't be all that difficult. Master Vane had shown her how once. And she had gone there lots of times in her sleep, in her mind, to speak with Khai, using their astral crystals.

Before her friend Khai had vanished without a trace.

Yet she had never been completely trained in astral travel, and didn't know that much about exploring or moving around. Master Vane had taken her there once, just to teach her the basics and give her his marker. Many other times later to spar with her.

If nothing else, she could probably focus on his marker and locate him.

Zhen had roused Naero and reminded her it was time. And that she and Shalaen would monitor her while she was in the astral trance.

Naero focused her mind and abilities, controlling her breathing. Remembering the little she had recently learned.

Within several minutes of focused meditation, she open her eyes and found herself floating in the Astral Miasma, the nebulae of energy. She hugged her knees to her chest in her astral form.

Om spoke to her, even more easily here than in her own mind before.

I have accessed some of the Kexxian Matrix's data files on The Astral Plane. Like everything else, they explored it quite extensively.

Om, I'm naked here. I'm not complaining–but just tell me–how do I put astral clothing on again?

You control everything here by imagination, and force of will. Concentrate on your favorite clothing and they'll appear.

That's easy.

She looked down and saw her favorite Nytex flight togs, programmed just the way she liked them.

Naero blinked, spinning and twirling in one spot, turning upside down.

Why can't I move more than a meter at a time in front of us?

You're not used to this reality. So it's not clear to you.

The air around her looked opaque. Not mist. Not smoke or vapor. And it glowed slightly with its own bluish-gray light.

In the twilight she glowed softly blue-white with her own light. From within.

"I once heard rumors that the Mystics could travel and send messages this way, but I thought it was all just a myth."

Since the other planes are entire universes within themselves, it is said, they are all nearly infinite. Thus, it is difficult to pin point any kind of location or person unless you already know them.

Naero instinctively tried to stand up, but there was nothing to stand on.

Then she recalled Master Vane's Marker, and it appeared right before her. Where she found him, she would find the other High Masters.

At least she deserved a chance to be heard by them all. To try to explain herself and her actions. What happened with the obelisk was clearly not her fault.

But they would still blame her for it–especially Mater Vane, who seemed to blame her for everything since Hashiko's death.

Naero could not simply stand by and let the High Masters decide her fate without herself being present at her trial, in some way at least.

She focused on the crimson and black star more and swept forward, seemingly at great speed.

She came to an abrupt halt, like a starship coming out of jump at its destination.

The opacity around her partially melted away. She proceeded forward, opening her visual field far wider. She made out the area around her as the miasma peeled back.

Slightly below her, she saw spheres within glowing spheres, all spinning within greater spheres.

Her own sphere, glowing white-blue, suddenly surrounded her like a glittering soap bubble.

Yet it did not pop when she poked at it.

One sphere in particular, the largest, glowed and pulsed blood red, containing a withered old man with a long beard, pacing impatiently.

Burning eyes vanished and re-appeared at random all over his bald head. The red sphere absorbed Master Vane's marker.

Was this his true form? What he really looked like?

His scarlet sphere was also flanked by two smaller spheres with figures inside them.

Om made a calculated guess.

His current guardian adepts, no doubt. The ones you rescued from the enemy Darkforce generators on Janosha.

I think so, Om.

At most times, every High Master had at least two champion adepts protecting him or her, each of them very close to mastery themselves. Just as Hashiko had been.

Naero studied Vane's new guardians for the very first time, and tried to see into their spheres.

Something about each of them did seem strangely familiar.

One of Vane's adepts, the male, appeared to be so deep dark black, he could be a singularity. This adept's sphere was flat black on the surface and barely transparent.

If Naero had been able to breathe, she would have gasped.

Instead she simply raised her hand to her mouth.

She recalled that she had seen many of these adepts long before.

In her dreams, nightmares, and crazed visions. Perhaps even on the Astral Plane somehow.

Vane's other adept was the white female, the exact opposite of the other. So brilliant and blindingly radiant, she could be a pulsar. Her orb was like a high intensity bulb, blinding and almost completely crystal clear.

It occurred to Naero that during her initial testing, Klyne had male and female assistants as well.

She couldn't guess what the significance of that pattern was all about. Perhaps just some weird Mystic, egalitarian tradition.

Then why weren't any of the High Masters female?

Everyone seemed to ignore her where she floated.

The next larger sphere, farther away, glowed silver-blue.

If she focused intently on it, she discovered she could zoom in with her third eye–her mind's eye.

Within that silver-blue sphere, a silver man sat serenely, neither young nor old. Master Tree, in his purest form of order.

Two smaller guardian spheres flanked him.

Master Tree's female adept glowed with intense blue energy in a deep blue sphere.

The male likewise glowed with vibrant green force within a green sphere, a shining sword sheathed down his broad, athletic back. He seemed very familiar somehow.

Naero did a double-take. Long blond hair. Green skin. Big glowing sword.

Yep. In the flesh–or–astral form at least.

It was Khai! She was sure of it. He was alive.

Had he actually succeeded in his great task of forging his mystic sword in the heart of a gigantic pulsar? Was that it on his back?

Naero gasped again. Now that she knew what he looked like, Khai was also the dreamy green hunk from many past, pent up nightmares. The one who kept sticking his astral sword through her head.

What did it all mean? She wasn't nuts enough yet?

Now she knew for certain she needed serious help.

And to do some serious dating at some point, once-and-for-all.

If the Mystics continued to let her live.

Khai must have sensed her inner turmoil, or thoughts, or maybe just her concentration on him.

Mr. Green-god even glanced her way for a second, looking just as confused and puzzled by her sudden appearance.

Neither of them had ever met the other in person.

Naero covered her face with one hand and looked aside, withdrawing her sphere suddenly further away.

How fricking embarrassing.

She crept forward again. Slowly.

The third and final sphere glowed golden, and contained an equally golden child within, energetic and bristling with lightning. He bounced back and forth inside like a gigantic electron.

Master Jo of course.

Two flanking spheres.

One of his adepts had no clear form, eyes gleaming within a shifting, flickering miasma like the Astral Plane itself. His female counterpart shifted shape from one fantastic creature to another.

When she suddenly made out their voices, she could sense that an intense debate had been doing on. One that still continued.

"We cannot be certain in this matter," the golden child insisted. "We do not dare act in any rash way."

"Agreed, High Master Jo," the serene silver man added. "She might yet be another Trickster from what I can tell."

"Yes. Quite possible, High Master Tree."

The old man in the blood red sphere blustered impatiently. "Fools! Always conspiring against me. Taking positions opposite of mine for no reason but to anger me. I've been telling you all along, this child is clearly the Great Destroyer–long foretold. Our duty is clear. She is a threat to all existence. To multiple dimensions. She must be eliminated, at once, before she can grow even more powerful."

"High Master Vane," Tree said. "None of us can be sure of that fact. Including you."

"I am."

"You are always certain when it comes to destroying someone," Jo added. "Your pure Chaos answer to everything. Destruction or Creation."

"It works."

"No. It doesn't. It only delays and worsens the inevitable," Tree said. "The Universe shall have its way. We all know this. You were mistaken with the last savant when he appeared, and now he remains at large–a renegade beyond even our control."

Baeven? We're they referring to her uncle?

Vane rolled his eyes. "Idiots! The Renegade is the Trickster, I say. This child must in fact be the Great Destroyer. Just look at the powers roiling within her. They will surely corrupt and overwhelm her entirely and drive her mad in the end. She will go berserk on a scale that makes her recent outbursts feeble and puny by comparison. She must perish now, while we have a chance to put an end to her. While the only crimes she has committed include destroying an entire planet, and another of the vital obelisks!"

"We still don't understand the purpose of the ancient obelisks. And we've studied the mysterious disappearance of Janosha, and we still cannot be certain in any conclusive way, that she had anything to do with it."

"Really? Who else could it be then? Planets like Janosha aren't in the habit of just obliterating themselves suddenly for no reason at all. Everywhere she goes, destruction follows!"

I cannot allow this.

Quiet, Om. Don't do anything. I'm trying to listen.

Naero…they're discussing our destruction. The Chaos Master means to destroy us.

Master Jo continued to protest. "You can't just kill off every entity that manifests Cosmic Abilities such as these. Our universe is peppered with them. We must continue to locate and guide them–not find excuses to execute them. Like the Others have told us, Tricksters often appear to oppose Great Destroyers. Without the former, final victory is never possible. "

"High Masters," Tree said. "This young woman also possesses the Kexxian Data Matrix. We cannot destroy her without destroying it. Intel and The Spacer Council of Elders value our wisdom, but even they would not agree to such action."

"Regrettable," Vane said. "Yet I cannot take the risk. I have decided this matter on my own."

"You have no such authority on your own," Tree insisted.

"Idiots! I cannot stand by and allow our galaxy–perhaps our entire universe to be destroyed–just to satisfy your foolish, philosophical, and theoretical whims."

Master Vane turned to his adepts. "My finest students, obey me. Delay these fools. Keep them occupied whilst I act for the good of all existence."

More rapid than thought, the male dark ensnared the blue sphere and its satellites in coils and tendrils of darkness. While the bright female enveloped the golden sphere and its companions in waves of of pure light.

Naero tried to pull away, but in her panic she did not know where to go.

High Master Vane sped straight at her with impossible speed.

I must act, Naero.

No, Om. Please, this is already bad enough. Don't do anything.

I cannot comply. I must defend us!

Naero went down on her hands and knees before Master Vane. She called out, using *the voice* to project her words.

"Please, Master Vane. Do not attack me. I only wish to be trained to control my abilities. I have struggled hard to do so. I still don't understand what happened with the obelisk."

Vane bore down on her, arcs of pure scarlet energy bristling around him.

"Far too late for that, monster. Nothing is ever your fault, is it? Now, you must perish for the good of all. I told you this hour would come."

Instinctively, Naero drew back again, trying to evade his attack. She rose within her receding sphere.

Vane closed in once more, gathering his powers.

"Don't do this," Naero begged. "Please. Help me. I know I can't fully control all of my abilities yet. I'm trying as hard as I can. I can't be responsible for what will happen if you attack me. I can't control myself."

"Yes, and look at the results? Countless lives crushed and eradicated. Janosha vaporized–an entire planet. You must never be allowed to reach your full potential. Now–monster–hold still and embrace your fate."

Naero put her hands out before her, holding her palms out defensively. Pleading.

"No. Don't. I can't–"

"I know, Maeris. You can't help yourself. That is why you are *an abomination!*"

Vane smashed into her, piercing all of her defenses as if they were shattering glass.

In the distance, she sensed that Master Jo and Master Tree finally broke free.

Too late.

Master Vane attacked, trying to overwhelm her with raw power.

He pummeled her with impossible blows.

In the end, he beat her up badly, but only succeeded in knocking her around once more.

Om roared in their mind.

Kexxian defense protocols unlocked and on line.

An energized, glowing armor of some advanced origin formed around Naero like a hi-tek battle suit.

Naero saw out of her third eye as it awoke and burst into radiance like a blue-white star.

Master Vane came at her once more, all of his powers focused through his primary scarlet, burning eye, centered in his forehead.

All of his other flaming eyes closed as he concentrated, his skull wreathed in weird cosmic flames like a mane of cosmic fire.

"See how powerful you have already become? No adept could have withstood those lethal attacks. We must finish this now, before the others can interfere."

"Please, Master Vane. Please–I'm begging you–please, don't do this."

"Maeris, just as I foretold–you shall fall before the greatest of all Cosmic attack techniques. And I am one of the few who have ever learned to master it: The Eye of Annihilation!"

The same Chaos technique that had destroyed Hashiko–even she couldn't control it properly.

A massive blood red beam of destroying Cosmic force shot straight at her.

It all happened so fast. Naero heard Om screaming.

Reflection defense. Analyze incoming cosmic assault. Duplicate and reflect attack tenfold!

Just before the incoming blast vaporized her, a blue-white beam shot out of her own third eye to war against Master Vane's powers.

The Cosmic flows flared intensely.

Naero screamed as if her body and soul were being sucked through the eye of a black hole's needle.

The wide blue beam quickly drove the red beam back to its source.

At the last instant, High Master Vane cried out in terror.

"Impossible! There can be no such–"

The destroying energy ignited on contact.

A massive detonation on the Astral Plane blinded the area within a few light years.

High Masters Jo and Tree barely managed to withdraw and shield the others. All of their spheres shattered.

Pure cosmic energy punched into High Master Vane right before Naero's eyes.

It drove him back like a white-hot comet.

He struggled against it with all his might.

To no avail.

The reflected attack obliterated High Master Vane to glowing ash and dust, screaming in the wake of his own annihilation.

Vane's dying force of will echoed off into the universe.

Naero would have caught her breath if she had any.

The outcome left her completely stunned for a shuddering instant.

Om…what did we just do?

We had no choice, Naero. My sole purpose is to defend our current form.

Naero stared down at her hands in terror. Tendrils of Cosmic energy rippled and still curled off of her body and her sphere like smoke.

Om…*Haisha!* We just killed a High Master of the Spacer Mystics!

Amazon Link to Naero's Fury: smarturl.it/NaerosFury

Please enjoy this teaser for The Citation Series, Book 3:

NAERO'S
TRIAL

Amazon Link: smarturl.it/NaerosTrial

NAERO'S WAR:

NAERO'S TRIAL

Amazon link: smarturl.it/NaerosTrial

by Mason Elliott

On the third day of Naero's trial, the Prosecution and the Defense made their final, closing statements.

Master Jo spoke first, for the Defense.

"In the final analysis, I would both conclude and insist that Naero Amashin Maeris has proven herself time and time again to be an honorable Spacer, and that her word is without question. She is also vital to the survival of her people in many important ways. Naero Amashin Maeris is a noble, invaluable warrior and a proven leader who has served the Clans and the Alliance well, in both peacetime and war. A Mystic Champion who is now part of the great and mysterious Cosmic Prophecy, long foretold. There is still so little that we do not know about those prophecies; who can say what her role will be in the end?"

Master Jo paced a bit. "And on a very basic level, she is a Spacer. As such, she has the right of all Spacers and all sentients to defend herself, to the death, against anyone who attempts to kill her. Reluctantly, she only resorted to lethal force when High Master Vane attacked her with the intent to destroy her, and take her life. Even after she had tried to get away from him, and begged him repeatedly not to attack her.

"She cannot not be convicted of murder for defending her own life against someone trying to kill her. Those are all many good reasons why you must see fit to exonerate her of these erroneous charges. We cannot take the life of this hero."

The Defense finally rested.

Master Tree was given the final word in the trial for the prosecution.

"Hero? First, let me also revisit the reckless side of this renegade, outlaw Spacer, who fled from justice and had to be brought back by force to face her crimes in shackles, in order to keep her from getting away once again. On several occasions, Naero Amashin Maeris has proven herself to be dangerous, unpredictable, and out of control. By her own words, she has more than once declared that if she ever lost control and became a threat to any of her people, that she herself agreed that she should be put down–and destroyed.

"The cold blooded murder of a High Mystic Master has not demonstrated this fact readily enough? Beyond all doubt? If she can slay a High Master of the Mystics so easily, how much more is she a danger to all? And she even admits that she cannot control her abilities. Her very existence has become such a clear and present threat that it cannot be ignored and must be dealt with. I repeat, she has admitted on several occasions that her powers can go out of control and be very dangerous.

"Next, she also clearly admits that she killed Master Vane. Now, of her own accord, she claims that she killed him in self defense. But she has thus far presented no single shred of proof of that. She claims that Master Vane attacked her, attempted to kill her, and that she killed him, as she now conveniently claims–in so-called self defense. And I remind everyone in this court, once again. It does not matter who she is, what she is, or whatever else she has done. No one is above Spacer Law.

"Not even the infamous, Naero Amashin Maeris."

Tree took in a breath and clasped his hands behind his back. "What are the facts, therefore? A High Mystic Master lies dead, murdered by his own student, who openly stated that she could not stand him. Who openly admitted that she killed him. Nothing else can be proven, beyond those facts. Nothing else exists as fact. And this case must only be decided, based solely upon the facts. Nothing else.

"A Spacer on trial for her life could readily claim and say anything. Merely stating something does not make it true. That does not prove it to be fact. According to the facts of what is known, Naero Amashin Maeris is clearly guilty of murder, and will undoubtedly say and do anything possible in order to get away with her crime. As anyone logically would, in order to escape punishment, justice, and execution."

Naero fumed. Haisha! What the hell did they expect her to say? Yes, I offed the asshole, I loved it, and I'm a fricking monster. Go ahead and kill me?

I wish that weren't so painfully funny, Naero.

Me too, Om.

Master Tree went on to demand that the jury uphold one of the key tenets of Spacer Law and Spacer society:

"Spacers do not murder other Spacers and take their lives! Naero Amashin Maeris is not above that law. Naero Amashin Maeris broke that solemn law. And like it or not, the law demands justice. There is no way around that law and no way to escape it. That law demands that she face the ultimate punishment for her being guilty of committing the ultimate crime!"

Tree emphasized his final point with a single, upraised index finger. "That punishment is immediate Death, by execution. To be carried out by beheading, at the hands and the blade of the Mystic Enforcer!"

The Prosecution rested its case.

Admiral Klyne looked slightly pale as he instructed the jury of Mystic Elders to decide the case and announce their decision after their period of deliberation.

Naero went back to her cell in silence feeling sick, unable to meet Khai's utterly heartbroken glance. She felt stunned and numb. She didn't know what to think. All that she could do was await the jury's decision, along with everyone else.

Yet it was her fate alone that was being decided.

But when she thought about it further it wasn't just her fate.

Everyone waited for eight long hours.

Naero could neither rest nor sleep.

Then everyone was summoned back to the court room.

A decision had been made. The jury had arrived at a verdict in her case.

Admiral Klyne announced, "All rise for the verdict to be read."

They did so.

The jury leader stood up and read their decision.

"According to Spacer Law, and based upon all of the facts and evidence presented, we the jury find the defendant, Naero Amashin Maeris, of Clan Maeris...guilty of murder in the death of another Spacer."

Naero gasped, nailed to the bedrock of the planet itself in almost complete shock.

Guilty meant...

Master Tree rose up. "This Mystic trial has ended; it is over. A verdict has been reached. Without question, this grim crime is punishable among our people by death. Under the circumstances, the sentence is to be carried out immediately and without delay."

Naero, I can–

Shut up, Om.

Naero gasped and covered her mouth with both hands as she sobbed and went down on one knee.

Then she dropped her hands to her abdomen and her eyes met Khai's in explosive waves of desperate horror and regret.

Their child from their love within that distant star barely grew within her. Now, no time remained to tell Khai all that she needed to before he performed his duty as the Mystic Enforcer.

Before he took her head…ended her life, and the lives of his own family.

Naero Amashin Maeris clenched her fists, and rose up with her head held high to meet her fate with her eyes clear and wide open, if that was what must be.

Amazon Link for *Naero's Trial*: smarturl.it/NaerosTrial

Please Join my Readers List

http://eepurl.com/BltPD

Be first to learn about my new releases. I promise that I will not share your info or spam you. I will use the list only to inform you about my publishing projects and book events.

About the Author

Mason Elliott grew up loving Science Fiction and Fantasy in all of their myriad forms. That love has transferred into his dedicated writing. Like most writers, he lives a Spartan lifestyle and yearns to devote his life even more to his writing. So be a fan, buy his stuff, and enjoy!

Mason's Amazon Author Page:

smarturl.it/BooksbyMasonElliott

Friend Mason on FB at this link:

http://on.fb.me/1qnBfJd

Like and follow Mason on Facebook, where he does most of his blogging at

https://www.facebook.com/masonelliott731

And on Twitter at

http://bit.ly/1nsqOSs.

Join Mason's Readers List Publishing to get the latest progress on his latest books:

http://eepurl.com/FgQzv
Visit Mason Elliott's website at

http://masonelliott.authorcontacts.com

Mason's Acknowledgements

I am forever grateful to my friends on the staff at High Mark Publishing SF.

And always let me thank all of my best friends among my beta readers, my amazing online writer's group, and of course, the rest of my family.

www.ingramcontent.com/pod-product-compliance
Lightning Source LLC
Chambersburg PA
CBHW060549260626
47161CB00003B/1125